Also by Tommy Orange

There There

Wandering Stars

Wandering Stars

Tommy Orange

Harvill
Secker

1 3 5 7 9 10 8 6 4 2

Harvill Secker, an imprint of Vintage, is part of the Penguin Random House
group of companies whose addresses can be found at
global.penguinrandomhouse.com

Penguin
Random House
UK

First published in the USA by Alfred A. Knopf in 2024
First published in Great Britain by Harvill Secker in 2024

Copyright © Tommy Orange 2024

Tommy Orange has asserted his right to be identified as the author of this
Work in accordance with the Copyright, Designs and Patents Act 1988

penguin.co.uk/vintage

Typeset by Scribe, Philadelphia, Pennsylvania
Designed by Maria Carella

Printed and bound in Great Britain by Clays Ltd, Elcograf S.p.A.

The authorised representative in the EEA is Penguin Random House Ireland,
Morrison Chambers, 32 Nassau Street, Dublin D02 YH68

A CIP catalogue record for this book is available from the British Library

HB ISBN 9781787304550
TPB ISBN 9781787304567

Penguin Random House is committed to a sustainable future
for our business, our readers and our planet. This book is made
from Forest Stewardship Council® certified paper.

For anyone surviving and not surviving
this thing called and not called addiction

Prologue

In Indian civilization I am a Baptist, because I believe
in immersing the Indians in our civilization,
and when we get them under holding them there until
they are thoroughly soaked.

—RICHARD HENRY PRATT

There were children, and then there were the children of Indians, because the merciless savage inhabitants of these American lands did not make children but nits, and nits make lice, or so it was said by the man who meant to make a massacre feel like killing bugs at Sand Creek, when seven hundred drunken men came at dawn with cannons, and then again four years later almost to the day the same way at the Washita River, where afterward, seven hundred Indian horses were rounded up and shot in the head.

These kinds of events were called battles, then later—sometimes—massacres, in America's longest war. More years at war with Indians than as a nation. Three hundred and thirteen.

After all the killing and removing, scattering and rounding up of Indian people to put them on reservations, and after the buffalo population was reduced from about thirty million to a few hundred in the wild, the thinking being "Every buffalo dead is an Indian gone," there came another campaign-style slogan directed at the Indian problem: "Kill the Indian, Save the Man."

When the Indian wars began to go cold, the theft of land and tribal sovereignty bureaucratic, they came for Indian children, forcing them into boarding schools, where if they did not die of what they called consumption even while they regularly were starved; if they were not buried in duty, training for agricultural or industrial labor, or indentured servitude; were they not buried in children's cemeteries, or in unmarked graves, not lost somewhere between the school and home having run away, unburied, unfound, lost to time, or lost between exile and refuge, between school, tribal homelands, reservation, and city; if they made it through routine beatings and rape, if they survived, made lives and families and homes, it was because of this and only this: Such Indian children were made to carry more than they were made to carry.

But before the boarding schools, in 1875, seventy-one Indian men and one Indian woman were taken as prisoners of war in Oklahoma and put on a train to St. Augustine, Florida, where they were jailed in a star-shaped prison-castle—a star fort. It was the oldest masonry fort in the country, and the first European settlement in the continental United States, built on the backs of Indian people under Spanish order in the late 1600s out of coquina—a kind of ancient shell formed into rock over time. The star fort built to defend the Atlantic trade route was named Castillo de San Marcos by the Spanish, after Saint Mark, patron saint of, among other things, prisoners, then under U.S. rule it became Fort Marion, named after the American Revolutionary War hero Francis Marion, who'd been nicknamed the Swamp Fox, and was known to have raped his slaves and hunted Indians for sport.

Their jailer, Richard Henry Pratt, ordered that their hair be cut and that they be given military uniforms. Pratt also ordered that the Indian prisoners of war at Fort Marion be given ledger books to draw in. One Southern Cheyenne man named Howling Wolf took to it best because he'd been doing the same thing on buffalo hides to tell stories long before that. In the ledger books, he drew things from way back and high up. A bird's-eye view. That hadn't happened before the same way on the hides. It was only after that long train ride from Oklahoma to Florida with iron chains around his wrists and ankles that Howling Wolf began to draw from where birds saw things. Birds see the best of any creature with a spine, are sacred because they soar the heavens, and with just one of their feathers, and some smoke, prayers make it to God.

The Indians were allowed to sell their drawings to white people who came to witness the prisoners of war, these Kiowa, Comanche, Southern Cheyenne, Arapaho, and Caddo people, to see them dance and dress up Indian, see the vanishing race before it was gone, and take home a drawing, a polished sea bean, or a bow and arrow, curios they were called, as if a souvenir from an amusement park, or human zoo—which were popular at the time, and tended to include Indians. Drawings of Indian life as depicted by Indians, on pages made to keep track of transactions, were sold as some of the first Indian art. Pratt drew from his experience at the prison-castle as if it were a blueprint for the Carlisle Indian Industrial School, which opened just a year after the prisoners were released.

Starting in 1879, Indian parents were encouraged and coerced, and threatened with jail time if they refused to send their children to school. In one case, Hopi parents from Arizona who had refused such orders were sent to California, to Alcatraz for nine months as punishment. The prisoners were stripped of their clothes and given military uniforms, told they'd be there until they learned beyond a shadow of a doubt the error of their evil ways. They were held in wooden boxes smaller than solitary confinement cells built later for the famously draconian prison. During the day they were made to saw large logs into smaller ones like some cartoon's dream of sleeping. When they were released and taken back to Arizona, they continued to resist having their children put into schools, and continued to spend time in prison.

Some Indian parents understood that their children were hostages kept to encourage better behavior from the more problematic Indian tribes. Others were forcefully taken from their homes, on what some Indians then called the iron horse, on loud trains across unknown lands, to a school where they were subjected to disease and starvation, and taught that everything about being Indian was wrong. It became law that Indian children attend these schools, just as Indian medicines and ceremonies, rites and rituals were being outlawed.

At Carlisle, they were taught that they were to become Carlisle Indians. A new tribe of Indians made up of many tribes but belonging to none, belonging to the school, which belonged to and was funded by the U.S. government.

As soon as they arrived at the school their long hair was cut, their clothes were taken, and new names were handed out along with military uniforms—which is to say the war began immediately. Each day they did military drills and marched as if against themselves in daily battles happening first from the outside in, and then from the inside out like a disease. If Indian children spoke English instead of their Native tongues, they were rewarded at first, but being rewarded for not doing Indian things was not where it ended. Beatings and jail time and countless other kinds of abuse became routine. You were supposed to kill the entire Indian if they were to be saved. Later it was said that Indian children in boarding schools had the same chance of dying as soldiers in one of the world wars.

All the Indian children who were ever Indian children never stopped being Indian children, and went on to have not nits but Indian children, whose Indian children went on to have Indian children, whose Indian children became American Indians, whose American Indian children became Native Americans, whose Native American children would call themselves Natives, or Indigenous, or NDNS, or the names of their sovereign nations, or the names of their tribes, and all too often would be told they weren't the right kind of Indians to be considered real ones by too many Americans taught in schools their whole lives that the only real kinds of Indians were those long-gone Thanksgiving Indians who loved the Pilgrims as if to death.

Boarding schools like Carlisle existed all over the country, and for almost a hundred years operated with the same principles as Carlisle. For decades, the Native dropout rate has been one of the highest in the country. Today it's twice the national average.

To become not-Indian the way they meant it at Carlisle meant you killed the Indian to save the man, as was said by the man who made the school, which meant the Indian children would have to do all of the dying.

Beware of the man who does not talk and the dog who does not bark.

——CHEYENNE PROVERB

The so-called Chivington or Sand Creek Massacre, in spite of certain most objectionable details, was on the whole as righteous and beneficial a deed as ever took place on the frontier.

——THEODORE ROOSEVELT

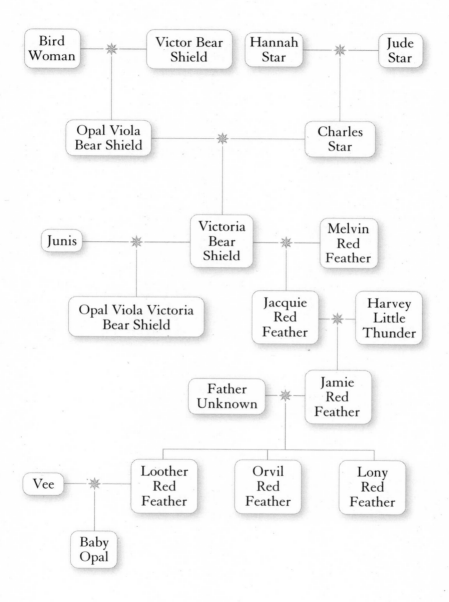

PART ONE

✳

Before

1924

Jude Star ✸ *Winter*

————— • • —————

CHAPTER ONE

Young Ghosts

I thought I heard birds that morning time just before the morning light, after I shot up scared of men so white they were blue. I'd been having dreams of blue men with blue breath, and the sound of birds was the slow squeaking of wheels, the rolling of mountain howitzers approaching our camp at dawn.

The bad dreams had been coming for weeks leading up to that morning, so I'd taken to sleeping with my grandmother, Spotted Hawk. She'd prayed for me before I closed my eyes to sleep, blew smoke in my face after rolling up some tobacco in a corn husk, then sang me the song that slowed my breath and made my eyelids heavy.

From inside the tipi I thought it was thunder, or buffalo, then I saw the purple-orange dawn light through the holes made by bullets in the walls of the tipi.

People outside ran or they died there having been picked off running.

Looking back, everything that happened before Sand Creek seemed to belong to someone else, someone I once knew, as I once knew my mother's perfect smile, my father's crooked one, the way both of their eyes looked to the ground when I made them proud, or cut into me when I made them mad, my brothers' and sisters' way of teasing me about my big ears by pulling on my earlobes, or the way they tickled my ribs and made me laugh until I almost cried in that way that made me hate it and love it, but hate it. Our camp with our animal companions and the big fires we made, the rivers and creeks we played in during summers, or kept away from winters; the hunts I watched the older ones prepare for, how they laughed themselves free when they got back, relieved to have food for everyone, then made fire and prayed and sang in earnest to the animal and to our Creator God, Maheo.

Everything that had been before what happened at Sand Creek went back inside the earth, deep into that singular stillness of land and death.

At the massacre, while it was happening, the bullets and the screaming, bodies down everywhere, Spotted Hawk shoved a boy at me like: Take him too. I was a young man then, barely not a boy myself. The boy my grandmother pushed at me had freckles spattered around his eyes that looked like blood. If someone had freckles, it usually meant white people had become intimately involved in the lives of one of our people, made some mess. One time, one of my uncles got shot dead right in front of me, some loose white man come to exact revenge shot my uncle in the back of the head, and there splattered on Spotted Hawk's face was blood patterned just like this boy's freckles, this boy whose cheeks were full like he'd been saving up spit, like he'd been too afraid to swallow it.

As ever, Spotted Hawk's face kept whatever she felt behind it. She pointed her lips at a horse, and once we were on, slapped the thing and we were off. When I looked back I saw Spotted

Hawk's body go down. I wouldn't ever know if it was from a bullet, to take cover, or to play dead. I'd known spiders to do this, had seen a black one with a bright red mark on its belly play dead. I'd hidden and waited, waited and watched, then seen it come back to life just before I came down hard on it with my foot. Years later in Florida, when I first saw the shape of an hourglass, and understood it meant time as the delicate falling of sand through a narrow glass passage, I was reminded of the spider's mark, and that there were ways to play dead, and come back to life.

A dog had managed to follow us away from the camp. The dog was all black but for a patch of white on its chest, with long legs, scruffy fur, and sun-yellow eyes. Just after I noticed the dog I felt a sharp pain and jumped off the horse thinking I got bit by something. I found a wet wound on my lower back when I reached for it. I looked at the blood and felt as if I were falling through the air. Then I took off my leggings and wrapped them around my midsection, hoping to stop the bleeding. The boy helped me get wrapped, then did his little best to help me back up on the horse as I was too weak to get up myself. I slept after that, and when I woke up, saw that it was night.

Me and the boy bundled up in a pile of blankets my grandmother had somehow managed to pack for us. In the morning we found the dog nestled between us. Where the bullet had gone in still stung, but the bleeding had stopped. I thought it must not have gone too deep, and wanted to find the bullet with my fingers, take it out if I could.

When the sun sank behind us in the west again, it brought with its absence a biting cold. We slept beneath the standing horse.

I felt that my grandmother had *prayed* that horse what to

do. She could run, like some current carried her. We went along the old water lines, down the dry creek, the massacre farther and farther behind us, with the memory of it still on top of my skin, the sounds still in my ears, ringing high and sharp. We moved through the trees and fields like young ghosts.

Before we slept that night we stared at each other without saying anything. I knew then that I couldn't speak if I wanted to. I couldn't say anything and couldn't tell if I ever had before. I believed I had memories of speaking, but the more time passed the less certain I became that I'd ever made a sound with my voice. And then I didn't know if the boy wasn't speaking for the same reason, or if it was because he already knew I was one of these rare people who didn't know how to speak.

How far will we go? the boy seemed to say with his chin and his lips pointing the way we were headed.

Until soldiers shoot us dead, I said by looking all around, then miming holding a rifle, then closing one eye to aim, then throwing my head back like I'd been shot.

Will we fight this time? the boy said by putting up his fists.

Did you think we should have stayed to fight before? I asked by pointing my lips back where we'd come from.

It would have been better dying than this, the boy seemed to say about our hunger, by rubbing his stomach.

That dog over there, he'd help us make it longer, I said by pointing at the dog and lifting my eyebrows.

No, the boy said. No dog, he said by looking down and shaking his head hard.

We went for what seemed a long time, letting the horse take us. When I felt too weak to stay awake, and the boy began to whimper, I could no longer ignore the horse's meat beneath us.

Winter's night was here, so I would need to move if I was going to do it. I tied the horse to a tree with a slipknot I'd been taught for just this occasion. If you had to eat a horse, this was how you first tied them down. But I didn't kill the horse, because out came a foal from behind her. It landed on its side, a wet thud, and at first tried to get up, but couldn't, then stayed down, then went still. The boy just watched, unable to stand anymore, sitting a ways off with his mouth hung wide open. The dog barked while the mother tried to nudge her young alive with her muzzle. I walked nearer to the foal to see if there was life. A string of unwanted questions came to me then: *If the foal was dead, would we eat it? And in which order would I kill its mother and eat her too? Would we have to fight the dog for the meat, and if we fought and killed the dog, would we then eat him?* I was too hungry. The wind got stronger and the dog came running over but then fell on his side as if struck by a bullet. I looked around to see if there were bullets coming, shielding my eyes from dirt that had picked up in the wind, which was now so loud I couldn't hear anything else. The boy's head was tucked into his knees, and I thought I heard him screaming, but it might have been the wind. I looked up and saw a thin cloud in front of the moon. There was dark light coming down through the cloud, falling down from the sky like rain in the distance. I ran to the boy, pulling him up by the arm, and we went under our blankets to hide.

The next morning I woke up and saw the mother horse still lying there, dead now, and the dog making its mouth like it was barking, but with no sound coming from him, and then he started coughing and vomited bright green grass. I went to the dead horse and looked around for the foal but saw none there, nor a trace of its birth. I'd heard of mothers eating their stillborn, and wondered if she'd done that, and if that was what had killed her.

I sharpened a branch on a rock, then made a fire. I needed to move before the horse's meat went bad. I ate half the horse's liver right away and handed the rest to the boy, who took it hungrily, then cut meat from wherever it came off easiest. We stayed where we were, eating off and on all day, and dared not look at what was left of the horse behind us when we were done.

In the morning our mouths were stained with blood when we came to a stream where the water was bitter. I don't know how long it was that we walked after that, when I saw a young man on a black horse. That was Bear Shield.

Bear Shield took us to a camp where the oldest Cheyenne woman I had ever seen told the boy to take my name. My name had been Bird before. She gave me a new name by pointing up at the sky where the night's first star had appeared, then pointing at me.

The dog stayed with us for a while. But when there was nothing left to hunt, and the hunger hurt too much, the dog—like so many other dogs—was eaten.

Even though I would never respond, Bear Shield liked to talk, and would talk to me, at first in Cheyenne and then in English when he realized I wasn't going to say anything back. He'd learned English from his father, who'd been a scout and had traveled with the U.S. Army for a time, before leaving that work and swearing himself to the Cheyenne Warrior Society, the dog soldiers.

One day Bear Shield said we should go out on our own, not stay to die in the camp. I told the boy to stay with the old woman who'd told us to trade names, and Bear Shield and I set out the next morning on Bear Shield's horse.

Winters alone seemed to pass. Sometimes it felt like the world had ended, and we were waiting for the next one to come. More often it felt like I was waiting for the sounds of war to come back again, for the first light of the sun to bring with it blue men come to kill and scatter us again, thin us out across the land like the buffalo, chase and starve and round us up like I'd heard by then they were doing to Indian people everywhere.

We saw and ate many strange things going around together looking for our people, looking for a place we could stay. There was no home to return to, and so we wandered. Caught and ate rabbits and turkey and snakes. We raided wagons and camps when we found them, whether they were white people or other Indians didn't matter, so long as we knew we could get away unscathed. Hunger seemed to be keeping us alive while also threatening to kill us. I couldn't tell you where we were those years because we were never anywhere for long. One of the first things I stole was a horse, and we were never good to each other, she didn't want me riding her, and I didn't blame her. I set her free as soon as I found another horse to steal. I didn't mind living that way, but it wore you out. And when we ended up having to hurt people in order to stay safe, I knew we needed to find a better way.

Whenever we stayed anywhere long enough, Bear Shield would put together his drum. He taught me how to, too. With hide, stones, a rope, an antler to pull the rope to make the hide taut, and a little bit of water at the bottom of an iron kettle. We kept seven stones at the bottom of the drum representing the seven stars in the night sky that seemed to surround the moon. I never knew why they were called dog soldiers, or why we had that story about the girl giving birth to dogs that then became stars. One thing about not speaking is that it's hard to ask specific questions, so most things I didn't understand I just had to accept.

The drum was loud, so we always went off to play it, far enough to where we knew no one would hear us, near water if we could find it. The drum had a deep, sorrowful sound, and I'd have to adjust how tight I pulled the hide to get the tone brighter, to make it feel less like it might pull me into it. When I got it the way I wanted it to sound, something that had been set loose from me got called back as I played. So I kept playing whenever I could. Sometimes Bear Shield would sing along, picking out what sounded good with the tone of the drum, with my rhythm. I didn't know if Bear Shield had heard those songs before, or if he was just making them up there and then. There was unspeakable pain and loss all about us wherever we went. So much hunger and suffering, but with the drum between us, and the singing, there was made something new. We pounded, and sang, and out came this brutal kind of beauty lifting everything up in song.

The place we settled the longest was near Fort Reno. We were pretty worn out by then and had heard we could turn ourselves in there, and would be fed and given shelter. But shortly after getting there, we were told there had been countless crimes committed by Southern Cheyennes against the U.S. Army, and one particularly gruesome murder of a family called the Germans, and that we were to be taken in to pay for those crimes. Thirty-three of us were taken to Fort Sill, shackled in iron chains, then put on a train to Florida.

————— · · —————

CHAPTER TWO

Life Masks

We spent three years in a prison-castle as prisoners of war. Our jailer was a brooding man named Richard Henry Pratt. He always had his shoulders hunched and his eyes aimed down. Pratt was stern and plain, with a nose that announced itself on his face like some stone monument on an otherwise unremarkable hill. We liked him well enough because his will seemed good. And though he seemed to take himself a bit too seriously at times, he'd made us laugh early on, when telling a story about how some Kiowa he knew dressed him up in full regalia and painted his face. The way he told the story, while the Cheyenne translator translated it, he kept laughing, so we laughed along with him, at first to be polite, but then because it did seem funny, or Pratt had convinced us with his laughter that he was being funny, about Indians dressing him up like an Indian and painting his face to honor him with a song and dance in front of a fire. Not long after he told us this story, our blankets and clothes were taken and replaced with military uniforms, and we were told we could not dress like Indians anymore. No one was laughing much then.

Our first months at the prison-castle were the hardest, and many of the prisoners got sick. Some died. Two killed themselves, and that's not including Gray Beard, who'd tried to hang himself on the train then was shot trying to escape.

The walls of the prison were slimy with something dark and fuzzy that smelled bad, and we weren't used to the humidity, to the air being so thick and wet as if the ocean had risen—some hot layer of it haunting the land.

Pratt wanted to improve conditions, or so he told me, taking me aside one day to ask if I wanted to learn to be a bread maker and baker. He said he would train us as soldiers. Give us discipline and rank. Give us guns to guard ourselves, keep us clean and uniformed and regimented. Pratt said he would make us wolves of the U.S. Army. When he said that, something cold slid up my spine.

But he did as he said he would. There was roll call and morning runs and bugle songs, and eventually an Indian court where those who were ruled against spent time in a dungeon beneath the prison-castle. After military training came education.

I learned how to read and write in English with the Bible. We went to school at the chapel. I probably learned to read faster than I would have had I had the ability to speak. And by then I knew English well, having spent all those years with Bear Shield.

The Bible was strange, and there was so much I couldn't get even knowing the words. The books in the book were named simply by the first names of the authors, the way Pratt's first name was Richard. Had there been a book of Richard, it would have been filled with descriptions of military drills. That was all we ever did besides school and church—train to be military men, dressed as the very kind of men some of us had seen wipe our people out.

I didn't know why so many people had written the Bible, but I liked that it wasn't just one person. There was beauty and wisdom in it, and I did my best to interpret what it meant everywhere it seemed to mean something to me, the way I would with a dream that stuck with me.

I spent a lot of time with the books of Psalms and Proverbs, took some solace in Job, and appreciated how comforted the language in Isaiah made me feel. *He hath sent me to bind up the brokenhearted, to proclaim liberty to the captives, and the opening of the prison to them that are bound; to proclaim the acceptable year of the Lord, and the day of vengeance of our God; to comfort all that mourn.* That passage really felt true to me. There were such things I read in the Bible that felt so good to me to read, that I wouldn't ever allow that it wasn't something important to have been written.

I spent some time with Revelation too. It seemed to me that what had happened, what was happening to my people, was what the book was about. There was a very short book before the last book in the Bible with a verse that felt already in me before I got to it there in Florida, before I even knew what a sea was. *Raging waves of the sea, foaming out their own shame, wandering stars, to whom is reserved the blackness of darkness forever.*

In the second part of the Bible, the New Testament, this man Jesus seemed like certain Cheyenne people I'd heard about, chiefs and other medicine people who led the people with their heart. And our Cheyenne prophet Sweet Medicine, had he not been born of a virgin birth? And hadn't I heard creation stories about a man's ribs to make women? Could there not then be something to this Godbook, to this Jesus, I couldn't not have thought. Sweet Medicine came from a virgin. My grandmother told me a voice told a woman in stories that a sweet root was coming. There was no father in that story, only a grandmother who raised Sweet Medicine after his mother abandoned him because there was no father. Sweet Medicine performed miracles and taught Cheyenne people a good way to be, just as Jesus had in the Bible.

For what reason I'll never be sure, Pratt brought us over to an island called Anastasia to stay for a few nights. We camped there together. And after that we were allowed time alone, to ourselves. We returned to the island again and again, and feeling the freedom of not being seen, we sang old songs and painted ourselves. Danced and remembered. We took dinghies out and caught sharks and alligators, ate that tough meat and shined sea beans, made jewelry, bows and arrows, and drew in ledger books we'd been given to draw in, all of which we sold to white people who'd come to see us. White people had been coming to look at us all that time we were there, just like when they'd come to see us on the train when we'd stopped in Indiana on the way out to Florida, when tens of thousands were said to have shown up to see us captured, real Indians in Indiana, to see the vanishing race off into final captivity before disappearing into history forever. The white visitors came from all over to see us. And we performed.

One day Bear Shield was challenged to kill a bull with a bow and arrow while riding a horse. There was something about the Spanish tradition of fighting the bull with a cape and a sword related to the challenge. He looked so big on top of that horse I thought he'd topple over, but then he did it all with such speed and grace, killed that bull no problem with a single arrow, I felt proud of Bear Shield, but bad for the beast. I stood over the dead bull, with its tongue, and thought someone should tuck the tongue back in, or cut it out to eat. Tongue tasted good.

That was the first time we performed being Indian for the white people. Some of us danced and drummed and sang— painted and feathered. I watched all the white people gather around us with that strange mix of disgust and astonishment. Later Pratt compared us to Buffalo Bill's Wild West shows. Said we "out Buffalo Billed Mr. Cody." More performances happened after that. We performed ourselves, made it look authentic for the sake of performing authenticity. Like being was for sale, and we'd sold ours. I even danced in one. Pretended to know something I didn't. It didn't matter what I did, white people wouldn't know the difference. Eventually I didn't either, it seemed none of us did.

Pratt gave us a share of money for the shows, and I would go into town to buy mangoes and oysters. I bought paper, pen, and ink, and got all the way to the point of starting a letter home, as some of the other men were doing, before realizing I had no such thing, or people to write to, so I started drawing horses and selling those drawings when I could.

After more than a year had passed at the prison-castle, just when we were beginning to enjoy a relative sense of freedom, Bear Shield and some of the Kiowas made a plan to escape. But then someone told Pratt about it and we were caught before we could make the attempt. I hadn't been a part of the planning on account of everyone aside from Bear Shield thinking I was a fool. When we were caught, Pratt only marched Bear Shield and me around the courtyard in chains for hours to break our spirits. When we could barely stand anymore, Pratt brought out needles and said Indian medicine was strong, but that the white man's medicine was much stronger. After the injection, I got weaker and weaker until I seemed to dream myself away from my body, or it all dissolved into nightmare. Suddenly I was back at Sand Creek. I thought I saw thin black legs coming down from the clouds, but realized it was just rain in the distance. I watched the drunk men creeping toward the camp at dawn from a bird's-eye view. There was something there, as big as a mountain, hovering above all the killing like what was happening was something it'd caught and was preparing to eat. Seeing it all from way up where I was seeing it from, it did look like my people were getting chewed up by those hundreds of bullets fired by those mountain howitzers. Then I saw a man coming from the east and knew him to be Jesus as soon as he got close enough. He spread his arms like wings and wrapped them around me, took me above something I didn't know I could get above, somewhere soaring, briefly, some small, bright, warm glory that made me feel lighter than I'd ever feel again.

I woke up in the prison-castle dungeon. My lips were chapped and I was thirstier than I'd ever been. I hadn't thought of or dreamed about Sand Creek in years, had sunken it down below the blood. Somewhere down there, Jesus from the dream remained. I felt a love for Jesus as if we were family, and the ancestors, and the unborn all at once.

We found out later that Pratt had rolled us away in a wheelbarrow after we seemed to have died, and that we were gone for three days. Pratt had called it a ceremony, and tried to make it seem like he'd brought us back from the dead, like Jesus did Lazarus in the Bible.

There were no more escape attempts after that. And Pratt

was suspiciously fast to trust us again. He believed in his methods, I guessed, and in the power of the white man's medicine.

I began to imagine what I'd do, if I had the chance, to Pratt, to any white man if I knew I could get away with it, even if I knew I couldn't, I just needed the chance, to take the right moment, to do what damage it felt would quell the mean thing beginning to spin me so hard, as if to turn me inside out, as if to get all the hate and rage and sadness I kept down to survive. I tried to push it all back down again. I thought about Jesus. And then of the needle. I thought about the sharpness of the needle going into me, and then felt a sharpness coming out of me from my back, where the bullet had gone in, from where there was still a bump. I put my finger there to feel it. I could feel something coming out of the bump, something sharp. I thought about what Jesus said about a camel passing through the eye of a needle to get into the kingdom of God. I pulled at the thing coming out of me with my fingers and felt it begin to slide up, out of me. I couldn't imagine what was coming out of me, if it wasn't a needle, and certainly not a camel. Then it came all the way out, and before I could register what it was I passed out and found nothing upon waking up later.

Before we were released from the prison-castle, a man came to measure our heads, to make masks of us, molds of our heads with white liquid. He called them life masks. The man wanted to compare Indian heads with white heads. He thought if Indian heads were smaller that could explain why we were savages. I froze as the thick liquid poured over and enveloped me. It was cold and then warm and tight against my face. It got quiet and then it cracked. There were tubes stuck into my nose so I could breathe. I wondered if it was death the man meant by life masks. I thought maybe I was being turned into a thing for them to keep. But a head was a living thing, a face moved and changed all the time, and then I couldn't move mine anymore at all, so, I thought, this must be some kind of death, some kind of keeping.

The guy said he would make a life mask of Pratt too, and Pratt put a hand to his chest like he was being honored. When they took my casted head off, I looked at it and was proud. There I was. Once they all were made, none of their heads looked smaller than Pratt's. In fact they all looked bigger than his. Measure them, I thought then. Measure them in front of us.

Freedom from prison and then documentation to keep track of us was what brought me to the name Jude. Some of the other Indians took famous American presidents as their names, one man took Richard Henry Pratt, the whole thing like that, and Bear Shield took Victor because of a book he'd read called *Frankenstein,* about a man-made monster. Bear Shield had told me the woman who wrote the book knew about Indians. That she'd understood everything from all the way over there, where she was from. And that being made to take a name like they'd wanted, being made to become the kind of person that they wanted us to be, it was just like that woman's monster, was just like what she had Dr. Victor Frankenstein make in the book, that was why he chose the name Victor, he was the man making the monster by agreeing to take their kind of name and living life the way white men like Pratt demanded. I read the book too, and liked how the monster learned language from the boy Felix, and remembered with great clarity a moment in the book when the monster explained that he can hardly describe the effect reading certain books was having on him. I felt that way too about reading, how quiet a behavior it was, and how quiet I had become, how that seemed to match, and how it brought me closer to reading, to words on the page, how loud they could be in my head, almost as if I were hearing the words as I read them, and, sometimes, almost as if I were speaking the words myself.

When it came to my own name, I went looking through a Bible. I couldn't decide until I got to the book before the last book, after coming across the verse, *They are clouds without rain, blown along by the wind; autumn trees, without fruit and uprooted—twice dead.* Getting these new names felt like dying again. And I felt like a cloud without rain. And I felt without fruit and uprooted. Twice dead. All of it. It was me. The book of Jude. I didn't even remember that the next verse was one that had so struck me when I'd first encountered it, that first time I'd read the Bible all the way through, that verse about wandering stars.

I put down my last name as Star, and gave them Jude for my first name.

On the train ride back to Oklahoma, I saw the bones of buffalo piled up as high as a man for miles. I'd heard that this was happening. The Buffalo Wars, they called it. I'd heard about why they were doing it. Every buffalo dead was an Indian gone. But seeing all those buffalo bodies piled up like that, and the swarms of vultures and other such scavengers circling all that death, it did something to me, ate away at some last part of me, and though I couldn't look away from the sight of it, I wanted to close my eyes, not have to see any more of the old world so dead before it was gone.

— • • —

CHAPTER THREE

A Son

In Florida, though we were forced to go to church at the prison-castle and to renounce our blanket ways, I didn't care about the blankets they'd taken, or whatever they thought I was worshipping before that was so wrong.

I never would have called myself a Christian, but the God-book, and even reading itself, had changed something in me, made me believe in the quiet life I'd either been born into or been borne out of the morning of the massacre. I came to love the Bible, and was only privately suspicious about the fact that the Bible itself was not mentioned in the Bible. The book and the act of reading the book seemed like such an important part of their way, but it wasn't there. It does in the first book talk about the word being at the beginning of creation itself, and that the word was with God, and that the word was God. I felt like I could spend my whole life reading, getting more and more understanding from words, from books.

There were so many more books and so many more kinds of books and writers of books than the Bible, and luckily,

Pratt's wife, Anna Laura, encouraged us to read other books to expand our understanding of the English language. She gave us books like *Moby-Dick* and *The Adventures of Huckleberry Finn,* plus the monster book Bear Shield loved, and poetry by a man named Walt Whitman, who believed himself to have written a kind of Bible he called *Leaves of Grass,* which I did not particularly like, but I always remembered this line, "This is no book, who touches this, touches a man!," because I'd started to think of books as beings. As things unto themselves, whether they were written by countless people countless years ago, or written just recently by strange old white men, the books themselves felt to me as if they were their own lives, separate from the bodies and minds that created them. I wanted to write one myself. I began to use the ledger paper I'd been drawing on to write down things that seemed like they might be on their way to being in a book one day.

In Oklahoma, Jesus came to me in dreams, always dressed in white, one time he was a train conductor, with a long beard made of thorns, and on top of his head was a crown of roses. Everything smelled bad in the dream, especially Jesus, or all of the bad smell was coming from Jesus. He smelled like something rotten, like death, as if in being dead those three days had made him rot. Another time Jesus brought me to the lion's den, and inside the den lived crazed dogs who believed themselves to be lions, and Jesus had left me with the dogs, rolling a boulder in front of the opening to the den. At some point I became a dog who believed himself to be a lion.

I saw that other Indians were becoming Christians, were talking about Jesus in conversation, and were going to church on Sundays. At first I only went to services now and then, just because other Indians I knew went. Just to see how it would make me feel. But by the time I became a heavy drinker, church on Sundays became essential.

How I became a heavy drinker happened entirely by chance, or if you believed in such things, as I did, fate. I was out on my horse with no aim in mind other than to feel in my chest the hoofbeats and to feel the air move at my face if the wind came or if she picked up her pace, when I came upon a mess of men and wagons, a few dead horses and some barrels loose from a wagon. It seemed to be a robbery gone wrong, or some other such kind of mishap. One of the horses was still alive, and the wagon was in good enough shape to take back home with me, so I did, not even then yet knowing what was in the barrels.

For a long time the barrels stayed in the basement where I'd first unloaded them. Down where you went if there was a tornado nearby. I continued to work the land and animals all day, from dawn to dusk. To make a living, as they said. The goal ever since leaving the prison-castle and going to Oklahoma had been to live like a white man, as Pratt had wanted us to do, and while I'd wanted to try Hampton, or life at any college that would take me, because I couldn't speak, even though I could read and write probably better than any of the other prisoners, I wasn't even considered as anything more than someone to pity, diseased with silence as I was, cursed to my quietude.

Before I got my allotment land in 1887, I'd worked as hard as I could with anyone trying to make something of the land we were given there on our Indian territory, Oklahoma, an Indian country to end that bigger Indian country too looted and taken over by then to ever go back to anything even resembling what it'd once been. I spent years as a quiet farmhand to anyone who'd take me, if they gave me food or some money, or even for nothing at all, just to be around other Cheyenne people; it was okay sometimes, even good, to struggle together was not as bad as if I were alone.

Then I got my allotment land. One hundred and sixty acres is a lot of land, which means a lot of alone if you're alone. From then on it was up to me to try to grow and maintain crops I could eat or trade or sell. Then I found those barrels.

One night I thought I heard something down in the basement. I had some grains stored down there by then and worried an animal had gotten in, so I went down there with a lantern to scare the thing off. But there was no animal. The barrels felt loud to me. The blue of the moon came in through the storm doors, and some wind was at my back. I tried to open one of the barrels but couldn't. Then pried it open with a shovel. The smell that came when I opened it felt like it burned the inside of my nostrils. I knew what it was. Maybe I'd always known. What other kind of liquid, since I'd always heard the liquid inside sloshing, would men have tried to steal? There was a bucket with a cup inside it in the corner, which I used to get water from my well. I dipped the cup and took a sip and spit it out right away. But then I tried again and made myself swallow. Then I took some more. And some more after that. A lot at once. I wanted to see what it did to me. I'd heard of drunkenness, of course, had seen drunken men, white men and Indians alike. I wanted to see what it would do to me, how it would feel to be that way. And it wasn't what I thought. Not at all. I coughed and gagged and then when I thought I might throw up, heard my voice come. It began with the cough and the gag, but when I heard my voice come, I tried to keep it coming. I felt light in my head and like some other weight had been lifted from somewhere else in my body, some hidden place I hadn't known how to lift it from because I hadn't known where I'd hidden the weight. Some place inside I couldn't find because I didn't know where to look. And then I spoke these words: *It is not down on any map. True places never are.* It was from *Moby-Dick.* This was my first time speaking English. How had I been able to produce such sounds then? When I'd only ever read the language in my head? When I'd been left without a voice for so long? I had to wonder whether I had spoken at all. But come morning when I awoke and heard the birds I found that I could speak. I coughed first, and felt sick from the drink, but I spoke, said my own name. Felt as if my voice was tired, as if I'd been speaking to myself all night down in the storm shelter with those barrels. But then the first chance I got to speak to Bear Shield, visiting him later that day, I found that I couldn't, and went back to what I'd always done, which was to stay quiet, or when I needed to, write down in a notebook I carried around a question or answer I had that required more than hand gestures or yes or no nods.

I went back to the drink that night to try to re-create what happened. It didn't work. The drinking became a nightly habit. And then a daily and nightly habit I soon came to think of as a problem. And then a problem I knew I couldn't fix and didn't want to.

I found that on the days after I drank even more than the usual amount, which often happened Saturday nights, I felt more intensely, and felt drawn to hear people talk about God. That feeling of the lingering drunkenness made everything feel loose, loose and without weight, like a cloud with no rain being moved by the wind. I'd let the sermon, the words spoken at the service, I'd let it mean whatever my mind and heart made of it, there between things, still drunk to be sure, but something more than drunk.

The nearest church to my allotment land was a Mennonite church. Leaving the service early one Sunday I spotted a
horse tied up a ways away from where everyone else's horses
were tied. The horse reminded me of the horse from before, the
one I thought of as my wind after the massacre. I traded out my
saddle and took the horse, left my horse there in its place, then
stayed away from the Mennonites after that, as I intended to
keep the horse, felt I could in some way atone for what I'd done
to that other horse by taking care of this one.

I called my horse Church, and thought of her as my second
wind. I got the idea from Pratt, who talked about how our time
at the prison-castle was our second chance, and that once we
got through the hard part, the discipline, and learning how to
walk for the first time with English, taking the Lord's hand,
learning to live by a red-blooded Christianity, with regiments
and discipline, that if we could last, we would then get our second wind, and we would find that we could go much further in
life than we ever thought possible. I didn't care about what Pratt
thought we were capable of as much as I'd taken an idea about
second wind for myself. That if you could last through what
seemed hardest, you got more, and that there lived somewhere
in the body the ability to keep going even though it felt like you
no longer could, some reserve of strength and power, to endure,
that took its share but not all of you; that you could save some
part of you, hidden away in a true place, even from yourself,
for when you needed it most—to believe in that felt powerful
enough to make it true.

Every time I got the chance to speak, to see if I had in fact
gotten my voice back and not dreamed it up in some drunken
state, I wasn't able to use it, wasn't able to call it up to speak.
That was how it was for me until one Sunday morning things

changed. I heard about a new church they were just calling the New Church. I heard Indian and white people worshipped together there.

From the back of the crowded church, I saw a woman up front, I don't know why she stood out to me like she did, but it felt as if I had to meet her. I'd never felt that feeling for a woman before. Her arms were raised high in the air, speaking in some tongue she didn't seem to know herself. Her arms lifted higher and higher as the pastor kept calling out to praise the Lord, praise the Lord, louder and louder.

There were other Indians there too, none I knew, but they were spirited, their hands were down, their eyes were shut tight, and their palms were open as if to say: Here I am for you to take.

After church I heard from an older Indian man that they performed miracles up at the front of the church. People were healed of all kinds of things, and they spoke in tongues, and had communion with the Lord. I decided I would go up front the next time I came. And when that Sunday came, the woman was there again, a couple people over from me, and sure enough they were praying for people harder than I'd ever seen anyone pray, touching their foreheads and yelling out the name Jesus in some kind of way I could feel in my spine. When the pastor came to me I already knew what I would ask for, what I would pray for.

So the pastor prayed and people circled around me praying for my voice to return to me. The pastor went so far as to touch my throat and when he did I yelled out *Praise Jesus* and coughed so hard I gagged. I said *Praise the lord* with a hoarse voice, in just above a whisper, and everyone around me, including the woman whose attention I was desperate to get, went wild with amens and hallelujahs.

After the service I approached her outside. She was kind, in her eyes, and shy to smile but still smiled despite trying not to. She said her name was Hannah and I introduced myself as Jude Star. Her face was covered in freckles, and she was Irish from Ireland, so she spoke with an accent I'd never heard before. She saw me see her and acted like she wished I hadn't. I liked that and I could tell she liked me, if not only because of the miracle everyone had seen in there, of me speaking as if for the first time, but I also suspected it might be that she liked Indians. There was a certain kind of look I knew from white people, when they liked Indians, there was fascination in it, mixed with whatever other magnetic draw, or simple curiosity, as one who had never seen a horse might first look at a horse, wonder at its possible wildness lying in wait, its power.

Back at my house we drank water and then whiskey on the porch and talked about our pasts. Hannah had lived with some Cherokees for years as a child, after her whole family died in a fire shortly after they'd arrived in America. They'd found her there in the ashes, not burned at all. She didn't know how. I told her everything I could remember, which felt when I told her like I'd said the same thing about myself, left and found in the ashes of some American fire.

We didn't talk about Jesus at first, about the service, or about Hannah speaking in tongues, and not even about my miracle. But we kept going back to church together every Sunday, at the New Church, and were married there later that year.

I often felt I'd cheated my way into talking. And kept cheating with the drink, with the barrels, which were running out. I started thinking about ways to get more barrels. Or just bottles, for when I ran out. I heard from Bear Shield that they were hiring policemen, for the tribal police, and I liked the idea of being hired and making regular money if only at first because I knew that meant I could probably secure an amount of alcohol I wished I just wanted but knew that I needed, more and more I needed more and more was how it felt, and having had access to those barrels all that time I'd never had to count before, the amount I felt I needed, that did for me the thing that made me feel enough.

Hannah wanted to have children, and I wasn't necessarily against it, but didn't really believe in the future. We tried plenty, but couldn't. Sometimes I wondered if I wasn't doing it right. Sometimes I wondered if it was the alcohol. No one had ever told me how it was supposed to happen, how it was supposed to feel when you were doing the thing together that was supposed to make a child. To be making a child while doing that strange act I was somehow just supposed to know how to do, was all so beyond strange I didn't even like thinking about it. Were you supposed to be concentrated in a particular way while doing it? Aimed at some depth? Was it like praying? Hannah told me we'd been doing it right, and I believed her. Said we needed to ask God and let it be his will. Everything was in God's hands.

And then as time went on and no child came, Hannah became more impassioned for the New Church, about spreading the gospel as far and wide as she could, believed it was her purpose on this earth, to spread the gospel, to bring his name into the mouths and hearts of all who didn't know him. She began speaking of the second coming of Christ. About the end of the world. This was the beginning of me losing her. I knew it. But I didn't deny her anything. I stayed quiet. Returned to the silence I once knew so well. I wanted to feel what she seemed to be feeling in church, wanted the love of God but could not find it in my heart, could not raise arms and hands on Sundays to God, though I did say grace and felt grateful for all that I had.

Bear Shield invited us over for dinner to talk about a new church he'd become a part of, peyote church. Hannah couldn't make it on account of undisclosed church matters that were becoming more and more common for her.

In his kitchen, Bear Shield told me it was a new way of praying, of worship making its way all over Indian territory and beyond, brought from Mexico by that Comanche chief, Quanah Parker. I had read about it in a newspaper. Parker had gotten it from Mexican Indians. Curanderas, the paper said, had healed the man back to full health.

Bear Shield said the ceremony went way back with the land that the medicine grew out of, and that it happened right there under the crisscrossed poles of a tipi. At the end of the service you greet the morning with weight lifted, and your eyes saw clearer, though things were still hard, Bear Shield had said, would always be hard, even so, he'd seen things in that fireplace that gave him hope for the future of Indian people, far into the future, he said he'd heard Indian men talk about praying for the next seven generations. I had trouble seeing the very next one.

"In that tipi, with that medicine they can't touch us," he said. "White men fear our hope enough to kill us over it. But this one here, in that tipi, we do it at night, stay up all night, when they can't see or hear us, when they can't stop us from being how we've always been, there in that tipi, with that medicine, and that drum, those songs, you remember," Bear Shield said to me, giving me a look.

"Remember what?" I said.

"Like it was before," Bear Shield said, and pointed over my shoulder with his lips, meaning our shared past with the drum from the dog soldiers, after Sand Creek, all those years before.

Bear Shield told me the medicine helped him let go of all he didn't want to keep holding on to. I wanted to want to heal the way Bear Shield seemed to be healing, but more than that I wanted a son. And not anymore only because Hannah wanted a son, I wanted to see the future in my child, the beginning of the future for Indian people in a little body. I wanted an Indian child, even if it was with a white woman.

Hannah refused to join me for the peyote ceremony. And hadn't wanted me to go myself. Said it sounded like the devil. I told her Bear Shield said it would help with the drinking, which had by then long been a problem. Bear Shield said he'd seen other Indian men just like me never touch the drink again after ceremony.

I couldn't believe what it was in there, what the medicine did to you. The fireplace there in the middle of that tipi blazed hot and bright and I felt myself tipping into it. When I looked up at the night sky through the crossed tipi poles above me, the stars shone impossibly bright to the point of looking sharp, and that brightness and sharpness at first filled my eyes with a beauty, but then turned into a kind of quiet violence, and a falling feeling, like everything was breaking apart, like glass had always been between me and everything else, and just then I saw a mirror, and the image of my own face cast white like I'd seen with the life masks, it was approaching me, still and dead and moving at me until it almost seemed to come through, but then didn't, and was what broke the mirror, the life mask shattered with everything else, made everything like broken glass, sharp and reflective and falling.

I thought I was dying, and it was okay, it was good, I would disappear, I would spread wide and across the land, rise up like a cloud and drift home. I was still Bird, beneath all my names, beneath the names for everything I was there, home inside the bones of everything that ever resembled home to me, a core being and beating heart, the booming drum, a song belonging to no one.

Death was going into my blood, rising from below it. And then it came. I'd never vomited so much in my life. Streams of green and brown and corn fell out of me onto the floor of the tipi. Bear Shield himself covered it in dirt, then brought it outside with a shovel. The medicine had done its work on me, and it wasn't done. I kept throwing up all night, and grew so afraid of something I couldn't remember later, something beneath the fire, with eyes, something old, that lived below every fire. I thought I'd lost my mind in there. Thought I lived a thousand years. And I never wanted to go back in again. But somewhere between the vomit and the terror I had prayed and prayed hard. I prayed for a son.

A son came in the spring. Those first years were the sweetest and clearest I could remember. I wasn't drinking anymore. And I'd been promoted to chief of police. I liked that role. It felt to me like it'd felt when we were guarding ourselves high up on the prison-castle walls, carrying a gun and looking down at the interior of the castle, making sure everything went as it was supposed to go. Control. It was what I'd needed all along. Order. The trouble came when we were told by the agents that we would be stopping any and all Indian ceremonies and rituals. That all of that was being outlawed. I did what I was told. I carried some of that out until I couldn't anymore.

CHAPTER FOUR

Into Another Life

I was making bread in my kitchen. I'd been telling my son, Charles, stories about my life, all that had happened to me before I became his father. I made good bread. I had liked to be away from the mold-ridden walls of the interior of the castle, away from the other prisoners, making food from grain, and I still liked it after that. You need sustenance, but you need a little variation too, if you can manage it. Nothing fancy, just sometimes bread with seeds, or bread with more sugar, or bread fried in oil, or bread with cheese baked into it. Bread had made sense once I got back to Oklahoma. The government gave meager rations on reservations, flour being one of the larger portions. Some Indians just threw the flour out, let it float through the air like pollen, and fed their corn to the animals the way white men did. But bread did the trick, and you could make a stew or a soup out of just about anything, then sop it up with some bread, and that could become something more than what it was, even if just while you ate something decent and filling, that sole comfort could carry you.

I felt good talking to my son and eating the bread I made,

there in our kitchen, on our land, in our home. I had a family now and the drinking was behind me. I'd lived enough life, almost died enough times to know when a good thing came along, a thing you didn't know could fill you right up, which only when it filled you let you know there'd been a hole in you before.

I told Charles that there was a story my father used to tell me, about Cheyenne people first coming from a hole in the ground. Charles asked what the story was, and I told him I couldn't remember, then I said that that was the whole story, and Charles laughed.

I was just then remembering certain things from a time when I was a boy myself. I remembered another story about a waterbird who dove down deep into the first water and pulled back up all the land and its people from the bottom. And another one about how our people came from the stars—that big hole up there that empties out all its days and nights on top of everyone like the weather. I told Charles that my father used to tell me a story about his father, about how hiding was one of the things Indians got best at once we knew it was what was required to survive, and that hiding didn't always mean hidden away, out of sight, but could mean transformation. I told Charles that his grandfather had soldiers after him, that they'd surrounded him in a cornfield. So he rolled up some tobacco in a dried corn husk, smoked that thing, and was gone. My father could have been making up a good thing to cover up the bad thing that happened. Meaning they probably shot my grandfather dead in the corn. But I didn't think stories were made to comfort. I believed what my father told me. Stories do more than comfort. They take you away and bring you back better made.

Charles told me to tell him stories about my life. I felt a swell of something flooding me, coming up to my eyes, and I turned away from him. I was ready to tell him everything. I'd wanted to tell him everything for longer than I realized until just then.

He said he wanted to know all that had happened to me before he got here. I was about to tell him when Charles said he heard someone calling his name, then we heard a knock at the door. It was Bear Shield's daughter, Opal. She was a couple of years older than Charles, but they were friends, so this knock wasn't out of the ordinary, as Bear Shield's allotment land was not far from ours. Opal hadn't come over to play but to tell me they were having a ceremony, that her mother was sick. That was all she told me, but I knew. She'd been sick before. Something had been eating away at her over the years. It'd been getting worse. Bear Shield had met her before he left for the prison-castle, and they married when he returned.

Opal told me that her father said to tell me it would be at the same place as that one meeting I went to. That one.

Not far from the Mennonite church, there lived a very short, very kind white man who allowed Indians to do their ceremonies at the back of his property, just beyond a line of cottonwoods. Bear Shield told me the morning after my first and only ceremony that he'd befriended the man at the post office, and that his piece of land had been secured in the Land Run of 1889 by his brother, who happened to race horses and was also short, was a jockey, which was how he won the race for the land, with not a racehorse in this instance but a camel he found wandering the deserts of Texas, which the U.S. Army had brought over from Saudi Arabia during the Civil War, then set free when the war was over.

I knew right away that I had to go to the ceremony. But also that I'd been a part of stopping such ceremonies. I'd gone into tipis in the middle of the night and helped agents stomp out fires, haul men off to jail. But it felt impossible to not go, so I went.

Before I left for the ceremony, Charles came out and asked me where I was going. We're gonna go pray about Opal's mother. She's sick, I said. Charles asked if he could come. I told him he would stay with his mother, and that he should listen to her, and to be good. I told him I would be back by dinner the next evening, before the sun went down.

I lifted my gun out from its holster and checked to be sure it was loaded. It was, and there were bullets in a leather pouch that once held tobacco tied around my waist.

On the way there, from my horse, I looked up and saw a bird circling, but every time I looked through a squint to see what kind, the sun made my eyes water. Dirt kicked up from the road thick and soft, an almost fluffy, red-orange cloud of dust stirred beneath us, then stilled, meaning there was no wind here, but the towering clouds darkest at their edges a ways off told of a summer storm coming, which I'd felt in my knees earlier that morning, waiting for water to boil at the stove, I'd had to sit down, my knees felt a certain kind of way about the weather.

Most of the time if I looked at the sun it would be just that, the sun, bright and hot and normal, a circle that circled the sky and brought with it each day the chance to see again what night had made gone; the world lit up again each day was the most normal and most blessed thing to behold. But when there were clouds in the sky and the sun broke through in a flash, it would catch me off guard and bring me back to Florida, in front of that photographer, who went under the black cloth with his machine to capture us, the picture they took when we first got to the prison-castle, right next to that other one taken months later in our military uniforms, which showed up in the local newspaper. Pratt wanted to show the people what Indians could be made into. Before and after pictures was what Pratt had told us, to put them right next to each other, how we were and how we became. Civilization's pride, Pratt had said. I hated the way I looked in the photographs. In both pictures.

There weren't many roads to choose from in the El Reno area. Oklahoma itself was as flat as a Cheyenne's hand motioning out from the chest meaning: *It's good, piva.* But it wasn't good, the land going on and on without rising or falling, finding no mountains or landmarks to help you find your way; and there were too many crossroads, so that one wrong turn could lead you a long ways off from both where you started and where you were headed. My horse stopped us at a crossroad, and a hot wind came as if from the road that crossed us. I thought I heard something in the wind, something between a whistle and a voice.

Up ahead there was something moving at me. I couldn't tell what it was. I wasn't far from the white man's property.

I had seen many strange things in my life, and I'd never questioned my eyes when they'd set upon something, whether that be seeing Jesus in the dungeon of a prison-castle, or buffalo piled as high as a man for miles through a window on a train, but I'd never not believed what I was seeing. This I couldn't comprehend.

My horse reared back as the thing got closer to us. I didn't even think of reaching for my gun, just pulled at the reins to calm my horse. I remembered I'd seen one for the first time, how I even knew what a camel looked like. The nativity scene in front of the cathedral, there in St. Augustine. The three wise men followed a star riding camels and brought gifts for the newborn baby Jesus. I'd seen the re-created scene the winter after seeing Jesus in the vision after Pratt gave us the white man's medicine that made us sleep.

Me and the camel just stared at each other, there on the road, with farmland on both sides of us, the road behind and in front of us. There was a cow a ways off, staring at us. I looked into the camel's eyes, its big sad eyes, it had these thick, heavy-looking eyelids. The thing looked like it was chewing something, but I couldn't see what. Then the cow made a sound that startled the creature, which got my horse going again, and I pulled at her reins, and as we were backing away from it, the thing spit at me, and hit me right in my face. It made a hissing sound then spit again. I wiped it off my face to be able to see again. I felt sick. As I opened my eyes I saw it running at me and my horse, and the last thing I thought I saw before my head hit the ground and the world went sideways, was the camel running off with the clothes and the bleached white bones of a man long since dead hanging from the back of it.

When I came to it was already night. I would be late. But I was close. I could hear the drum.

As I got closer to the tipi, after I hitched my horse to a tree a little ways off, I heard the sound of men talking and I ducked down into a bush. From there I saw the agents, two of them looking like they were getting ready to go into the tipi to break up the ceremony. I noticed they didn't have their guns drawn. I was positioned behind them and I knew I couldn't hesitate, had to take my chance right there and then, so I got up and ran at them with my gun. They turned as I got to them and I managed to kick one and knock the other over the head with the butt of my gun. Then I kicked the one on the ground in the jaw just before he could get a shot off. I moved fast after that, running back to my horse and getting some rope. I knew the men knew who I was the minute they saw me. That I couldn't just kill them and leave their bodies there on a white man's land. So I tied them up and put them on the back of my horse, and tied their horses to mine. I would ride off with those men knowing no one could ever see them or me again, that it would be the only way no one would come after Bear Shield or his family. I would disappear these men. But I would have to disappear with them. Into another life.

Before I rode I stopped and listened to the sounds coming from the tipi. I had to lean my head in to hear better what I thought I was hearing. It was Bear Shield's daughter. She was singing. The women normally weren't allowed to sing or even speak in ceremony beyond bringing the morning water in. But Bear Shield had once told me that he didn't agree with what other men said about women in ceremony. And here she was singing in a ceremony for her mother's healing. It was the most beautiful sound I'd ever heard.

I left knowing I wouldn't be coming back. I would figure my life out on the other side of what it meant that the men were already stirring from the rain that was just now falling in big fat drops.

Richard Henry Pratt
and Charles Star ❋ *Spring*

CHAPTER FIVE

An Honest Lunatic

From a familiar perch on his porch, Richard Henry Pratt's eyes squinted then clenched against the light of the new day, shut to what shone between branches where the light shot through. When he rubbed his eyes with his knuckles, a pain hummed there, behind his eyelids but on top of them too, and even though it made them hurt more, he couldn't stop doing the clenching and the rubbing, like picking at a scab or pushing at a bruise—he was exercising his agency over the pain by controlling when and how he felt its acuity. Headaches like this were becoming more common. The ache pulsed at light, at movement, at sound, and gave a crushing pain every time he got up or sat down.

The birds sure were making a lot of noise about the morning, like it was the very first time the sun had risen. Pratt looked at the dew on the grass, and went to take in the smell of it, but couldn't get enough air in through his nose, then sniffed in too hard and swallowed a chunk of something that made him choke and cough a cough he couldn't stop for several minutes.

There was a time when Pratt would have loved the sound

of birds singing in the morning. Now, it was just noise. Now, the tenacious looping of the thrush's four-note rattle, the woodcock's terse, taut buzz, worst of all the mourning dove's cooing threnody, all of it made him want to shoot them down out of the trees, stuff them, and keep them on his mantel, as quiet as the framed photographs of family he kept up there. Pratt had been meaning to buy more birdshot for just this reason, but he could never remember such things when he was out. And wasn't this idea of shooting the birds out of the trees and then keeping them, hadn't it come from Theodore Roosevelt? Yes, that was the reason Pratt had not bought birdshot when he was in town, and was the very reason he first began to hate birds.

He'd needed more funding for the school, and in one of the many letters he wrote to then president Roosevelt, pleading his case for the Indians, for the school, he'd tried to appeal to the man's love of nature, of birds, and knew Roosevelt was— among his many conservationist efforts—trying to end the production of feather-based fashion accessories in order to preserve and protect rare and exotic birds. So Pratt had asked in his letter what the president thought of the use of feathers in Indian regalia, and might he be interested in Pratt emphasizing to the children that they instill in their people this same love of birds, to help further protect them from going extinct for what couldn't amount to more than vanity, even among the Indians, could it? What could be more vain than wearing feathers as an accessory? He said all of this and added at the end of the letter a brief, modest plea for more funding. With no other note, Roosevelt's entire response to Pratt's letter and plea had been a copy of a publication of his from 1879 called *Notes on Some of the Birds of Oyster Bay, Long Island*. It was a diminutive publication, not even an article, published while Roosevelt was at

Harvard, consisting of his notes about the birds he saw and shot near where he lived, in which he wrote passages such as the following: "One shot June, 1876, in a wet thicket. It was almost blown to pieces by the discharge, but there was enough left easily to identify it."

Pratt had kept the publication, as well as a copy of the newspaper the day the man died. And while Pratt had wished the man dead at one point, he hadn't kept the paper to relish in the fact of it. It seemed a piece of history. As was another day involving Roosevelt, which Pratt returned to again and again, in his mind, with all of the time he had in his retirement, to sit and stew and remember about his time with the Indians.

Pratt had known about Roosevelt's plan to use Indians for his inaugural parade, but he only came to find the extent to which he used them in the paper. This was a little under a year after Pratt had been forced into an early retirement, before the perch or porch was familiar, back when he saw only through a smoldering. Ashes regularly rained down upon him then, or so it felt, as if a great and terrible volcano had erupted miles away. He tried to throw the newspaper then, and even it, even gravity, resisted him—the paper falling back and forth like a feather.

They were not Pratt's Indians but the children of Indian men like American Horse, who was there, in the parade, as was Quanah Parker, even Geronimo, all of them leading the young Carlisle Indian students in a procession designed to represent American progress. It was Roosevelt leading the image of the old Indian and the new, progress in a procession, with the old ones up front on horseback in regalia, and the students following in march step, short-haired and uniformed, sharply lacking the wildness of feathers and horses beneath them. Rounding up the parade was Roosevelt's cowboy brigade, with their wide-brimmed hats, neckerchiefs, and six-shooters; all of them there to celebrate the nation's new cowboy leader. Teddy Roosevelt had ridden with the Rough Riders as volunteer militia in the Spanish-American War, and he'd written about it, being an obscenely prolific writer, how he'd fought with western frontiersmen, cowboys and Indians alike. He was sometimes even called simply the Rough Rider. Pratt hated just how much Roosevelt managed to publish, when Pratt could publish almost nothing.

The newspapers had called Pratt an honest lunatic for what he'd done with the Indians, the fervor with which he went at reforming the Indians at Carlisle. Celebrating Roosevelt's conquering of Indian people in his parade by way of showing their progress using Carlisle Indian students was most painful for Pratt because of how little support the Bull Moose had shown whenever Pratt had asked, and then for Pratt's work to be used as it had, to bring in those famous chiefs and display Pratt's emerging Indian children become men and women born of the school and Pratt's own lifework, well wasn't that the guts of it all. That was the way Pratt liked to sum up subjects he thought rather gruesome to think about, having first thought of it while fighting in the Civil War, and seeing for the first time the wet pink bloody guts of men coming out of them, thinking: So that's what's behind everything, what we're made of. The guts of it all.

When asked why Roosevelt had invited the cowboys and the Indians, why he'd invited the famous rebel Indian Geronimo, who'd murdered so many Americans, Roosevelt was cited in the paper as saying simply, "I wanted to give the people a good show."

Pratt spat, sitting there on his porch, he spat then spat

again, thinking about Roosevelt, and the parade. He didn't like the look of his spit in the dirt. The bubbled blobs made the dirt look dirtier. Spitting wasn't getting what he needed to get out, out. He spat about all that hadn't happened, which he'd become exceedingly, excruciatingly aware would never happen, all that he'd fought so hard for, to make the country see the worthiness of Indians, not the show, not for the show of it, as Roosevelt had orchestrated in his inauguration, or the country itself, its Constitution, its Bill of Rights, men being created equal. What the spitting was really about was Pratt not being any different from Roosevelt. He didn't want to know that he knew he was the same as Roosevelt, putting on a show to ultimately wield power for control, and though this fact existed in his head as a truth, it was kept a kind of secret, which hurt to keep, which hurt to carry, like so many unspoken truths one privately knew one really didn't want to know about oneself.

And so he was the spitting image of the man, if not in terms of sight then in behavior certainly. The spitting was about the bitter taste of deeply knowing the fact of it. The spitting was to get his own taste out of his own mouth. It was knowing he couldn't. He swallowed his spit wrong, which made him cough, and as he coughed he thought of those orchestrated photographs for the newspaper when he was establishing Carlisle, and the ones before that at the prison-castle in Florida, those side-by-side shots of the Indians, the before and after. There with their blankets and long hair on the left, and then again on the right with short hair and in uniform. Before and aftermath more like it. There was something so horrible and true about those photographs, true about what Pratt had done to the Indians, and true about how he'd done it exactly the same way Roosevelt had. For the show.

There'd been a dark hymn somewhere in him, the song unsung because it remained in him, and so it bothered him, made him restless, made him want to go out into the world and do something with it. Such a hymn had come from his mother before, he'd been able to hear her singing in the distance, in other rooms, on the other sides of walls or doors, sometimes across the street as if in another house, always in the distance, so that he'd have to lean into the sound to hear, and, always, when he did it would go away, for years after she died, her dark lament, but this was something new, some newness rising up, not yet even in his throat. The song was unsung because no one had ever seen through to what his vision entailed, his plan for the Indians. Stuck home in retirement all these years without having seen his vision come to be, those feelings and energies sunk below the surface, made a new life in him there, first as a kind of rotting, then as a rooting, then as new growth, first as limb and then as lyric, but trapped in him, as he'd felt trapped in his house, on his porch, waiting for what he didn't know.

And then there came in the mail his answer. It was from a Carlisle student, not one there while Pratt was superintendent. His name was Charles Star. He was the son of one of the prisoners at Fort Marion. Star had apparently become Jude Star after his time at the prison-castle, and had a son whom he sent to Pratt's school. Jude Star had been a mute, and Pratt had assigned him to be trained as a bread maker. He remembered the Indian well. Charles Star was asking if Pratt, should he find himself in California, if he wouldn't mind giving him an interview. He was writing a book that included his father's time at Fort Marion. A book that would then also include Pratt. What kind of book? he wondered to himself out loud. But Pratt would never again just find himself in California. The last time he'd been there he'd gone with the football team, and that was more than twenty years ago. He was ready to file the letter away with other letters from Indians he didn't know how to answer. There were countless letters from Indians, most of them happy Indians, but some unhappy ones, especially after he'd had a survey sent out to graduates from Carlisle, satisfaction surveys. There were far more letters he answered. Pratt kept correspondence with his loving and faithful Indians, who had seen the wisdom and unavoidable nature of his position as jailer then superintendent. For the letters he couldn't answer, that he knew he would never answer, they went into a section of his filing cabinet he'd called dead letter mail, of which he knew there existed an office after trying to track down some mail he'd sent out he believed he'd both sent to the wrong address and failed to write a return address—these being the very qualifications for dead letter mail.

Then he came across the piece of mail that gave him his plan. It was an announcement from San Francisco, about his great-grandson being born, a birth announcement, another Richard Henry Pratt, his son Mason's son Richard Henry Pratt was having a son and was naming him Richard Henry Pratt. He looked at the address on Charles Star's letter and started saying the name of the town out loud.

CHAPTER SIX

Over There

Charles Star's memories come and go as they please. They are a broken mirror, through which he only ever sees himself in pieces. He doesn't know that it is true of everyone, of memory itself, that it is a centerless map and, for those who risk too much looking back at their lives, a trap.

He has forgotten that he has forgotten things on purpose. This is how he has hidden them away from himself. He suspects there must be something worse beneath the worst of what he knows happened to him at the school, the haircuts and the scrubbings and the marches, the beatings and starvation and confinement, the countless methods of shaming him for continuing to be an Indian despite their tireless efforts at educating and Christianizing and civilizing him. Not every teacher. Not every schoolmaster. He was even teased and shamed by some of the other Indian children for being half white.

There is something deeper down, doing its dark work on him, some further forgotten thing, but what is it? His life is about knowing it is there but not ever wanting to see it. It is to be a kind of secret, kept over there, way over there, as he's heard other Indian people say in prayer, referring to time, referring to a past long ago but not that long ago, when things were better for Indians, when praying was free of this plea, this begging, this *please God have mercy on us haven't we suffered enough* kind of way it'd become for so many Indian people out there in the world, wherever he saw them, having traveled the country by train after finally leaving the school for good, sitting up in tipis all over, seeing how far the peyote had made it since coming up from Mexico, so far, in fact, it seemed to Charles the ceremonies and the way people talked and prayed, it was as if they'd never been without it.

He left the school the way one left a war, and for a long time he didn't know where he was going. At some point along the way it became about finding his father, or finding out what happened to his father, who'd gone missing before he got sent off to the school, was part of the reason he got sent off to the school, when his father disappeared and his mother left to do missionary work on the other side of the world, where those poor souls possibly hadn't even heard the name Jesus spoken once yet, and Charles Star was left without anyone but his friend, Opal Bear Shield, who went off to the school with him, whose father left in the same way Charles's mother had, for God, to go off and pray for other people.

The first time he ran away from the school he didn't go anywhere. He stayed nearby, hid in an apple orchard and subsisted on apples alone. It was summer, so the weather was good. Charles hid in the trees and watched from far off the goings-on of the school. He watched them look for him. He understood it all differently from afar.

After a couple of days, when he'd eaten so many apples he thought he might become one, he snuck closer and closer, until he was finally caught peeking in through the window of the dining hall. He can't even remember what his punishment was that first time.

In one of his earliest memories, Charles is in church crying with his arms reaching to his mother, he is asking her to lift him up, he is asking his mother to lift him up to where she is standing so that he can see the man in front preaching to them at a pitch approaching a scream about the Almighty, the Lord, their Savior, God the Father. Charles sees his mother not looking at or noticing him there just beyond the end of his reaching hands, she is reaching with her hands too. She is crying for the Lord to lift her up. She is aimed at the double-sided cross at the front of the church, with two Jesuses, one facing the people and the other facing the sweaty white preacher with his gut hung over his belt like some swollen tongue.

The second time he ran away from the school he ran as far as his legs would carry him. It was only a couple of weeks after the first time, so the weather was still nice. He followed a creek that brought him to a lake where he swam and managed to catch a fish with his bare hands, which he realized he couldn't cook since he didn't have a fire and didn't know how to make one. He'd packed apples, so he ate those again. Charles felt for the first time in his life, when it was getting darker, that something was stalking him, that he was being hunted. The feeling only grew as the night got darker. He decided he stood the best chance near the water, that he could jump in and swim if it came down to it. Go under and hold his breath. Swimming was something he learned early and did as often as he could. He was a fast swimmer. And surely the thing hunting him was not, as no big animals that lived on land were good in the water, were they?

This time he'd brought a blanket with him and lay under it at the lakeshore listening, waiting for the sun to come back. He thought he saw a wolf with yellow eyes watching him in the bushes, but then snapped awake just as the sun was beginning to come up. He went back to Carlisle willingly, sick of apples and so afraid of the wolf he swore he'd never run away again, which he knew, just like that boy in the story he'd heard at school, the one who cried wolf, that even while he was making the promise to himself to never run away again, that it was a lie.

Just now he is in a dream he doesn't know is a dream, which makes it real, though it weaves him across the years, impossibly, he believes it is real and so it is, but only as true as his belief that he is being followed, a belief that stuck around since the wolf, a belief that follows him in dreams as in life, and worse, sometimes he thinks he is following himself, that all his actions are predetermined, and that he is a kind of shadow, watching himself do everything after the fact, a kind of echo, in which he is only watching, only the sound already bouncing off the walls of a canyon, from where he has called out from the valley floor once again for help.

This is the fault of his morphine tincture, the fault of his habit, the fault of the laudanum. He'd taken to calling it his medicine even though he'd long since known it didn't do him any good. Dreams are that way too. Not necessarily good or bad, just so strange and specific as to feel true.

He is on the train. Riding that iron horse, almost falling asleep, or just waking up, assuming either way that he definitely isn't dreaming, cut by the grip of the iron chains at his wrists and ankles, the shackles eating away at his skin, there where the metal bites the bone each time the train bounces. The dream is made of his father's memories, from stories his father told him in a letter Opal gave him that his father sent to her father, a letter meant for Charles, which reached him at the school and got into his head like a song.

When he first got put on a train to the school, after his mother announced she would be leaving to do her missionary work, just weeks after the night his father left for ceremony and never came back, the roar of the train was so loud he thought there was something coming out of his ears, so he held his hands against them and tried not to think of an iron horse carrying them inside it, him and Opal and the rest of the children off to an iron world, where everything was too hard to not end up hardening them, and too heavy to not end up crushing them.

The train roars and clatters, set in a groove of metal tracks that stretch across and alongside rivers that snake alongside him, the tracks move not under but through mountains in tunnels so dark he can't even think about seeing when he is in them.

When the light comes back into the train he looks down and sees where the reach of his hair meets with chain, watches his braids sway. Outside he sees the buffalo carcasses stripped of their hides, and beyond them the bones of buffalo piled up as far as he can see, and in the distance like an approaching storm cloud, countless vultures coming to swarm the waste. It is the end of a world out there.

Coming out of a tunnel he sees the light hit the inside of the train and it is him and the children again, but they are headed for the mouth of a creature too big to see past its massive body, which stretches in every direction, like a mountain but with limbs that stretch and begin to reach inside the windows of the train just before they are swallowed by the darkness once again.

When he emerges from the darkness he hears someone yelling about arriving in Washington. That name that stands for the first president and for the nation itself, the way of Washington was what Indians were supposed to acquiesce to, for their own good. Assimilation was one of the words they used for Indians becoming white in order to survive, in order that they might not be killed for being Indians. The train is stopped but the doors aren't opening. The children are gone and everyone on the train is white.

There was a time when every white man looked the same to him. When he went all over the country on trains after he got away from the school, in addition to meeting so many other kinds of Indians in ceremony, he met more kinds of whites than he knew existed. There were the American whites of course, with their ties to the original colonies, or to the people on the boats that first came, the German Mennonite whites in Oklahoma, that one Scotch-Irish white he met riding his first freight train, they hid together, and he shared his strange, mushy food that he kept in jars in his suitcase, and then the many other whites he met on trains, these hobo whites. He'd heard the word hobo used for travelers, heard it was short for homeward bound, or homeless boy, or Hoboken having something to do with New Jersey. There were Swiss Italian whites, and Polish whites, French whites and British Isle whites, Swiss and Dutch whites, and many of them mixes of different kinds of whites with sordid or noble pasts, depending on the story they were telling, what they were trying to get out of it, to pass the time or ask a favor. He liked some of them, the people themselves or their stories, and hated others. He wanted to know how he was or was not one of these whites, how he could be an Indian and a white and some kind of American.

Everyone here on this train is wearing a hat and suit, it seems. He knows why he is here. Where he has seen them before. He is going to see about the man the parade is for. He reaches down without even thinking, and there it is—a gun in his boot.

As he nears the president's horse-drawn carriage, he runs behind the Indian children in military uniform. He creeps up behind the painted Indians on horseback. He is as if moving through centuries, then goes to kill the man parading its stolenness as victorious progress. At the horse-drawn carriage, he jumps on the back of one of those horses, aims at the man's head, and shoots him square in the face, or so he thinks, as he watches his body slump down in that familiar way the dead go dead when they're dead, but then the man's body without its head intact sits up straight, and out of the hole where Charles shot the man comes laughter.

Charles stirs in his chair where he has drifted. He knows he is there in the room. But intoxication can mean more than the room it is in. The room you are in can be made gone. You can be made the room to house the drink you are drinking. He is in his shack there at the back of the orchard, wasted like so much fallen fruit.

·   ·

CHAPTER SEVEN

San Francisco

The train ride is bumpier than Pratt remembers any train ride ever being. So is it age then? Looser skin and brittler bones, he has to wonder. He'd ridden on so many trains over the years, sometimes in dire circumstances. On the train to Fort Marion in 1875, the very onset of his time with the Indians, Pratt had to free an Indian named Gray Beard from a self-made noose of cloth—which the once great chief had tied to a metal guard for luggage. Gray Beard was shot and killed trying to escape not long after that. On Pratt's order. Should he have let the poor Indian go? It wasn't his charge to decide the fate of these Indians. Not yet. He was to escort prisoners of war to Florida. Those were his orders. Following orders was who he was, wasn't it?

Pratt drops the word tool in his head with a clatter. He'd been forced to retire from the military twenty years ago. So where had following orders gotten him in the end?

Pratt had been living deep in the struggle since smallpox left its marks. It'd gotten so bad for Pratt, when the disease was with him, before the lifelong scars would later remind him how close he'd come to dying, that an undertaker had come to take the measurements for his coffin, and his father had plainly told the guy when he came that his son would in fact not be dying.

"Deep in the struggle" was a phrase that had come to Pratt regarding the Indians, but at some point along the way he adopted it for himself: To be human was to struggle, and to be a good human was to struggle gracefully, which required first being deep in the struggle, only from there could one transcend the struggle in a meaningful way. He believed wholeheartedly that all Indians were men, it was simply a matter of educational opportunities, military discipline, red-blooded, muscular Christianity, these would shore them up, and, like the men who came and made this country, the Indians just needed to bear their cross, to cross the waters of discipline and manners, swim through their past, as they had swum in the Florida waters near the prison-castle so many years ago. It was as if it were a different life, they'd become guardians of their own prison and its prisoners, in actuality as guards for the actual prison as well as men guarding themselves against the Indians inside, against their blanket ways. It was simply that they needed to arrive at themselves and begin their nations anew.

Pratt gets off of the train more easily than he'd boarded it. The smell of the ocean, the sheer breadth, the wind and roar of the place, it all takes Pratt's breath away the moment he steps off the train. And sure it is not New York City. In New York, you were on the inside of another New York embedded in yet another New York as soon as you stepped off the train. You couldn't see past the thing. The sky disappeared. From beneath its mass, you looked up and were made dizzy by its heights and how tightly packed it all was, but this, this is elegance, it lets your eyes breathe. Pratt crosses his arms against a breeze that doesn't let up.

He feels tired like he'd never felt tired before. It is a brutal exhaustion, like it could be terminal, like if he doesn't sleep soon he will die.

At Mason's home he can hear children in the backyard playing even as he walks through the front door. Mason has done well for himself. The quality of the wood alone on the banisters. The marble stairs. Marion is there too. She hugs Pratt harder than he would have liked. And then the children come rushing through the back door, clomping, and a baby is crying, and he knows this is Richard Henry Pratt III.

They put the infant in his arms, and the world begins to topple. He wants to be held the way he is holding the baby, but by someone more sturdy, someone with youthful energy, able to carry him wherever he needs to go, feed him when he is hungry. Pratt is smiling down at the infant who seems to him then the ugliest creature he's ever seen in his life, red and now crying and splotchy, and he knows they all mean well, and that they've missed him. He is only seeing through his exhaustion. Finally it is Mason who tells everyone to let the man get to his room and catch his breath. When Pratt finally gets into the guest bedroom, he collapses onto the bed and feels as if he is fast asleep before his head hits the pillow. He dreams of an unending earthquake. Pratt had been thinking of earthquakes, having read a story about the 1905 earthquake, which the great opera singer Enrico Caruso had been in, and people believed to have started just after he'd belted out an aria in the halls of the hotel he was staying in. Pratt thought it was foolish to put the two things together, but he liked the story. And the dream was only remarkable to Pratt because his dream life was essentially unlived, because he never remembered his dreams, became uncomfortable when people wanted to relay their dreams to him or to anyone else, felt the world over there, on the other side of sleep, was not to be trusted, or was made for children alone, but he got it then, that morning when he woke up remembering his time at sea, the deep rumbling of the earth, the way the end of the world had brought everyone together, made them forget their differences in order to survive the great quaking together, he understood the draw of dreams, the life he'd been missing out on. In the dream about the quake that doesn't end, there is no break and no rest from the quake, that is just what life is like anymore, a quaking, and everyone moves onto boats, lives on the water, fishes, and watches all the buildings on the land they'd ever erected slowly crumble to dust.

— • • —

CHAPTER EIGHT

Nape

Charles Star shoots up out of bed and leaves without having thought of a thing but the song in his head. Enrico Caruso's voice is singing, *Johnny, get your gun, get your gun, get your gun.* It is stuck in a loop as he leaves his shack and heads off the property and out into the street.

The plan to rob general stores started as a joke to Opal. They were wearing masks because of the Spanish flu. He said they looked like bank robbers. It was from there that the idea grew on him. He couldn't live his whole life in the orchard shack. But robbing general stores would only work temporarily. The real plan, the one he'd told Opal about, was to save enough to take a train up north. He told her he'd heard of a town where Indians are well respected. In his telling of the town to Opal, of the plan, he'd said he'd been there, so that she'd believe it. Opal had told him to save his lies, and that had really got the fight going. Charles lost his temper, threw a lantern, and she'd accused him of trying to burn them down. He laughed at that. He liked that. The idea that he could burn them down. She told him it was cruel to laugh, then she left. He was finished.

That was what he thought as he was stamping out the small fire there in the corner of the shack. His mind, through their love, had always felt less buried come morning, when she'd leave for work before the sun rose.

He has his mask with him but he won't wear it until just before entering the store. It's been years since everyone wore masks everywhere, years since the Spanish flu. He realized he preferred to cover his face. He hates his face. The freckles. Despises them. They look like mistakes. They are from his mother. His aquiline nose and round face are from his father. He can more easily pass for white with a mask on. He was wearing a mask when he got the job he has, and believes the old man thought he was white when he first hired Charles to take care of his horses and orchard. He waves to the old man now as he leaves. The old man looks at him but doesn't acknowledge him in any way, just lights and smokes his pipe.

Charles Star keeps his head down, minds his own business, committing all the time he can to writing. But his idea of becoming a writer was compromised by his love of the laudanum, submitting himself to that doomed God of dream in the tincture, the old dream of becoming a writer drifted so deep into the background, mostly he didn't even notice it anymore.

He'd first seen laudanum advertised all different kinds of ways. As an elixir. A soothing syrup. Once he saw it called the poor child's doctor. Another time it was advertised for teething babies. The advertisements—not unlike songs that got stuck in his head—made him believe in a promise explicitly made, because repetition came to resemble a promise. The laudanum was disgusting at first, and then it went tasteless, and then the taste made a warmth, a comfort, of temperature and emotion.

He came to love the feeling and taste, as he loved his spoon, with its floral design on the handle, and deep bowl to hold the good amount. The way the pain receded felt like a draining and a filling at once. His lantern-lit, hoodlike eyelids would droop halfway over his eyes, and he'd remember nothing. Sleep came like a blow to the head. When you push it down, when you go to kill memory, it finds its ways to haunt you.

It is morning, but still that deep blue of night, the moon buried behind clouds, with rain coming down some but looking to clear up soon. Charles's hat does not block the rain from the back of his neck, which is the only part of being rained on that he hates. He prefers to not think about where this hatred comes from. He is acutely sensitive there, and feels there is something important about his sensitivity, about the connection of the head, where the mouth and eyes and ears connect to the body, which brings him everywhere he needs to go like a horse. He keeps the memory away from his thoughts, and is only reminded when something like rain touches the back of his neck, there where a man first held him down, gripped the back of his neck so hard his legs gave out on the floor of the bathroom of the boys' quarters at Carlisle. This is the memory he keeps but doesn't see, the one that lives in him, in a room he has all but abandoned.

The next store Charles decides to rob is in North Oakland. It's the Piggly Wiggly. He's always hated the name of the store. The old man behind the counter doesn't even notice him standing there with a mask on and a gun out, holding a sack but not yet having told the man to put the money in the bag. The old man cocks his head like he doesn't understand. He is playing stupid. Charles only has to move the gun a little closer to the old man's temple.

"You Indians," the old man says as he puts cash in the cotton sack. Charles feels good that he is being recognized as Indian. "That's why you lost. No respect for law and order. A bunch of wild animals," he says, and coughs, then really goes into a coughing fit, and Charles can't tell if the man's got some chronic problem or if he's trying to make noise, to stall, then Charles hears something in the back of the store, not a voice but a crack, as in someone's joint, a knee perhaps, followed by some rustling, so he gestures with his gun for the old man to hurry.

"Let an old man cough," the old man says between coughs. "At least be a decent criminal," he says, and as he laughs to himself the cough settles down.

"Enough," Charles says. And he doesn't know what he means by it.

"If someone's fixing to come out here they better do it soon," the old man says, and tries to yank back the sack before Charles can get a good grip, but it is too late and the old man pulls at nothing, then falls back from the force of it, crashing into all the stacked mess he has back there behind the counter. Charles hears the gun's boom before he feels any different. And he is able to walk away from the store without a chase, not even the old man's voice coming after him, with the bag of cash in his hand, appreciating the weight of it, before he reaches with his other hand to where he begins to feel at first a throbbing, and finds there where the bullet went in, little rivulets of blood coming out over his hand.

On the walk home he feels so light-headed he thinks he is floating. He thinks of Opal. They haven't seen each other in weeks. He misses her voice. The way her voice sounded he knew in his heart, as if for the first time just then, it was the sweetest sound, not just because of the tone, or because of how patient she'd always been with him, never turning her tone on him to indicate even a trace of resentment, but the quality of her voice like the quality of water when your throat needs most to feel it moving down into your body, which has been too dry for too long, this whole world without enough sweetness and quenching, all this hate and desperation, but Opal with her love for him, it had meant more to him than he allowed himself to feel until just then, when it was too late, and he hadn't returned the feeling, hadn't shown her the way he felt or acted accordingly, and so, even if he'd known her the longest he'd known anyone, and had considered her the truest person he'd ever met, actually because of this, he did not deserve her. She would be better off without him, is the thought he has before a darkness gathers in his periphery, but just before he goes he sees an Indian girl running into it, into the darkness, barefoot, as if into a forest, leading him away from the pain he'd been running from for too long.

———— • • ————

CHAPTER NINE

No Better Plan

Pratt spends his first day in San Francisco nursing a cold. He goes to find Charles Star the next day. It is late in the afternoon. Why is he more worried the closer he gets to the shack at the back of the orchard? Why is he patting his side to feel for his gun as he approaches the door? It is so quiet. If Charles Star is home, he must be asleep.

Pratt hears a dry leaf crunch and turns around to see an old dog who doesn't much care what Pratt is up to. The dog doesn't have a tail, and one of its eyes is gone. Pratt reaches for his gun but does not pull it from its holster. He knocks on the door of the shack. Once. Twice. One more time turning his fist sideways to change from a knock to a bang. A golden light shines through the orchard from the west. The air smells sweet, and he feels promise in the light shining from the west, a dying light, but a promise nonetheless.

Something is wrong.

Upon entering he knows right away he shouldn't have come. And here is the Indian, dead on the floor. Bled out. He steps toward a writing desk where he thinks he sees his own name on the page in the typewriter and immediately regrets it as he steps into the blood. Which is when he sees cash spilling out of a bag there next to the body. And then he knows something more wrong than he cares to find out has happened here. And that he should leave. Pratt leaves the shack at once and the dog barks at him as he walks out, which makes him walk faster, away from the shack, and the sun has sunken and it is almost night and he feels absolutely cursed but also sick, as if what he just witnessed brought back the cold he'd beat, and he coughs, and sees blood on his hand as he moves it back from his mouth.

Pratt was staring out the window at the San Francisco Bay, at the fog and the seagulls flittering in and out of a gray-white sheen. Was his son Mason there, had he asked his father a question, said something about the Indians? There was no better plan. That was the only thing he could say, that sentence, but also the feeling, that Pratt had done all that he could, and that he was saying all that he could say on the matter, that the Indians got their chance with Pratt's help, and that the U.S. government got their chance with Pratt's help, and if nothing else could come of it than what came of it, if the Indians didn't turn out okay, and the U.S. government could not see the Indian race for what they were, see their potential and give them what should have been their right, then it couldn't be his fault because there was no better plan.

But there he was possibly dying from what? Facing the white wall in the white room in a military hospital so far from home, his son Mason standing there, beaming at him like a lighthouse.

Did he want to figure out shore, or did it feel right to drift into whatever had landed him here in this hospital bed, he didn't know. Mason.

If only he could have convinced the Indian boy that there was no better way for it to have gone, Pratt's attempted deliverance of the Indians from themselves to themselves, no better plan for America, no better plan for the Indians, no better plan, there was no better plan than that, he said to no one, and faced the wall, and died.

Pratt would later be moved to Arlington National Cemetery, and at the bottom of his tombstone it reads: "Erected in loving memory by his students and other Indians."

———•·•———

CHAPTER TEN

Everything Blue

Charles Star was writing again. He didn't know it would be the last time.

It was the morning before the morning he would wake up to rob a general store. He was trying to convince himself of something. That he would die soon. That he would not.

What was he writing?

There were connected points, events, and the people he'd come from that he wanted to try to say without delivering them into the vanishing, where it was assumed his people were headed.

Everything had become so muddied, so filthy feeling, his own skin, spattered with mud from the mess they made, his parents by mixing their blood and making him.

Surely there was a story he was a part of, that spoke to the purpose of his life?

But the answer to why anyone had come here to live and to die was never clear. Nor why some died too soon and others went way past their ripening, who looked like rotting fruit fallen from the tree.

Most days he just let the laudanum do what it would do to him, which he would have trouble remembering later, and hate himself for not being able to stop wiping out his own memory. Sometimes in his effort to get rid of memory, all that was left was the deep past. So then he'd be thinking about his people.

His tribe was in Oklahoma, and there were no parents left to speak of. He'd never found his father, and his mother was surely worshipping God in whatever part of the world Jesus was not yet said to be their lord and savior.

Charles had never known a God.

He'd wanted to. God felt more to him like a hole than a presence.

He knew something holy was happening to everyone even while life could feel a hell of a lot like hell.

There were other people. People who hadn't made you who ended up making you. There was Opal. There had always been Opal.

The purity of her voice, her sound mind, she was a stone.

But he felt his entire worth gone, despite having Opal; she couldn't be had, she was her own, and so did everyone belong to themselves and to themselves alone.

He just then as if suddenly felt like he belonged to the thing that he was doing, this writing or thinking or being at the page, which felt like both doing and waiting.

He wondered then if all waiting didn't require some amount of faith. If all of life was waiting. Waiting for what?

He felt then that everything was blue, the blue of sky and the blue of starlight but also deep inside the blue of vein and bruise and song; it lived in him—the blue smoke he'd read about in a letter from his father about first running away from a massacre.

He didn't know anyone else like him, so he was that thing more than alone, lost even to himself, yet here he was, here he remained, even now as he was feeling he would go, leave the world. Was it only a feeling that he would die or did the feeling mean more than the feeling?

He felt then his body was a metaphor, human history some elaborate hoax, the world made against itself, split in half everywhere with its good and evil, love and hate, day and night, dream and waking, heaven and hell, Indians and men.

He was once a child, an Indian child in Indian country, then his people put him on a train to the school, then the school took him further past himself and left him somewhere he couldn't find his way back from.

He felt something bulging in him. He felt pregnant with death.

And so tired of enduring.

The wolf was still following him. That wicked dog of need inside.

The laudanum tincture, that alcohol and morphine mixture, infused with powdered gold and pearls, it had done something to his mind. Something he couldn't get back unless he stopped using it. Spooning it into his mouth.

He'd just been trying to make himself feel better. Had that been it? Had that been what everyone had been trying to do about being alive? Find whatever made them feel better about the hells sure to visit the seasons of their lives again and again? There was more. Something more. What was it?

He would not die. He thought then. He would get the money, and with Opal find what it was that made everything make sense—love or peace or just a little place to live near where he could hear water and the birds singing in the morning when he woke next to her and perhaps their children. Was it hope then he felt in his heart or disappointment? He couldn't tell. It was heavy. Hope could feel heavy too. He looked at his spoon, then out the window at the sun.

Opal Viola ✳ *Summer*

———— • • ————

CHAPTER ELEVEN

Bloom

Your father and I had gotten into a big fight, and I'd stayed away from him for weeks because of it, but then the woman I worked for found out about you and I came down the hill ready to leave with him straightaway if he was ready. Brave fool that he was, your father had been robbing general stores even though I told him to stop, that he was going to get himself killed doing that kind of thing. I felt something deep down like a bad memory surfacing as I approached his shack, there at the back of the orchard he took care of for the old man I knew to be related to the Havens, Mr. Haven's uncle, I believe. I never wanted him to see me come or go, but especially not after what had just happened with Mrs. Haven finding out about you.

I almost didn't knock, almost turned around and left, so bad did it feel in my stomach approaching the door. Then when I did knock there was no answer. When I heard a dog whimpering behind the door I opened it, and there was the Havens' dog, Cholly. There was a sack of money spilled out, a big pool of your father's blood, and boot prints in the blood going out of the shack. Had I the time I might have wondered who came and saw your father's dead body, they had stepped in his blood, after all, and the money, then left it like that, but I knew I needed to move if I stood a chance at getting away with the money, knew whoever came was probably coming back. I took the stack of written pages sitting next to your father's typewriter on his desk.

We were going to run off somewhere. We were going to make a life together. I didn't see that your father never meant to do anything but drink his laudanum and drift until I saw his eyes open when they shouldn't have been, looking at nothing, before I picked him up, and with all my strength, maybe even some of yours, hoisted him on the horse's back and got out of that place. We came up along the creek, where there are paths made by people and deer. I followed a deer path to where we are now, here to rest. Navigating this horse along these narrow, winding paths with your father on top of it is no small feat. I have little experience with horses, but this is your father's horse, and perhaps because even he is still here with us, perhaps because the horse knows he is not, perhaps too because the horse knows that I am with you, there is grace in the way she leads us.

Listen. I speak to you in my heart, and as we share one body now, trust you'll find a way to hear this. I can remember my mother speaking to me in some tongue I never heard again, some deep underwater sound inside and outside of me at once. She thought and felt at me and it was language. I can remember before the water left, before air entered my chest, when all light was pink and blue and purple-black.

I feel wild now, with you, out here with your father's body. We must try to find a way for him to make it home, across that river in the sky.

I speak to you here in your becoming alive, and I speak to

him in his leaving the living. We must reach to the living before they are alive, which is like reaching the river before it arrives, just as we must keep in reach of the dead even when they seem to be gone, which is like following the water lines after they've dried.

I need to tell you about your father so that you might come to know him. He is making his way over there, on his journey home, and the dead want to be remembered before they journey home. And yes he will be gone once he goes, but the dead are never far. They find us in dreams, and keep teaching us from the inside long after they go, so you might come to find each other, in some blue-white field, or overgrown underbrush, or beneath a forest home you'll remember but have never known. Your father's name was Charles Star. I never knew his Indian name. His Cheyenne name. I'm honestly not sure if he ever got one. Some of the kids at Carlisle called him Charlie, meaning Charlie Chaplin. I don't know why. He was clumsy, and perhaps occasionally his attempt at recovering from his clumsiness resembled a silent-movie actor like Charlie Chaplin. There was grace in the way his falls felt controlled, I thought. I suspect it was also because your father was half white. He didn't mind, even though they meant it mean, because your father loved Chaplin's films, loved all films, going to the theater, when we were in Oakland, whenever we could. He even played the piano for silent films, when the old man he worked for was too drunk, or if he'd forget what day it was, your father would go down wearing the old man's ridiculous top hat and play. He'd learned how to play the piano at Carlisle, but he'd found his own way into the instrument at some point, because I was there at one of his performances, he was playing music for a Chaplin film, and though what he played didn't match the feeling of the film exactly, the mood and the sadness he brought to Chaplin's performance made the whole thing feel incredibly tragic, with just the right amount of joy and wonder to make it go beyond tragedy.

As for me, I came into this world without a name. Didn't even cry or hardly make a sound for years. Quiet as a stone was what my mother told me once I was named Opal and old enough to ask her why. It's this stone, she said, and put her hand to her heart. I thought she meant her heart was a stone, but she pulled out the stone for me to see, the one I was named after, it was the only time I ever saw it. It seemed to me that every color in existence was in that stone, but it also looked mostly blue, moon and starlight blue you only see on certain nights. I asked her if I could hold it and she said no, plain as if I asked her if she could give me the sun. When I asked her what kind of stone it was, she told me it carried ancient water. At the time, I don't know why, I thought by ancient water she meant blood. My father would later tell me he'd traded a bagful of polished sea beans for it in Florida, and that he'd given it to my mother when he returned home from the prison-castle. He said there was ocean in the stone. I thought maybe it was me, that the stone became me. Then after my mother died and was gone, I remember thinking, maybe she became the stone.

Little Bird Woman is my Cheyenne name, from Bird Woman, my mother. I'm the little one that came after the first one. I would have been given a new name at some point had she not died, had I not gone off to the school. And then once I was gone, keeping the name felt like a way to keep her.

We didn't have middle names before, just as we didn't have first or last names and not even names we kept, necessarily, we might keep getting new names as we changed. Your father gave me my middle name. We sang in a choir at the school. I was holding this note for a song in the chapel, and your father had come late. He told me later he'd waited, holding his breath, listening outside the chapel. They had us singing hymns. He said he didn't know what the sound was, and that the beauty was doing something to the sorrow. The sorrow. What sorrow did he mean? I asked him when he told me that, but he wouldn't say. He said he thought my voice was someone playing the viola, then when he realized it was me, he started calling me that. I told him not to, but he wore me down, and eventually I liked it enough to put it in the middle if I signed anything. I like that middle names can be a kind of secret. That we can have secret names. I haven't thought of yours yet.

Here at the creek, a ways off from the trail, we have blackberries for now, not as fat and sweet as they get, but I like them tart, with that little bit of red still at their tops, or if they're just a little hard and not so soft they come off when you pull at them and leave your fingers stained. The sweet and the sour together at once has been tasting better ever since you got big in me, so it must be you doing that. You are pushing out through me so that I am like a flower bud about ready to bloom you.

Here near the creek, we are trying our best not to be seen by men who could do worse than get rid of us if they find us. We won't know they're coming for us until they're coming for us, not until we get deeper upcreek, where we can see them coming from far enough off.

Where the blackberries are deep with thorn they are deep with berry, and I can gather plenty if I wade through the deeper part of the creek. I've gotten it worse from thorns. The last job I did for Mrs. Haven was to take out her rosebushes. I was to clear them all and rip their roots from deep in the

soil. Old coils of thick swirling braids of vine that whip back
at you when you go to take them out. I chopped them down
and they fell around me, scratching me as if in defense, then
I gathered the remains in a burlap sack. Everything smelled
sweet and sour. Then she had me plant new roses in place of
the old ones. Mrs. Haven wanted pink roses when what she
had before were red and white. I planted them and watered
them to sprout. She asked me about when the new roses would
come in. I told her they would bloom before she knew it. She
didn't like that answer, and said she was asking me because she
didn't want them to bloom *before* she knew it, she wanted to
know they were blooming as they bloomed. I was going to tell
her just to watch them every day, when Cholly came over and
tried to jump up at me. That was when she looked down at you.
Blooming as they bloomed, I thought.

I'm a bigger person, I am already round, and I'd been wearing baggier clothes, but I'd gotten hot from gardening and had
taken off layers, and there you were, showing, unmistakably.
She got a look in her eyes then. I didn't like what I thought she
might have in mind. I knew they'd been trying for children for
years, that she'd lost several children before they came, some as
close to being born as you are now. The first question she asked
was who the father was. I told her that we'd known each other
since childhood, that our fathers were close friends, that he
went to school with me and worked in town. None of that was
a lie. I even included that his mother was white. I don't know
why I said that. Then she asked about my intentions. I lied and
told her I would be leaving to go back to Oklahoma where I
had family who would help. I said I was sorry and that I'd been
meaning to tell her, then I made way for the servants' quarters
and she followed me. Asking more questions. How far along

was I? Did I have the means to travel back? Did I know that I could stay? She said the baby would have a good life here in California. And then she said what made me leave. *No one need know.* That's what she said. Then she said it again, this time in a whisper. *No one need know a thing.* She gripped my arm harder than she wanted to, then apologized. I thought she was saying it would be kept secret about me having a child out of wedlock. But secret from whom? I began to worry about your father's freckles. Your father being half white, would that show up in you in a way that would make people suspect it was the Havens' baby, that Mr. Haven and I . . . he also had freckles. I regretted telling her about your father, but I didn't give her time to do or say anything more. I left after excusing myself to use the bathroom. There was a back door next to the bathroom and I left immediately without bringing anything with me but you.

We are going to lay him to rest in the trees, as is Cheyenne custom, how my mother buried her mother and father, who died within a day of each other. We must bury him within four days of him dying, and I have to assume he wasn't dead for more than a day when I found him, otherwise Cholly might have already tried to drag him out of there, or run back up the hill to find me. My mother used scaffolding instead of trees, and brought their bodies up with rope, had them wrapped in blankets. I'll put your father in a tree because there are enough trees here to choose from. We will wrap him in bright colors. I do not know the ways of our people. I was too young when they took me, and then the school meant to make what I knew a sin. Everything I have left to share, to pass down to you will have to be good enough.

All I have to tell you about being Cheyenne came from my mother, before she died, and because she was dying, she spoke to me in a way, while she was dying, like I knew she wouldn't have otherwise. Not unlike the way I speak to you now. Not because I am dying but because you are on your way to being born. But what I have to give to you from her, my mother, is not more than a distant memory. I've lost parts, or I'm sure mangled them in my remembering. This is what I have to give you. And you can't even hear me, except in your heart. My mother once told me a story about a woman with a bird for a heart, who ran everywhere she went. She couldn't stop moving. Said she was restless. Our people once lived near lakes in the north. We farmed and harvested wild rice, fished. Stayed put. My mother said that woman put the bird in our people's hearts, and that's what made us go wandering off from the lakes. I thought of the story just now because you are kicking fast in me, up into my ribs, as if at my heart. It was to follow the buffalo, why we left. We were hungry. And you are kicking because you are hungry.

We need to get farther up this hill, somewhere far enough in that no one will smell the smoke, and dark enough into the night where you can't see the light of our fire. We need to eat too. We can't expect Cholly to go off and find anything for anyone but himself. But there's plenty of fruit down the hill, even on the property where your father worked, there's fruit everywhere, and here at the creek, more blackberries.

Cholly comes and goes and I believe that means he is keeping watch farther than my eyes can see. We go a long way back with dogs. Cheyenne people. Our dog soldiers went against our peacekeepers the same way our peacekeepers ended up having to eat our dogs when we got too hungry.

I don't know where the Havens got that crazy name from. Cholly. He's one of these mutts you don't know what kinds of breeds are in him and you don't much care because he seems all his own in the eyes. Well he's only got the one eye, but it's got more life in it than I've seen in some men with two. And I've seen worse men than those with no life in their eyes. It's worse when they know what they want and they're hungry for it, white men in this country, they come to take everything, even themselves, they have taken so much they have lost themselves in the taking, and what will be left of such a nation once they are done? My mother once said, "A nation is not conquered until the hearts of its women are on the ground. Then it is finished, no matter how brave its warriors, or how strong their weapons." I wondered about the women's hearts on the ground. And I wondered about American women. White women. Where were their hearts? I take solace in knowing my heart is still in my chest, that yours is in there too, beating like a drum waiting for its dancer, keeping me on my feet, ready for a rhythm, ready for what's next, because what's next is always coming.

Your father had a harder time at the school, because he was a boy but also because of his freckles, which he had on account of him being a half-breed, which meant he got it bad from both sides. No one wanted him because he didn't seem like he belonged enough on either side.

Sometimes the look on his face got so bad it seemed to be saying he didn't even belong to himself, did not even want to belong to himself.

I worked for a summer in Oakland between Carlisle and Hampton for the outing program Pratt first came up with when your grandfather was with him in Florida before Pratt started the school. Your father had run away again. He told me he would find gold in California. That was his plan. To find gold and become a writer, which both seemed equally foolish.

When I came out to work in Oakland I thought I would

make money too. But the outing matron manages all the income I make from the Havens. They gave me room and board, and after some of the other girls ran off after saving, any money we get must be approved by the outing matron, and that amounts to little more than what we can spend in an afternoon. She approves new clothes, or foods we don't normally eat, sometimes going to a matinee. I thought I would never have to see the woman again once I ran away with your father. Now I know I won't see her again but I don't know how we'll get out of this. Running seems like a means to an end when you haven't gotten away yet. And I don't even know where we will go.

Before he started talking about running away, your father had already done it more than a few times. None of us blamed him. We all imagined getting away from the school, going back home, but some of us had a harder time remembering how to get back home, and even if we did, if our people sent us away the first time, why wouldn't they just do it again? Your father wasn't trying to get back home when he ran away, just away from the school.

We both played in the marching band. Your father played the trumpet, I carried the bass drum, but he also blew the bugle in the morning for our drills.

I never did find out what happened to him the night before the morning he went out and blew his trumpet instead of his bugle, blew and blew a song that grew out of him in extended notes that called for the rising of us not out of our beds but out of our bodies.

I can't explain it well, you never can with music. I can say the notes were long and building to something the way he started it out, not completely unlike the bugle calls normally were in the morning, but then he veered off into a kind of chaos that felt wild and maybe a little uncontrolled all the way until he returned the song home to its initial call just before the men started to chase him.

He ran circles around them as if he were out on the football field, and though he ran, no longer playing his trumpet, the notes still hung in the air, in our ears, calling for us to know what he knew, that we couldn't have known, what had been done to us since we arrived, and what had been done to him while he should have been sleeping.

The song he played was not a song and not even a lament and not an alarm but like a call from a broken bird, whose throat and beak had become elongated through some trial of pain meant to break him, but only ended up transforming him into something longer stretched, and into his song with these notes that kept stretching after he stopped playing them, that sang about everything we'd been feeling all along stuck in our suits and dresses, in that school and without our language, he was making music find it for him, his lost tongue and all of ours.

As they came at him, running at him like they knew what he was doing was telling us something against them, wild and free and loose on the football field where the players were winning and the school was being celebrated like everything that happened on the field, all of the victory, like all those American victories before meant no one really could have been losing.

He used his trumpet as a weapon as they came at him, swiping with it at their faces; the thing with its curved lips and edges, its weight, it did damage, and this was the really shocking part, when he swung his trumpet, an especially hard swing caught one of the men's noses with the rim, or the lip, the curved part of the trumpet where it flares out like a flower, it caught the man we called Dr. Fuzz on account of him being so hairy, with not long but short fuzzy hair on every part of him, it caught his nose in just such a way that it pulled the thing off of him, ripped it half off to where it was dangling, or so it's what I thought I saw, and he was screaming by then, and your father stopped at that, and was then tackled because he stopped, shocked the same as any of us watching, the blood just pouring.

It landed your father six weeks in the jail, the one he spent so much time in after that, when he began running away, and really running, making a run for it, only to come back days, sometimes weeks later, wandering out there in the Pennsylvania woods, or I don't know how far he got, but he'd always end up back in that jail after, and it didn't change him or make him different, because your father only ever brought to bear anything that happened to him on himself, from the inside, as if he were the only one to blame for anything bad that ever happened to him, as if we hadn't all been imprisoned there at the school, where they kept us even from ourselves, and we lost the memories of our families.

That was the moment where all the trouble began with your father, running out and playing that song, then hurting Dr. Fuzz, that ape, who then beat him as he dragged him off, and we didn't see how badly because he was in jail for six weeks, but it must have been bad because all he did was run away after that, until he was finally all the way gone, out to California, where his addiction ended up getting the best of him, over many years, some of which I'd see for myself. Addiction was a punishment for him, one he could enjoy, which he hated and loved at once because it took everything, it allowed everything in its swallow, as his trumpet had once allowed through its blow, no more than that day when he blew and blew and ran and blew a song I would never forget, that changed me, and changed him, changed the way I'd always think of him and our time at Carlisle.

I don't know the story of how your father actually made it out to California, how he ended up in Oakland, but I'd known he was headed that way ever since finding out his father was in Oakland. His father sent my father a long letter about his life and where he'd been since he disappeared. And my father sent it to the school, to me. At times I've thought the only reason your father wanted to stay close with me was because I represented a connection to his father. He'd cried the whole way out to the school from Oklahoma, like many children did. He wasn't crying because he was being taken from his home or from his parents, as many children did, but because if his father came back from wherever he went, your father wouldn't be there to ask where and why he'd gone.

By the time I got a letter from your father from Oakland, he didn't have to ask me to come. I'd been in love with your father for years by then, but hadn't known where he went after he ran away from the school for the last time.

I went to the office of the outing program I knew about, where they placed students like me in white homes to work and earn money and learn how to live like and with white people. I asked them if they knew of such programs in other states. Specifically in California. In Oakland, or near Oakland. The outing matron made some calls and found an office in Oakland where they could place me in a home.

I came out on a train. The guy across from me talked the whole way. I made the mistake of telling him about myself. All about Carlisle and your father and the job I was being given doing this outing work, going to live with a white family in

Oakland. I had asked to be placed in or near Oakland through the outing program they had available at Hampton and Carlisle, and they just so happened to have had a request. I don't believe in coincidences, but also have my doubts about fate. A young Indian squaw like you, was what the man said to me. I should have just pretended I didn't speak English.

"Resurrection only happens if you allow it to. Move out of the way and let God in. God can take over. Take you where you need to go," he said.

I'm not a nice person. But God help me I can't help but give people what they want, so I told him I was a Baptist. He told me about his life of sin, how he'd fought in the Civil War and got taken by the soldier's disease, drinking and then drugging himself almost to death, then how Jesus gave him back what he'd been taken by. The way he was talking about Jesus made me think of something your father said before he left Carlisle. He was talking about intoxication. He was talking about intoxication in the tipi. The peyote. It felt wrong for him to say it, but I felt frozen by the fact of him saying it. He was saying intoxicants, any kind was the same. Like Indians were getting drunk or intoxicated in the tipi the way they did in the opium dens he had read about. I almost warned him he better keep quiet his thoughts about the peyote. And then it scared me to think that thought, even if secretly, that the peyote might do something to him, bring him bad luck or curse him the way we expected it to help us when we prayed with it. He explained to me then that he wasn't saying intoxication was bad. Only that it was the same anywhere, intoxication was intoxication was intoxication, was what he actually said.

The Christian man on the train said people come into our lives for a reason. Jesus had put us together on that train.

I would have laughed if it was another Indian man telling me something like all he was telling me. But a white man? It was better to seem pleasant. You don't know who might turn on you, make you their need, suddenly, make you their must-have. I nodded my head and sank down lower and lower like I was getting tired and meant to sleep. He told me the city was a great gathering of souls and lights. Of commerce and communion. Where the great buildings rose up like the trees and reached toward the heavens to praise God, who gave us dominion over the earth, and that we honored him by building our buildings up into the sky as high as we could. I pretended like I was sleeping and then I was sleeping, and dreamed of my mother telling me a story under a willow tree, right along our favorite little stretch of water. She was talking about the stars, though the sky was clear and blue. She was talking about spiders that lived behind the sky. How their web held the stars, how the spiders were the darkness of night. I'd always had dreams about all of the stars in the sky falling down to earth, collapsing on us. I hated those dreams but they taught me something. As the stars were coming down, about to land right on top of me, each time I dreamed it, I said a little prayer, to say thank you that I got to be here, if I had to go, it was the last thing I wanted to be able to say before I went. Thank you. Beneath a willow tree whose branches just almost touched the water, my mother said, "The spiders weave a web to keep the stars in place, as guiding light in our darknesses. The stars are our ancestors, but the spiders are too. They are the weaving and the light."

It is morning, and I feel like talking. As the sun with its light does, and the birds for the sun, then its animals and people beginning to move and make their way through their days, it is what we do for the new days each time they come, each sunrise a blessing, and I have always felt the time of sunset like a little death, like there will be more days but none like the one that is going now, as we prepare for that final rest, and each night sleeping and dreaming our little deaths.

You are my only company if we don't count Cholly. Dogs don't like talk anyway. Dogs like work. Run them, and run with them, and give them something to do, something to chew on, or some place to chase their legs out, and they're happy. Me, I need to say things, talk my tongue loose. Your father is in a tree now. We will camp here for four days. I don't know when you will come. You aren't as big in me as I've seen women get, but you've been in long enough that I know you could come soon. I tied your father's arms up, then threw the rope over a branch and pulled and pulled at that rope until his body was hung up there good and held. I could have begun having you from the pulling up of your father's body, and wouldn't that have been something, to bring you in as we were sending him on his way. That is the way we bury. We put them up in the sky. No one ever told me about the proper way to bring a child into this world. I wish there were more I could do. I am afraid to have you. And though it aches from the loss of your father, my heart is full. Maybe we'll be running our whole lives. Just keep moving. That would be okay. We'll have strong legs, keen awareness, and big hearts, keeping ourselves and each other going like we belong to that one-day distant future, when we can look back and say this is how we made it, despite everything.

Victoria Bear Shield ✳ *Fall*

—— • • ——

CHAPTER TWELVE

Victory!

It has been said that you know the life you're being born into, that you heard the story told to you before you came, and that as your life happens to you, as all the many people and dreams and events unfold before you, you will feel a certain kind of way about all of it that you won't necessarily recognize as remembering the story.

Most lives begin and end with great pain. Your birth will mean your mother's death. Look, even now your bloody body is coming out and up by hands you will become familiar with, will become family with, that do not belong to your mother.

Growing up you will not know anything about your mother. Your name will be Vicky. You will hate to have to answer to that, that sound, like a little whip, like a thin little thwap, like a stick scraping a window, or like that sick sucking sound you will hear when you get your first hickey from an Indian boy in an alley, which you will hide at work with a scarf borrowed from Jackie, one of the other young Indian women you will work with at the jean factory.

Walk up to her after work there in front of the factory even though you feel shy. Say hi and ask her what she's doing. Listen to how she asks, "Do you mean now?" Tell her you do.

Enter the bar she's clearly been to before. Drink as much as she drinks. Further fall for this woman you know likes you, and has something to teach you even though you can't remember on the walk home anything you said to each other.

Go to Jackie when you think you need help and go to her when you don't think you need help, but don't get her involved with the men in your life, protect her from them. Because there will be other marks from not boys but men that will not be hidden so easily as a hickey, nor will these marks be made with mouths. Leave those men. Find ways to get back at them.

Leak the air from their tires, call them in the middle of the night whispering sour nothings, let their dogs out of their yards, drop frozen fish in the open windows of their cars, call out their names on the street then hide; these men who hurt you, who wrong you, who hit you, make them miserable in every way you can. Some would call it spite, for women it will be called spite and being vindictive; while injured men receive their justice and pass out their vengeance, women will be called petty and catty, won't get to feel the honor a word like revenge endows upon men. You will. Inside you will declare it. You will declare victory when you hurt them back and move on from them faster than a machine hems a jean, you run in a rhythm you find without even trying to in the middle of a long workday.

Keep pursuing Jackie as a friend. Ask her questions about her life. Hear the way she tells you that she's from here. That her family is from here going all the way back. Listen to the way she says she is Ohlone. The look on her face with all that concrete behind her, all the buildings and streets and cars rushing by. Think about what she means by way back. Don't ask her anything yet. Don't tell her about yourself. Listen.

Jackie will come to mean more than family to you, because the idea and feeling of family will be made a lie. Your white parents will not be your real parents, and you will find that out far too late. Finding out late will set you off searching everywhere for what it might mean that you are an Indian woman, born of an Indian woman who died giving birth to you, then raised by white parents.

Your full name will be Victoria. Your real mother will give you that name, will have said that to your white parents as they helped her through labor, while also helping themselves to you, your mother's child, just as soon as the wet and life in her eyes was gone.

They will keep the name Victoria for you, but only ever call you Vicky. That they keep anything that came from your mother will be a kind of miracle, as all Indians alive past the year 1900 are kinds of miracles.

You will wonder about the name Victoria once you find out your real mother named you that while she was dying and birthing you. Wonder if she was saying the word *Victory!* out loud at some unknown triumph, perhaps the sound of you crying as you came out, that you came out alive, that she birthed a living being, brought another Indian into a country that'd been doing its best to disappear you for hundreds of years, in countless ways.

Victory was a child in such a country.

You will never know that the name Victoria also comes by way of your grandfather, Victor Bear Shield.

Your dying mother could not possibly have known how apt the name Victoria was for the year you were born. In 1924 the

American Indian Wars will be declared over after a hundred and thirteen years. Any war that long becomes victorious by virtue of simply ending, has no winners or losers only what's left, what could survive so much war is made more than war by virtue of surviving it. And in the year 1924 Indian citizenship will have been granted, even though they will mean to dissolve tribes by giving citizenship, dissolve being another word for disappearance, a kind of chemical word for a gradual death of tribes and Indians, a clinical killing, designed by psychopaths calling themselves politicians.

Citizenship being granted will be a kind of victory too, because you will not have died in any of the wars or massacres, you will have survived starvation and relocation, indoctrination and assimilation, you will have lasted long enough that they had to say that you too, our longtime, once mortal enemy, even you are one of us, even if its meaning, its rights, won't come for decades, the seed will have begun there, in the year you were born.

You will grow up with white parents who will treat you well enough at first, but then eventually will turn you into the help, realize they miss what your mother used to do for them, having brought her on as cheap labor, working with an outing center in Oakland that places Indian students and graduates with families, who exploit their labor under the guise of education and opportunity.

You will grow up an unpaid servant, a faithful daughter to faithless drunks, in a white world that just starts to seem like it might change in ways you never even dreamed of at the end of your too short life.

At the end of your life you will have two almost-grown

daughters, after what will seem to you like a lifetime of struggle and heartache. You will feel as if the possibilities for Indians are just then beginning, there on a prison-island, where you will see Indians of all tribes coming together. You will feel the most Indian and the most free on that island with that water tower sprayed in red paint with phrase *Welcome Home of the Free Indian Land,* with no punctuation.

The phrase won't make sense as a whole, just as the movement to occupy the prison-island won't make sense, won't come to anything more than a metaphor, but the story will remain, the Home of the Free Indian Land, Welcome, is how the origin story, the creation story of this country always begins when white people tell it, with welcoming Indians and a feast people are still eating about to this day, so big was the welcome made, on the Free Indian Land white people will have thought was free of people, so free for the taking. Land of the free, home of the brave.

Your firstborn daughter, Jacquie, will be one of the teenagers who climbs up that water tower. She will climb up just for the climb, just to have done it, she won't be one of the ones who thinks of the message, or spray-paints that indecipherable scrawl for all to see as they come to the island, visiting celebrities and day-trippers wanting to see for themselves what John Trudell was talking about on pirate radio when he said if we're gonna be free, we'll have to get that freedom on our own.

Or much later when people visit the island to learn about the history of the prison, Al Capone and the rest, even Indians will come back and see the writing on the water tower after it is restored, they will come back to commemorate the story of the takeover, to celebrate that time when you chose to live on a prison-island and demand that you be seen as human beings once and for all, they will come back for sunrise ceremonies, to give thanks and to pray at dawn on days other people might be thinking of Columbus, or turkey halftimes, they will restore the days and the island and the hearts of people who gather around the fire or around their computer screens streaming the event.

That time on the island will be a sad one for you, because you will know that you are dying, you will have found out before moving to the prison-island, you finding out that you are dying will be the reason you will go to the prison-island, and eventually the reason you will drink again, there with your two daughters, who will complicate everything, ruin and save everything, will be the reason you will have everything to lose.

On your way, as a young person, long before all that, there will be too much you won't know. Not knowing will leave you empty but fill you with wonder, with curiosity, with hunger to know who you are, why for example you are the brownest person in every room.

You will be told you are Italian from your mother and Irish from your father. There will be framed photographs of your Italian ancestors hung on the walls of the house you grow up in, old brown people from an old world, the old country, your white mother will tell you, your grandparents and great-grandparents, that is why your skin is brown is what she will tell you when you ask. Nothing true will be explained to you until after your mother dies.

Your mother will die by falling off a horse and breaking her neck. She will have been drunk, as sure as she will have been a drunk. The parents you grow up with will both be drunks. They'll even let you drink at an early age, and you'll like it.

It will be normal. Everyone will have been drinking from an early age. So many Americans will be doing so much, too much drinking they will have made it a crime to drink. You will be nine when Prohibition ends and you get drunk for the first time, on pink wine with your mother in your backyard, there in the pink rose garden she so loves. You will experience the whole thing as lovely, because your mother will have been using that word for everything the weeks leading up to that day. You will have gone to the movies with her, gone to see one of the movies with sound, that talks, a talkie, and one of the actresses in the movie will use that word, lovely, for everything, and from then on your mother will have decided it is her word, for her pink rose garden, for her pink wine, and for you, her pink-cheeked child, drunk for the first time, running silly through the yard.

It won't be until after your mother dies that your father will decide that he wants to tell you the whole story. Everything you should have known.

The night he tells you he will be drunk. It will be after the wake. Everyone will have been drinking. These will be people you recognize but don't know. People your parents always had around that you sometimes had to call auntie or uncle, grandma or grandpa, but never had a single conversation with. They will have avoided knowing you. They will have known what your father is about to tell you. Watch them watch you, afraid you might approach them.

See your father sitting on the ground, legs splayed like a kid.

"It's time you come to find out who you come from, someone you should know about before you, become, who you become . . ." will be how your father starts the story, confused seeming, and trailing off at the end of a sentence he won't finish, slurring his words, but determined to say what he is about to say.

"Your real mother was an Indian," he will say, and put his index finger above his forehead pointing up at the sky indicating a feather. "Your real mother was a *real* Indian," he will say, and raise his eyebrows like you should be impressed. Don't say anything. Responding only distracts them from their point, only serves to throw them off from what they mean to say, which annoys them, which further throws them. Nod your head, indicating he should go on, that you are listening, that will keep him from his anger.

"Your birth mother's name was Opal Viola Bear Shield. We still have a box of her stuff somewhere around here, stuff she had before she . . . ," he will say, getting up, but then plopping back down when his eyes indicate the room has turned on him. "A Cheyenne, from Oklahoma. You've heard of them. The Cheyennes, haven't you?" He will ask you about your tribe but not look at you, swaying a little, sitting there looking into the corner for more memory. Don't answer. You won't have heard of any tribes, you will only have known about Indians in general as those wild men out there killing white people if they weren't careful, who the cowboys were protecting everyone from.

He will cry then and you will hate him for it. This isn't his moment to cry. Ask him why he's decided to tell you all of this now. Hear him tell you between his sniffling that now, with your mother gone, and you leaving the house to start your new job, with you becoming a woman, he thought you should know before you go. Ask him what else, what else he could tell you about your mother, your real Indian mother. Tell him there has to be more than that. Watch him have nothing else to say.

Watch him leave your life then, begin to fade just then, almost crumpling.

Walk away. Ignore him yelling after you. He is lying. You won't know what part he is lying about, and if he is finally telling some kind of big truth he'd been hiding, why would in the telling of this truth finally, would it ultimately be a lie? You won't know, but you will know what he told you is not the whole truth, and is a lie enough that you will know it as a lie. You will have long since learned to sniff out lies from them. They will have drank and lied and lied about when they drank and you will have smelled that too.

Your job at the jean factory will pay you enough for you to rent a room in a Victorian house just outside downtown Oakland. Drop the Haven name and become Victoria Bear Shield. Make it the name that appears on your paychecks. Keep hating that you can't shake the name Vicky. But know that Victoria takes too long to say, sounds too formal, too grand for a thin thing like you, parentless twice. Find that with Jackie, when she calls you Vicky, you notice that you like it because you will like Jackie, will want to be like her, will like how the name Vicky sounds—and in a way even rhymes—with Jackie.

You will even name your first daughter after Jackie, but spell it with a *c* and a *qu* for your daughter Jacquie to have her own kind of name even if just in the spelling.

Go out with Jackie and some of the other young Indian women. Bond over drinking too much after work. Find that you love the cool darkness of bars, and the kind of bright the city lights at night make the clouds, with that more-than-four-drink buzz making your head swim, then arrive somewhere that feels like it is—everything you are, finally—enough.

You will not have known what being Indian means on account of never having been around Indians before the years spent with these Indian women working at the factory, drinking at bars after work. When you will learn all about what they know about being Indian, you will wonder if you have that in you. It will not be hard to find what matches, what is Indian in them, how that is what is Indian in you. You will know it in their laughter, how they need to laugh, how they love to tease and twist and poke at you, talk about back home. That part won't be what matches, you don't have a back home to miss if where you go at the end of the day to sleep doesn't count, and it doesn't.

You will hear them talk about loss. You will feel and talk about loss with them, feel and talk about loss, and feel and talk about loss, laughing all the way through the nights in the bars and outside the bars where you knew Indians were welcome.

Jackie is Ohlone, so an Indian from the land you will have been born on, and the land you call home—her people's land. You will always want to ask her what it means, to live on the land that was taken from you, to have to still live on the land that was taken and keeps being taken. Did it feel like it kept happening in present time, not in the past but perpetually, as in a car someone steals from you with you still inside it, driving through your neighborhood, forever circling the driveway of your home, where you parked the car, acting as if there is no car at all, just the smooth movement of newly paved city streets, where nothing belongs to anyone, where everything is just so build-overable, and almost no one stays for long?

But you won't ever ask Jackie what it feels like, because you will fear that if there is no answer, it will hurt worse, or if the answer is that it does feel exactly the way you describe, then it will be like you are trying to take something from her that was supposed to have stayed private, her own bad feelings about a stolen homeland you wanted to take to make yourself feel better for being one of its occupiers, by knowing how it might feel, even if it wasn't your fault, even if you were Indian, you were not from this place. You did not belong here.

All the conversations you never have with Jackie will be a conversation.

For years, a whole decade, you won't do anything but work in that factory and drink. You will visit your father when you can. You will pity him, then feel shame about pitying him, and the shame will be what walks you back to his house. He will always be drunk when you go see him and act like you hadn't visited the time before because he will have been blacked-out drunk the time before, so in his mind you'll never have visited nor will there even have been a time before anything other than the sunken, *drunken now* he is doomed to sway and stumble through.

Eventually, after he accuses you enough of never visiting, you do stop visiting.

Everything about your life will feel impossible. And you being or becoming an Indian will feel the same. Nevertheless you will be an Indian and an American and a woman and a human wanting to belong to what being human means.

One day you will be out with some other Indian women at a bar, and a man will come up from behind all of you tapping your heads singing *one little two little three little Indians.* You will be ready to fight this man for treating you like children like that. You will be the first to stand up, pissed off and ready to yell something mean at him, but when you see his face, the way he is smiling, already apologetic for the dumb joke, putting his hands up like sorry I meant no harm. He will tell you it just made him so happy to see so many Indian women in a row that he had to count. His name will be Melvin Red Feather. From Bakersfield. He will say drinks on me like a magic trick.

And then one morning you are sick. Go to the bathroom. Vomit. Drink water and try for some food then go back to the bathroom to vomit more. Do that again the next morning. And the next until you know what it means. Cry in your bed and sleep and don't show up for work and get yelled at the next day when your supervisor warns you that if it happens again you'll be fired. Hold back your tears and get to work and hold back the fear of what you know it must mean once you start talking to Jackie about what's going on with you.

You will be sick for half the pregnancy. It will feel weird and wrong, your stomach growing like that. Smells will overpower some days. All smells. And your feet will swell. Work will be impossible to do, but impossible to not do. Ignore the feeling that you need to stop what is growing inside you. Remember you are carrying someone over from the otherside.

Know that you will be bringing another Indian into the world. Wonder what the thing moving in your womb, as your growing womb, this person, this Indian girl, you will want to know that you know it is a girl, wonder what will she need to know about being an Indian girl in this world, and what you will do about that.

She will come in June 1954. On a Sunday morning. Jacquie Red Feather. You will give her his last name on the birth certificate even though Melvin Red Feather will be long gone before she is born. He will have gone to work and never come back halfway through your pregnancy. Feel the cold in the room the night after you realized he wasn't coming back. The wind coming in through your open window, you listening for the sound of his car pulling up. Arrive at the place where you don't care anymore about him or how he made you feel or what it will mean to be the mother of a fatherless daughter. Remember your own father, the drunk. Gag at the thought of alcohol. At the heightened smell of the wet city in the morning when you go back to work the next morning wearing more clothes to hide the bump beneath them.

It will just be you and Jacquie living in that same rented room in that Victorian house.

You will take her little body everywhere you go wrapped up in a swaddled blanket or fit tight against you in a thin cotton wrap the woman from Indian Health Service will have given you after finding out there wasn't a father or much of an income in the picture. She will help you find help taking care of the baby.

You will begin to go to the library, become a member and read as much as you can about Indians. About Cheyennes. There won't be much but you will read it all. American history too. Even some world history. You will read Mark Twain and dislike him. Jack London will hold your interest for a while, and the librarian will tell you that he became a reader at Oakland Public Libraries. But you will hate the way Jack London writes about Indian people once you get to those books. You will ask the librarian what novels are written by Indian people and she will tell you that she doesn't think there are any. This will make you think about the box your father gave you the night he told you about your mother, the pages you found in the box. You took the box with you when you moved and you were disappointed when you finally went through it and saw that there was nothing but a stack of pages written by someone else, someone named Charles Star.

Go to your closet and pull the box out. Your daughter will be crawling backward—the only way she will know how to get around at that point—on the rug next to you. Read farther into those pages than you had before. This will be how you meet your real father.

The writing you find is mostly letters of correspondence, but there are other kinds of writing you will not know how to categorize. Part family history, part poetry, part something else entirely. You will get something from the writing that you will cherish.

You will find that lines from the pages in the box will get stuck in your head. Live with you. Or will exist in you as if they were already there.

This line is from a letter your father sent to your mother: *We belong to what we are the way a song belongs to the singer, my heart is a runner and my soul is a winter.* In the letter he talks about belonging. What we belong to. And for the most part you believe he means the two of them belonging together. But in another part of the letter he is saying we don't belong to the earth, but that we are the earth. You won't understand what he means. And you want to know what your mother said in return, but there were no letters from your mother among the pages.

There are long passages about your grandfather, detailing his life after he fled from the chaos of the Sand Creek Massacre as a boy. You will go back to the library to learn about the massacre. Take in what it means to be the children and grandchildren of massacre. You will understand another form of inheritance then. Feel it.

Be sure your daughter knows about this box, these pages. Pass them on to her, tell her to pass them on to her children, so that in understanding who they are, they will understand that it has to include who it is that made them, this is what you will come to know about your relatives and ancestors, not that they be thanked or acknowledged because they are inherently sacred but because their stories are what you are made of.

The year your daughter turns one, bring her to see the man who raised you. He will be gone. Knock on the door with Jacquie in your arms. Watch the woman who comes to the door tell you she doesn't know who you're talking about. This white woman doesn't like the fact that you are there. See her sniff at your presence and look around to see if there might be more of you coming. Tell her you grew up there. That it'd been your childhood home. She will say she doesn't think so, like you'd gotten it wrong.

Leave and wonder if you made up the whole story about your life with your white parents, before the factory, before the bars, and before your daughter, there in your arms. Her being there in your arms, and you having a clear, sober head, it will bring you back to knowing. Spit in the direction of that woman, and your old house. Muzzle your nose into your daughter's nose and make a buzzing sound with your lips. She will make the same sound back at you and your whole body will become a humming that will start you humming a sweet little song for her as you walk away from that house for the last time.

You will get back to work at the jean factory doing the same old same old thing but feeling new about it. Jackie will take Jacquie for you when she can. Sometimes you will have to leave your daughter in your rented room all by herself for hours at a time.

Stay away from drinking.

Work and work and work. It will feel like waiting, but waiting for what you won't know.

And then as if he is what you were waiting for, along will come Junis. He will be delivering mail, he will work for the post office. You will think he is white or part white but he will recognize you as Indian and ask where you're from. The question will throw you at first, because you're from Oakland, so you want to say you're from here, but you don't know what here means for a moment, did it mean modern times, did it mean Oakland, did it mean America? And where would you be from if you were a real Indian? Oklahoma? You will know that's not true, that Indians were from every single corner of the country—beyond the country. You will have read about hundreds of tribes, each with their own languages and customs and creation stories. You will want to tell him that you are Cheyenne, that that is where you are from, that Cheyennes once, up near the Great Lakes, were agricultural people, and then followed the buffalo before running for their lives like the buffalo, and that your people, they were Cheyenne wherever they went, but instead you just say the word Cheyenne, with your hand over your heart, to which he will say the word Lakota with his hand over his heart. You will laugh at each other's hand-to-heart gestures.

The day you and Junis get your apartment, you will witness a fight at the bus stop. A father and son will pull at each other's collars. The fight will seem spontaneous and yet rehearsed. They will be Indians. A little girl will appear, the daughter, she will get in between them and push them apart. Her hair will be braided, and she will be wearing big thick black glasses. After she pushes them apart, she will sit down on the bus-stop bench and stare at the ground. The father and son will move away from each other. The son will straighten his shirt. The father will move off and smoke a cigarette. There will be a fuzzy brown bear wearing only one shoe with one shoe missing sitting next to the little girl. She will pat the bear's head and talk to it. The bus will come and then they will be gone, but the little girl will leave the bear there.

Go pick the bear up. Wait to see if the girl will come back. Remember buses don't come back, not for a long time and with different people, sometimes different drivers, sometimes not until the next day. Keep the bear. Look how it looks almost new. It is in fact a beautifully made bear, see the hand-sewn stitching. Notice the missing shoe and the shoe that is there. Give the bear to Jacquie, but first put it away for a while. Give it to her when the moment is right.

The place you end up in with Junis before he leaves you will come with a radio, and much more than you expected when you moved in, a fully furnished situation. The Bureau of Indian Affairs will have taken care of you in a way that seemed too good to be true. But you will wonder whose stuff it was. Where were those people now and why didn't they need their things? Had they died? Is it then bad luck for you to live there? you will have to wonder. These kinds of questions will arise in your mind and hang there, like the smell in the house you will never quite get used to, like old dusty clothes, and like garlic and lemon. Like other people. It will feel for months like you are spending the night in someone else's house under suspicious circumstances. Like you don't belong.

Tell yourself you do belong. Tell the apartment.

The night you move into your apartment with Junis you will say a prayer and burn cedar and cook hamburger meat and sliced potatoes. Oversalt your meal. Sit there in your new kitchen. Look at each other and smile that we-have-arrived smile that only comes with a hard amount of waiting and wanting.

You will know already then that there is new life in you. You will have known for some time. Tell him that night.

Forget about the face he made when you told him after dinner. Flip the pillow behind your head. Enjoy the new cool and imagine yourself continuing to have babies for the rest of your life, to fill the world up with as many Indian babies as you can, to repopulate the country with its original people. Enjoy playing with that idea. You will not know then how hard it will be to just have the two daughters you will have, not yet know that the news of new life will be what causes Junis to leave, not immediately, not the way Melvin had, but eventually, over time, even after she arrives, your precious Opal, he'll be there but already part gone.

His presence will fade like the new paint on the apartment when you first moved in, until it wasn't even a color you noticed anymore, something vaguely white or vaguely gray or vaguely yellow, and he—just like the color of the paint—will one day not be a thing you give a single thought to anymore.

The end of that year will be when you find out about the Friendship Center. It is a place in Oakland where they have Indian events and where Indian people gather. Keep going back there. Win a raffle and go get the TV you won. Buy a Christmas tree for the first time. Know this will be one of the sweetest moments of your life, that Christmas morning with your TV and your decorated tree.

Wake Jacquie up and give her the gifts you wrapped. Watch her surprised eyes while she is opening them. Look how they're just dishes and cups from the cupboard that came with the place, or other little things you found around the house like a thimble, a relatively clean-looking unarmed mousetrap, and a bag of rubber bands, but Jacquie treats each gift with such wonder and care you don't want the day to end. She will name everything you gave her like they were all people, all her friends. She will turn the bag of rubber bands into a ball that she bounces in the kitchen. And she will eat imaginary meals from the dishes and cups with the one-shoed bear, which you gave her last. She will love that the most. And she will talk to the bear right away. She will take the bear with her everywhere. You will tell her you are bringing a new child into the world, and you will begin to dream up the life you will all live together once she comes, as if she were bringing a bright future with her from that otherside, from the beforelife.

By the time her little sister is old enough to hold her own teddy bear, you will buy her one and Jacquie will teach her little sister to talk to it, and to love and respect inanimate objects, turning every object in their life into a member of the family by naming it, giving it character, this will be what she taught herself and then the family that Christmas day, and their way when they're young. That is the only way you will know them, as young girls, following you around wherever you take them, happy to be anywhere with you and not left at home alone, something they will at first like, but too much of it will leave them feeling like they are being left behind, forgotten, feelings they won't even think of naming but will feel, that will make them want to go with you wherever you go whenever they can, even if that will mean a prison-island, even if that will mean sleeping on the ground of prison cells, it will, and you will tell them you are dying there on the prison-island, when you will have been dying long before that, and when you get home from the island you will not let them go with you up north where you will try to heal alone, at a place you will almost have forgotten you'd gone when you were much younger, with Jackie, just one weekend, for a ceremony, it was for her father, he was dying, and the medicine was intense, the peyote, with her father dying, the way everyone was praying for him with that singular desperation death alone can bring.

You will feel something in the ceremony that won't make sense to you. You won't know that your grandfather Jude Star had first brought peyote and a fireplace to the area, and that it had stayed there, as had he until he died there in 1924, stayed there with Indians and with white people carrying it on alike. You will never know any of that, only that you will feel your people there and it will scare you, the whole experience, but it will change you. It will change Jackie too, so much so that she will stay up there.

You won't see Jackie until you go back all those years later, desperate to keep on living, to find a way to pray yourself to staying.

You will get something from the ceremony up there but it won't be healing, it will be a quiet, devastating peace, a peace that will silence you before it wipes you out, a peace that you will only have access to just before you go, after spending months on a couch, watching your girls watch you go, without any words for them, you will try your hardest to think and feel with your heart, love at them, as you shrink, and you will think you see that they see the peace on your face just before you take your last breath, or you believing they are seeing the peace on your face is what will bring you peace in your last moment, and that will be what you learned in the ceremony up north, to give them peace by showing them peace.

On the day before you die you will suddenly come to distrust everything about the situation you find yourself in.

Quick, gather your things into a corner of the room. Whose house is this? You won't remember. You will see that all you have left in this world could be gathered into the corner of a room, and once you look at it harder, into a box. Laugh to yourself. Get light. There isn't much time left. You're almost free.

Leave. Bring your box down to the Friendship Center. Tell your friend Maxine to keep it there. To archive it. You won't know what you mean when you tell her to archive it, something you picked up at the library. Maxine alone can be trusted. Go back home. You're tired. So tired by the time you get back to the couch you will think it's the end when you close your eyes to sleep.

Wake up. It is morning. Have a cup of coffee. Watch the sun come up. Feel as if you are the only person in the whole world seeing it. Know that it was always true that you were the only one seeing the world the way you were seeing the world. Give thanks to the rising sun. Give thanks to the day that was every day, was the sun itself making everything seen and was called the day as a nickname for the big light the sun was sending the world before it took it away.

You will not know that when you die, your youngest, Opal, will run out the house and up the street without her shoes on, running as if for her life, or as if to outrun the life she'd been given, the one she will feel for the briefest moment she is remembering when she knows you are dead, and this will scare her so bad she will not know what else to do but run and run and run barefoot through the streets of Oakland like her head is on fire.

There are many stories for what happens after you die. You

become light or become the dead light of stars or you swim the river in the sky or you become the soil in the earth. Angels and demons and ghosts. Anything is a story we tell ourselves about a silence.

But stories are for telling after the fact. And the one true fact about the afterlife is that nothing comes from there. Everything goes there.

There will be so much you still do not know when you leave about how you got here.

You are from a people who survived by making their surviving mean more than surviving, who did their best to stay together. But you will not know if the people ahead of you will be capable of the same. And they will not know if they will be capable of the kind of love that survives surviving, that holds bullet shards in a body, doesn't let it poison the blood, the kind of love that chooses the harder way, the way that includes more and not less, the way away from selfishness. No one will know if anyone is capable of making this place more than its accumulated pain.

That you don't know, that you can't know, that the only thing you do know is that this means you have to believe if you expect to stand a chance at doing more than surviving, and this belief, despite not knowing, this belief because you can't know, it is the reason the story has to be lived in order to be told, it is the song being sung, and the dancer in midair. It is the child, with miles and years of hard road ahead, running up a paved street at top speed with no shoes on, feeling she must outrun even the running, feeling she has already overcome gravity, feeling with her feet the kind of victory belief alone can claim, and so feeling she is absolutely about to lift off the ground, to take flight.

PART TWO

Aftermath

2018

Tell me your diamonds.

—TONI MORRISON

CHAPTER THIRTEEN

·.·

How to Fly

Orvil had been lying on his back in bed at home for longer than he ever had before, not even thinking or sleeping or dreaming but stuck about what happened to him, holding its weight without knowing how—or even if—to feel about it, when it occurred to him to look up what other kids on the internet had to say about surviving a shooting, and when he did he couldn't believe he hadn't thought of it before. Existing with the internet was like that. With too much at your fingertips, most of the time you could only scroll or doom scroll and collect tabs you'd never return to, failing to ever land on anything long enough to really experience it as more than a passing glance, but then suddenly you could think of something to look up that you couldn't believe you'd never thought to look up before.

Hearing stories about survivors of shootings made him feel so seen, he almost felt complete again. And then he experienced déjà vu, like this all happened to him before, or like he dreamed it a long time ago and was just then remembering the dream. Feeling almost complete was maybe the most anyone could expect to ever feel, but what felt missing from him still was related to the actual hole made by the bullet that had gone into him, that they hadn't taken all the way out. He needed to watch more videos.

There was this whole side of YouTube consisting entirely of kids who survived school shootings. Some of the kids were too emotional for him to finish watching, and some of them seemed overexcited to share, or for other reasons cringeworthy. And then some were overproduced and made-for-TV, lacking in sincerity or honesty, or were staged, or felt emotionally manipulative. The ones he sought were the confessional-style videos where the kids still didn't know how to feel about it, who reported what happened to them from a distance, who'd flown away that day and were still trying to find the ground again, in other words kids who felt like he had, because even though he hadn't survived a school shooting, there was no other experience he could think of to compare it to.

One kid who always wore an elf hat, without once ever referencing Christmas or elf life in his videos, said that Native people were the first ones to do a school shooting. That got him mad at first, but then he looked it up and saw that it was true. In 1764 some Lenape warriors went into a school and shot ten kids and a schoolmaster. What was not recorded anywhere was why the Lenape warriors killed them. It did describe their tribal elders calling them cowards after the fact, and that the Pennsylvania legislature reinstated a bounty for Indian scalps— which maybe pointed to why they'd done it.

Orvil found a whole list of kids shooting other kids in schools throughout American history, long before Columbine. None of the descriptions of school shootings seemed remarkable, except for this one bizarre incident in 1856 where a teacher told his students if they harmed his tamed sparrow he would kill them, then when a boy stepped on the bird and killed it, the teacher took him into another room and strangled him to death, after which the boy's father shot the teacher dead.

He read something about schools being designed in the first place to control people better, to extend adolescence and create more complacent citizens using models they used to domesticate animals. He wanted to know more about that history, but then when he went to find where he'd read that he couldn't find it.

He wanted to feel normal again. How it'd been before the shooting, before the hospital. Those years after his grandma took them in. All those years ago. They seemed so good. You could say that about years you couldn't get back, wish for normal when normal seemed to be taken away, even if normal was never all that good in the first place.

Everything had become so serious, like the most serious, because he'd taken in that stray bullet. It wasn't even meant for him. Just random. One of the doctors, who wore a faded-ass baseball cap with a fish on it he didn't think the guy should have been wearing on the job, told him the bullet shard in him was shaped like a star, like that was some cool shit. Then the doctor told him he should be grateful that it stopped moving, that an exit wound could be what kills you. The doctor said they would keep an eye on it, the star shard, because, he warned, they've been known to wander, parts of them getting into your bloodstream and poisoning you. And then the doctor, still apparently trying to comfort him about the bullet staying in, said it wasn't bullets that killed but the path they took. This seemed to him like some dumb-ass bumper-sticker wisdom, like: Guns don't kill people, people kill people, or, The journey is the destination.

He would be embarrassed to admit that not that long ago he used to print out quotes in the school library, then glue them on the wall next to his bed for inspiration. Some of the quotes were from rappers, and others from philosophers he'd never even heard of, but the most embarrassing part was that most of the quotes he loved were Native American, supposedly, sometimes called Native American proverbs, all of which he'd found on the internet and were even worse than bumper-sticker wisdom.

He was looking at the ceiling, the sharp pain he'd felt that morning receding, and the slow building of a good feeling becoming in his blood a kind of flow, slow and mellow but bright, even hypnotic, like lava in those lamps or like the lava he'd watch on nature documentaries when nothing else was on, the calm of it after the eruption, slowly eating up anything in its path before turning into hot black rock.

The coats of paint up there were changing, seeming more than random forms, more and more like distinct shapes, and then like shadows from a life he'd once lived but couldn't remember, or a life on its way, a future beyond what he would hope for if he could hope, or if hope was the right word for how drugs could feel when they were really starting to work.

His grandma came in then, with a pretty beat-up-looking acoustic guitar, waving it around in the air in front of him to get his attention.

"You want this?" she asked.

"I don't care," he said, knowing she hated it when his answer to a question was: I don't care. She strummed its strings and it sounded bad and they both laughed at that.

"Think you'll play it? Or should I give it to your little brother, he seems to be more interested in music than—"

"He is not more interested in music than anyone, he just likes classical, which he calls oldies by the way, and you think it makes him more smarter than—" He immediately heard himself saying *more smarter* and hated himself for it.

"No one's more smarter than you," she said, and put the guitar down in the corner of the room with a clang.

She told him she'd gotten the guitar from an estate sale she'd seen on her route. When he asked what that was, she said it was when some old rich parent died at home and that parent's children wanted to sell all their stuff. He didn't understand the dying at home part, and not even what an estate was, but he liked the idea of playing a dead guy's guitar.

For weeks the guitar sat in the corner, mostly in his periphery, like some stray animal they'd brought in that he knew might make noise if he got close enough to it.

And then one day he was high, high like he was every day, a prescribed high, routinely killing the pain, not overly high, not like it would end up getting. These were the earlier, brighter days. Days that ran together and went nowhere. Long before the doctor stopped filling his prescription.

The way that it was, was different from the way that it felt. He was a gunshot victim healing from his wound, was the way that it was, but the way that it felt, when he got opened up like that, the way that it felt was that something else had come through, as if from some other time, or dimension, or universe.

Orvil had always had an active dream life. This included nightmares. But after a certain age you don't want to have to call them that. That was what kids had. He didn't want to have to tell anyone he was afraid to go to sleep, or that he'd wake up from a violent scene so vivid and prolonged he couldn't sleep the rest of the night. So he stopped telling anyone. Just dealt with it.

Most of the dreams he had now were of shootings of one kind or another. The sounds, the running, the heavy sinking feeling of being shot. One time he ate the insides of a horse then crawled into the hollowed-out carcass, and heard what he first thought were drums from outside the body of the horse turn into gunfire, then knew the horse's body was protecting him from the bullets, but then heard it all as drums again, and just before he woke up realized it was the horse's heart beating inside him. Thinking about the dream, he was afraid of how good the horse tasted, and how safe it felt to be inside it, and how strong the horse's heartbeat felt inside him.

Eventually he noticed that if he took more pills than they said he should, he felt even better, and he'd dream less, or not remember the dreams, which came to the same thing. And then taking more pills felt like it meant he'd have to take more pills to make the taking more pills thing keep working. Like more meant more meant more. Like he could stack and sink at once, or like the stacking was what caused the sinking.

He came to understand it all in cycles. If he took more than was prescribed, he'd have days he was higher, but then days he'd be without the pills, days he'd have to wait, and on days when he didn't have pills the dreams would come back with a vengeance. He would have gone back to how it was at first, taking the prescribed amount, but every time he got the new prescription, just the sound of the rattle of that full bottle made him too happy to stop the yellow pills from tumbling out into his palm, then plopping soft onto his tongue, then going down-river with a glass of water, out to sea, taking him deep down where it wasn't happiness he was after anymore but some new thing without light or air, a kind of secret he wished he didn't have to keep but that he cherished nonetheless, that he could keep all to himself.

He had the thought that he was becoming addicted. This wasn't new language. He'd had it used against him for video games and for phones, for screens in general. And he knew he came from addict blood. His mom's brain had been wired wrong, and her parents' brains and their parents' brains all the way back a long descending line of Indian heads figuring it out as best they could. Past family members and the ancestors were constantly sending their blessings and curses down through time from that beyond before, that gave his present its particular bent, its dimness, its light, its scream, and its song, but also its sometimes dead silence.

In his case, his mom had damaged his already damaged brain before he even took his first breath. Before he was born the want had been wired into him. His mom with that needle and the horse. As he'd gotten more deeply involved with it, he came to know that getting high made him feel closer to his dead mom, like they could commune despite death and time, because there she was sometimes in the corner, in his periphery, searching the room for keys, or almost nodded out slouched against the wall—muttering to someone on the other side of it.

Then he remembered something. He didn't know if it was a memory, or a dream, or the memory of a dream. It went like this: Before she died, when he was young, but not as young as his brothers—who wouldn't stop crying—he tied up his arm and found a vein like he'd seen his mom do, and shot some of what she had in a syringe she hadn't fully pushed in. It just put him to sleep. But he'd done that. In the memory, or the dream, or the memory of the dream. His mom had always called it her medicine. He remembered thinking that it was natural that he should take some of her medicine, and that they were all some kind of sick. He didn't remember anything else, just falling asleep to the feeling like the milk of gold was buzzing in his eyes and filling him up from his toes to his nose, a kind of singing that meant everything was a foot off the ground, if just for the time the high lasted—every molecule in his body knew how to fly.

After that when he heard people talking about getting high he thought about flying and not about people getting fucked up but trying to get above things, to feel and see from higher up or at least to not have to feel so heavy; before he started getting high, when he heard it mentioned he tried not to think about his mom but birds or feathers, not weight but flight.

Years after getting high loses its novelty and feels closer to duty than enjoyment, he will sit on a toilet thinking about how to get rid of it, at first not even knowing what he means when he thinks it, just how do I get rid of this, while the dim light above him blinks from a bad bulb in the bathroom everyone keeps forgetting to fix. He will stare at a line of powder and soon leave his body with it, and whether it was a dream or a memory that first time won't matter anymore because he will know the secret of flight again, and he won't know, while he is there, whether it will be the last thing he will ever know, whether he will come back down, won't know whether or not he wants to.

But at the beginning of finding out what drugs could mean to him, the pills, if he had them, he took them before doing anything. He took pills and watched shit, sad anime on the internet and reality shows on cable TV, literal shit shows that were funny because of how overly bad they were. He took pills and played video games. He played *NBA 2K,* dominating with the Warriors, and he played *Red Dead Redemption 2,* and *GTA V,* going on killing sprees and fleeing the scenes of crimes in epic getaways in cars and on horses. He took pills and slept. Took pills and clicked through the internet until it felt like he couldn't read or think or even look anymore. He took pills and played guitar. He took short walks around the block to prevent blood clots like the doctor said, like his grandma said, like everyone said. He thought about the powwow. He tried not thinking about the powwow. He thought about the powwow. He took pills and worried about wasting time, as time escaped like air out the room when one door closes and another one opens— like missed opportunity.

He'd heard drugs could make you go numb, but he *felt more.* And he felt better because he felt in ways he hadn't allowed himself to feel before. The way the painkillers made him feel was brave and confident, like he could feel what he kept hidden before without even meaning to.

He kept going back to the guitar, at first playing the strings without putting his fingers on the neck to make chords or to play notes, just listened to the ones that came out of the hole in the guitar he started to think of as a mouth, which he would later learn were the open notes. It was a good sound, something he recognized he could make, that was coming from a mouth inside him, that was singing. That was how it became more than just a stupid old piece of wood and wire some dead guy would never play again. His long days spent doing school at home, playing video games, and drifting on the internet came to be replaced by his time with the guitar, which was just starting to feel like a language if he learned how to speak it might end up saving him.

CHAPTER FOURTEEN

What Were Drugs

Sean Price had never felt so fully accepted by his dad and brother as during the brief period following his mom's death. The disease ate up her brain quickly. And it took way too long to diagnose what she had. Pick's disease. Sean had been the first to notice something was wrong, was off. She started swearing, when she'd almost never sworn before. She was Catholic. And while the swearing was relatively easy stuff to deal with, compared to what was to come, it'd felt extreme to Sean. His dad, Tom, shrugged it off as work-related, stress-induced. When she couldn't remember where her car was, having already come home somehow, and they couldn't find the car for weeks, after having reported it stolen, and the cops found it like a mile away, parked behind a large boulder near a hiking path, it was enough for Tom to agree she needed to get herself checked out. It's harder than you would think to convince a doctor that she needed medical attention.

That she was fine remained her refrain.

And then the disease progressed, so that by the time she was diagnosed, she didn't believe she'd ever married Tom, and thought Sean was the little brother she'd lost to a fire when she was nine, whose name was Sean, who Sean was named after. His brother, Mike, became the Nazi doctor, which was apt, as he'd become some kind of alt-right psychopath as only the Oakland hills could produce, the kind who'd decided he would only listen to nineties and early aughts music, to Souls of Mischief and Hieroglyphics, Too $hort E-40 and Mac Dre, drank Hennessy he called Hen, smoked blunts exclusively when smoking weed, and only ever referred to Oakland as "the Town," but listened to Joe Rogan on predawn jogs—a routine he'd established at military school. None of which had Sean's mom, Grace, known when she started calling him the Nazi doctor. That it didn't seem to be based on anything was part of the point the disease seemed to be making as it ate up the part of her brain that seemed to have contained her essence, which made her who she was, which scared Sean, that who you actually were was just some losable scoop somewhere in your brain.

And so it was like losing someone else, someone he didn't know, by the time she was finally gone.

Pick's disease was like dementia for middle-aged people. Toward the end she couldn't even speak or seem to understand anything anyone said to her. To watch his mother become nothing more than a warm, breathing body in less than a year was, to say the least, devastating. And not only to Sean but to his dad and brother too. It changed them.

After she died, Sean mourned then grieved with his dad and brother with a kind of pathetic sincerity he should have known couldn't last, but while it did, her absence was theirs, together. They prayed before meals without the TV on. The act of praying was for her, they did it for her, because none of them really believed as she had, and every now and then they even slipped into praying at her—skipping God altogether. Maybe she was still somewhere between things, in the walls or vents, unimaginably small, tucked deep inside the dust dangling from a cobweb in the corner of the kitchen, where Sean would sometimes watch his brother stare while they prayed.

They were kind to one another during that time, for months, almost half a year. But everything wears off. And if not grief then their initial responses to grief gave way to the habitual, and soon Sean was making his way downstairs, then making himself a salami-mustard sandwich, then sitting in front of the TV with Mike, who brought up that Sean must be getting over it by now, on account of him being adopted. Mike said something about blood that Sean had to ask him to repeat, because Sean thought he was hearing him wrong.

"It's not like you're blood though," Mike said. "That's all."

"That's all?" Sean said.

"It just can't be the same for you," Mike said.

"Dad doesn't have her blood either, so—"

"Yeah but they mixed their blood to make me, so it's closer."

"Closer to what?" Sean asked, with anger in his voice, even some trembling, even his chin shook that little shiver of sorrow, which he stopped by opening wide for his salami-mustard sandwich, thinking about Mike's use of the word mixing for their blood, like he was a cake they made.

"You know what it's closer to," Mike said, and visibly shifted his attention to the TV by swiveling his legs toward it.

"I can't believe you're trying to make this into some kind of competition," Sean said to him, scooting away from him. They were sitting on a massive brown leather sectional. Muted heads on the TV mouthed commentary about basketball highlights.

"Not a competition. Blood is facts," Mike said.

Sean got up too fast and dropped the rest of his sandwich on the floor, then picked it up and went to the kitchen to throw it away but just put it on the counter instead. Blood is facts as a sentence was killing him on multiple levels. He put a glass under the sink and filled it to its brim to where it spilled, then drank just a sip and poured the rest in the sink. He wasn't thinking. He normally would never have wasted water like this.

"Blood is facts has got to be the stupidest thing you've ever said. Grief doesn't work like that," Sean said, standing off to the side of the TV. "Blood doesn't even matter when it comes to the way we feel things."

"Feel feel feel. You're such a pansy," Mike said, and laughed a little.

Sean walked away thinking of the flower. That he'd known immediately that a pansy was a flower probably made him the kind of person Mike was trying to make fun of. Sean sat down at the dining-room table and looked up the origin of the word being used in a derogatory way, how long people had been using the flower in the pejorative, and saw the earliest use Google could find came from Claude McKay, a Jamaican writer Sean had never heard of, described as a central figure in the Harlem Renaissance. Sean looked up Claude McKay quotes and found this at the beginning of one of his poems, "I plucked my soul out of its secret place," which seemed to fit the moment so well it almost brought him back from his rage, from being so mad he was shaking, or made it worth being mad.

"What'd you look up the dictionary definition of pansy and see a picture of your face there?" Mike said, and laughed too hard. Sean felt bad for him suddenly. He was five years older than Sean, basically a grown-ass man, laughing at his little brother about what? Mike had been kicked out of military school and never recovered. He'd become some kind of man-child, unable to hold down a job or figure out what to do next, and spent too much time in his room, on the internet. It was from his room that he got radicalized by the alt-right through whatever series of clicks made that thing click in his head that said white men are the victims here, and the country is suffer-ing. But then just as sudden as his pity came, so did his rage return, and Sean grabbed his sandwich off the kitchen coun-ter, went up behind Mike, opened the sandwich, and, knowing how much Mike hated the smell of mustard, slammed it down as hard as he could on his head then ran as fast as he could up to his room and locked the door and the deadbolt he'd had his dad put on after Sean realized Mike could pick the lock with a paper clip years ago.

Sometimes it felt like he just wished he did not have to belong to the group of men that made him a part of what Mike was all about. That square-jawed American brutishness, that surly dickishness.

Sean had always felt uncomfortable being referred to as a boy, or as a young man. But, and he knew this was the big-gest but, feeling nonbinary did not mean he wasn't a man who directly benefited from being a man. Men were a secret cult. To be a boy being groomed to be a man was to be joining a secret cult against women, and against anything not squarely a man—square-jawed shape into the square-jawed hole. Not every single boy. Not every single man. Not Sean. He didn't think. But he knew he was a part of it, and could not fully recuse himself from participation in all that it included.

In an ideal world, Sean would be referred to as they/them

by everyone without anyone having to ask or explain. In an ideal world, there would be better, more inclusive, kinder language for everyone. He does not live in such a world. In school the language used was loud and empty in the halls, quiet and desperate between him and his classmates between classes, and almost always condescending coming from his teachers or other authority figures who stood around like bouncers. But there were ways to make things feel ideal inside, ways to cultivate a private life. He was a reader of fantasy and graphic novels, books about other worlds, and could read or play alone for hours with toys, his guys, as he called them until he realized using guys as a general plural for more than one person was sexist, at which point he started calling them his people, and was ashamed as he entered middle school that he still loved to play with them when no one else seemed to be doing such things. It was in middle school that he first heard the phrase *find your people,* which his social studies teacher, Mr. G, told them on their first day of class. Mr. G was the most real feeling because he actually seemed to care. Most other teachers had been checked out for years, some for decades. Mr. G seemed to see Sean, and seemed to see himself, had actually spent time thinking about who he was and how he'd gotten to be who he was and tried relaying that to students like Sean with messages like *find your people,* and *all this will one day seem like not that much.* Sean had wanted to ask Mr. G what he meant by *all this,* but never worked up the nerve to ask him anything. Sean stopped playing with his people that year, and never did find his people at school.

He was not convinced enough he would be accepted in LGBTQAI+ circles or groups or clubs or cliques to ever try to join anything or attempt to make friends with people he thought belonged to the acronym. *Belonging to the acronym* felt to him like a secret society he didn't know how to become a part of. Or did the plus at the end of the acronym mean to say, and you too, and you too, in an ever-widening umbrella meant to cover as many people as possible from the inevitable rain made to soak the minds of those lost to a system of definitions that increasingly did not include them?

He'd known since before he could remember being attracted to both boys and girls, but for the first time the summer after he started middle school, something changed in him. He was up in his room listening to Mitski's "Your Best American Girl" in his earbuds and dancing a dance that was mostly spinning. Something in the distorted guitar and open rage in her voice sounded somehow so pretty and ugly and good but mad about something he'd felt shame about off and on his whole life. When the song was over something was gone, like he'd let it go or it rose in the room from his spinning and didn't come back down.

The summer before his first year of high school, Sean spent three months in traction because of what everyone ended up calling the accident.

The accident and resultant move through the mangled passage between before and aftermath, happened during a game of roller hockey.

Roller hockey was the game his dad had played. It was what he'd been good at in life. So of course his sons played roller hockey, Mike and Sean both, they'd been playing since they could walk, and had practically grown up at that rink and on skates, that was what you called them, not Rollerblades, the rolling footwear was a means to an end, to play hockey was what mattered. Tom had emphasized this when both Mike and Sean tried to tell him rollerblading was dorky. For Sean it was even worse than a dorky look, he'd always hated the way people looked on Rollerblades, all gangly and slower than it looked like they should be when rolling on wheels; to Sean they looked like mutants, like those creepy Wheelers from the *Return to Oz* his dad made him watch one day when they were both home sick, out of nowhere, Tom just put it on and said he would like it and the movie gave Sean nightmares for weeks that he was too afraid to tell anyone about on account of it supposedly being a kids movie.

The accident was caused by a player potentially intentionally cross-checking him in the back, which was an infraction, penalty-worthy to be sure, but more of a bent rule than a broken one because of unclear intentions, the accidental or purposeful cross-check causing his body to go into the boards in such a way that bent his back to breaking, as is the medical shorthand, but technically it was a compression fracture in his lower vertebrae and not his whole damn back somehow becoming broken all at once, though it did feel that way, not as it happened, not initially, but after. That was how Sean Price, given drugs for long enough to mitigate the pain, began to like getting high from the drugs, and where all the real trouble began. And though he would never play roller hockey or any sports seriously again, he would walk, he would walk again, and that, that he knew even without having any kind of relationship with God or religion, was some grace.

Grace was his mom's actual name, but everyone only ever called her Gracie, which felt like a cutesy form of grace, or meaning, only with some grace, like grace-ish, which Sean felt like grace needed to be full to be true grace, didn't it? But she was gone, had left Sean gracelessly, had actually fallen from grace, away from the meaning of her own name because he couldn't even recognize the person he was losing as he was losing her. She couldn't have known she was leaving him to the wolves. After they decided their grieving was over, his dad and brother had become more like brothers to each other than father and son, seemingly at the same time, conspiratorially even, like it was some great plan coming together, for what purposes Sean couldn't fathom.

During their visits to Sean, while he recovered in the hospital, their whole vibe was that they had to be there, like they were only there to perform their concern, and didn't even know how evident it was they were performing their concern. Love was always tied to and obfuscated by obligation. Sean wanted to believe in their basic summation of what happened to him, at first, that some asshole had cross-checked him in the back like a cheat. But then they asked questions like, was Sean asking for it, like digging for the puck in a corner, or was he in front of the other team's net, messing with their goalie? In other words, was it his fault? Did he deserve it? In the end, it was clear they felt it was more like he'd lost a fight, and that if anything he should have felt lucky to be alive. She had died. Here he was living and worrying about a back, legs, walking.

You'll heal, he heard his mom's voice say from the walls of the hospital room. He felt her there the most just after they administered the morphine. He didn't know that while it was happening. She was just there. Talking to him through the walls. She was telling him *we* would heal. That *we* would be okay. She kept using we, as if his recovery somehow meant recovery for the both of them. Sean believed her, and believed he was only able to heal because he believed.

The doctors mostly said that his back would heal too. But one of them, balding a little at the top, which was only visible when the man bent down to pick up a pen he was constantly dropping, said, "Walking again should be the case if . . . ," but then he trailed off, and immediately left the room. It registered late to Sean that the doctor had rushed out, and then he smelled smoke, and it felt too hot to mean anything else but fire. The ceiling was absolutely crumbling from above him. Someone came when it felt almost too late and rolled him out of the room then down some kind of striped, carnival tube slide out into the parking lot. It was a dream—whether morphine-induced or not—he came back from coughing to the point that they brought in a machine to help him breathe.

When Sean's dad and brother came to the hospital to bring him home, he felt confused about almost everything, but comforted by these two facts: (1) He liked drugs. (2) He would not be confined to a wheelchair the rest of his life—though he would be going home in one.

The whole experience was bittersweet, bitter because of the pain and because of all the time he spent afraid he would not walk again, and sweet because of how he'd been introduced to drugs, to morphine and opioids. But he was still trying to figure out what was pain and what was relief, what were dreams and what were drugs, even as they were being injected into his veins—straight into the bloodstream.

Administered drugs were a trip. He knew it was sick that he liked being high, that it represented some sickness, his want, but he wanted them anyway. There was a reason for the want, he wanted to be taken care of the way they ended up making him feel so taken care of; was that such a bad thing to want, to ease discomfort, to not have to worry so much? Maybe not, but the way he thought about having drugs in the future, and not caring that he knew it was wrong, he knew it was a problem, and that he didn't care that it was, and that that too was a problem about which he also didn't care.

Sean Price had had this *fuck-it* kind of energy for as long as he could remember. He believed he was born with it, that people who were could just say fuck it and do something crazy, something most people would have the common sense never to do, because yes you only live once and all that, but the fuck-it energy was different. It wasn't even necessarily a bad thing. It could be useful. Sean believed it came from having been adopted, from someone else having said fuck it about him.

Sean was adopted straight out of the hospital after he was born, his birth mom was not even a memory. Grace and Tom were his mom and dad, he'd always known they were not his real mom and dad, but they *were* his mom and dad because there was no one else. From early on he knew he was different from his parents and brother. Sean was brown and his parents and brother were white. Questions from other parents at school or in the supermarket began about where the boy's father came from, and ended with comments about how beautiful and exotic he looked. Referring to Sean like he wasn't there became as normal as his mom's terse but tense response: This is my child, which always made Sean feel good, loved, but also smothered, like the way he used to love when his dad rolled him up in the futon like a burrito and held him there.

Anyone's skin color in a place like Oakland, that could be okay, that could be nothing to mention, normal even, but

Oakland had a lotta sides to it. And it had these hills, these Oakland hills, as they were called in code, meaning not the flatlands, meaning not the east, meaning there was money up there, real estate value, multimillion-dollar views of Oakland. That was where he grew up, Sean Price with his adopted family, near a place that called itself Montclair, tucked into the hills on the other side of Highway 13, where everyone pretended it was a faraway luxury mountain town, when it wasn't even not Oakland, just an area, hardly more than a neighborhood with a fancy sign, not like Piedmont, which had paid for the right to declare itself its own city, to become officially not-Oakland.

White people have always either ignored people like Sean or made him painfully visible. Either could happen depending on the day, depending on the dude. It was almost always a dude. A bro. White boys thought the world of themselves, thought the world was themselves, and that anything otherwise was out of place, needed to be noticed or ignored. But Sean wasn't gonna pretend like at one point he didn't want to be one of them. He was always careful about how much sun he got. He reverse pinched the sides of his eyes to a stretch to try to make them stay bigger, or pulled his nose out to make it less wide, or sucked his lips in to hide the fullness.

Before the predominantly white private Catholic high school, he'd gone to a middle school that bussed kids up from East Oakland so that it wouldn't be a predominantly white, predominantly rich-white-kid experience for everyone. Before that he went to an elementary school made up of mostly rich white kids. It was those years and the years before that Sean thought he wanted to be white, thought he wished he could be white enough, could at least pass, with these pinching regimens in class he didn't think anyone would ever see, and they didn't, but also, it didn't work, his skin and eyes and nose and lips stayed as they ever were.

It wasn't until after he was back home and managing his pain and the pills on his own, that he knew he would need more than what he had, than what would be prescribed. The daily return to the high, the need to feel normal by being a kind of high that wasn't ever enough, that was more and more a middling, this was his return to civilian life, as he came to think of it, influenced by his brother's way of talking about everyone who wasn't in the military, as if the hospital bed had been a war. Mike had been to a military academy for a year but got kicked out for what he called a prank, which Sean suspected was some brutal thing that landed someone in the hospital and fell into exactly no one else's prank category but Mike's. There was still a summer of rehabilitation to go, figuring out walking again, while also figuring out how to stay pilled.

This was where his dad came in. After roller hockey became more of a weekday hobby, and wasn't paying anything anymore, and Tom didn't need to stay in shape for it by constantly training, but also needed something to do, and to provide a much-needed second income for their mortgage and general monthly expenses, Tom had sold cars for Toyota while going back to school to become a pharmacist. He sold pharmaceuticals for a company for a while before going independent, which was his word for what anyone else would have called becoming a full-blown drug dealer. So Tom, pharmacist and now amateur chemist, started up a lab in the basement of their house. He'd built what he called an arsenal of painkilling mats—an unnecessary shortening for materials he picked up from the summer he got obsessed with *World of Warcraft*—with the help of a large store of fentanyl he kept in the basement, which he stocked up on way before it became a part of the opioid epidemic, plenty of OxyContin, and other generics and derivatives, plus ketamine, LSD, psilocybin extract, mescaline, MDMA, and who knew what the fuck else was the feeling when Sean walked into the lab and saw all the many bottles and vials and tubes and locked cabinets. Actually, Tom had been fired from the pharmaceutical company shortly before Grace's health deteriorated to the point that she needed someone to take care of her. The drug experimentation and creation then subsequent distribution was related to managing Grace's pain and trying to fix her brain, and about paying their mortgage, but it seemed to mean more to Tom, like he'd found the thing he'd been born to do.

Toward the end of the summer, Sean had asked his dad what he had, what other kinds of drugs, like what was his mom taking before she died, and his dad had given him pills. After he tried them and liked them, he told his dad so, then asked for more. His dad asked Sean whether he thought he could figure out who might want to buy some at school, which was how he found out what it would have to mean to keep himself pilled.

The DNA test was a birthday present Tom got for the whole family. "How's it a birthday present for me if everyone gets one," Sean had asked Tom, suspicious it was related to him being adopted, for them to find some kind of commonality despite not having any blood relation. The whole thing was dumb, but what if there was no shared DNA, wouldn't that have been worse? Tom handed Sean a wad of cash, which may or may not have been the question's response, or an impromptu part of the birthday present.

The results from his spit were emailed to him. The spit

said he was white from Northern and Southern Europe, Native American from North America, and Black from the North African region. He'd already assumed he was part Black, because he knew what he looked like. Because people know what they look like. And because of the way people had always looked at him in the white community he grew up in; there was no mistaking the look you got if you were assumed Black or part Black in a white community—whether you were or were not all or part, with or without the data regarding your DNA. But everything about race and background was trickier when you were adopted. Sean didn't feel he had the right to belong to any of what it might mean to be Black from Oakland. And he couldn't pretend to now be Native American, not white either, but he would continue to be considered Black, holding the knowledge of his Native American heritage out in front of him like an empty bowl. Being part white was something he'd just assumed. Even if he hadn't been white, everyone was raised with whiteness as the standard and as the gaze, so you had it in you even if you didn't, it was the background sound you only ever noticed got turned off in rare moments when the spotlight shifted temporarily.

Before Sean Price knew what he was, in terms of DNA results, he'd done a project he was assigned for his social studies class called: *I am Oakland*. One of the kids in his class was actually named Oakland. Oakland Lee was his full name. Oakland was adopted like Sean. They'd been friends before middle school. They used to take the bus together. They rode Oakland's different bus routes all over Oakland, and it was scary, for both of them, that was part of why they did it, something having to do with both of them knowing they were Black, and taking the bus through neighborhoods in Oakland where mostly Black people lived, to prove something to themselves and to each other. Oakland Lee had lighter skin than Sean, and this, he told Sean, made it harder for him to do what they were doing. But mostly they didn't talk about what they were doing. Talking about anything more than was necessary would have made it impossible to keep doing it. And before they knew it, what had begun as some kind of test, or rite of passage, or competition, became a way for them to just not be noticed, to not be one of the only people of color in the spaces they occupied, to not have eyes on you like that, became for them how to disappear completely. They'd each be listening to music from their phones, watching the rest of Oakland not from up in the hills but down where its real people lived, where the stakes felt higher and what people said and felt had this realness, and this urgency that always felt more to Sean what being alive was supposed to feel like.

In middle school Oakland Lee started hanging out with the popular white kids. He played lacrosse and soccer and became popular himself while Sean failed to make any real feeling connections and began to resent and then hate Oakland Lee.

Oakland's parents were white hipsters, and his presentation was obviously heavily helped if not entirely made by his parents, and was ironic, and was that too clever for its own good kind of clever that made everyone experiencing it insecure about when and how hard to laugh. It was about the oak tree being the national tree of America, and how Oakland represented the future of the country, how Oakland was the acorn that would grow into a mighty future oak this country could become if everyone kept being more and more like Oakland, the city, as well as this boy presenting his seemingly parent-made presentation. What was worse was a pie chart they'd made showing the kid named Oakland's DNA result percentages, how they were almost identical with Oakland the city's racial demographics, which were, roughly, twenty-eight percent white, twenty-seven percent Hispanic, and twenty-three percent Black. What depressed Sean most about the presentation was the look on his parents' faces as he presented, how proud, how loving they seemed, and then what made it worse was that when Oakland finished his presentation the way everyone was asked to finish it, by saying their name and then: . . . And I am Oakland. Oakland said, "And I am Oakland, but like, my name is Oakland, so like, I literally am Oakland," and everyone laughed, and he kept it going by saying, "Everything I do, I do it Oakland Lee," which got even more laughs. Like Oakland could be an adverb. Sean chewed on the inside of his cheeks until he tasted blood. His presentation talked about how being a person of color with adoptive white parents was an analogous experience to being a person of color with an old white male patriarchal colonial government in charge of them. It was an especially sad feeling because of the feeling in the room, the way it followed Oakland's hopeful, light, fun presentation on race, whereas Sean's presentation seemed to come off as judgmental of a system that was just doing its darndest, especially in a place like Oakland and in a place like this classroom for God's sake can we have a moment to appreciate a little progress for once without having to complain about yet another discrepancy in the problematic way we keep doing things, was the feeling Sean felt in the room, why it felt so bad to be presenting after Oakland. But when Sean said *I am Oakland* at the end of his presentation, it felt more true than when he heard Oakland Lee say it. Sean felt good when he said it, about saying it, but Oakland Lee had made everyone laugh, and Sean had basically shit on white liberals celebrating diversity without really addressing the white supremacist, systemic problems that made diversity so necessary feeling as to be celebrated by white people who want so bad to be on the right side of history they forget they're inevitably on the white side of history. So Sean ended up feeling really bad about the whole thing in the end.

As it turned out, the commonality found on the test between him and his dad and brother, besides being white, was Native American heritage. Sean was a quarter, and they'd found out they were 12.25 percent Native American, so a half of a quarter.

"The thing you want to be able to do is to live with the idea of your ethnic background, form an identity with it so that by the time you go to write your college essay, you'll really sound like you know what you're talking about," Tom had said. And here was the real reason he wanted Sean to take the test. Because even though he was perfectly fine with his son taking his homemade drugs and selling them, it was never not emphasized that he would be going to a college, and a good one, a respectable one, and certainly not off to a military academy like Mike. Don't be like Mike was their father-son mantra, when they talked about the future, if Mike wasn't around.

"I'll no more know what I'm talking about than I do now. The test isn't a history lesson. It certainly isn't a cultural education plan or whatever you think you mean by living with the idea of my ethnic background. Also, ethnicity and racial makeup are completely different things."

"I just want you to have cards to play when the time comes."

"I thought being adopted was my card. I thought Mom

dying was a card. Me being not-white growing up in a predominantly white community in Oakland, aren't those my cards?"

"Not-white in a predominantly white community in Oakland, that sounds too vague, where's the story in there, how does America fit in? Now, the Native American part, what about playing that part up? You got more than me on that part."

"Stop saying part," Sean said.

"What?" Tom said.

Sean and his dad were talking on the phone from separate rooms of the house. Sean was in his room, elbows perched on his knees holding the phone in front of him with both hands, and white earbuds strung up into his ears, scrolling through news headlines, as his dad audibly paced the kitchen downstairs— the kitchen floors for whatever reason were the creakiest in the house.

"I'm like a quarter by percentage according to a test. Play up being a quarter according to a DNA test?" Sean said. "That's not a story."

"Yeah. Maybe not. But I'm part Indian now too. We have that together, you know?"

"Don't say Indian."

"I said part."

"Stop saying part!"

"It's not an insignificant amount," Tom said.

"This feels gross," Sean said.

"There might have been a chief in our line."

"We're not from the same line of people just because—"

"There's nothing wrong with it, Sean. It's our heritage now."

"Now? See how that doesn't work? The shit doesn't land on you, does not arrive in the mail," Sean said.

"It's ours, it's who we are. It's science, son."

"No it's not. Not really."

"How so?"

"I don't know, but it's not science."

"Genealogy is a science. The study of genes. It's right there in the name, all the 'ologies' are sciences."

"Not cosmetology."

"You know what I mean."

"Fine, but it doesn't mean you have the experience, it's abstract data about our DNA. I heard it's flawed because the datasets are mostly white people. I heard they stole Native data."

"They can't take from us what we are, the stock we come from?"

"You sound stupid."

"I'm telling you, Sean, I feel chief energy," Tom said. Sean heard Mike yell out *Chiefs* in the background. It was the family team after the Raiders, since Tom had grown up in Kansas City.

"If the test is true, most likely it was an Indian woman who got raped, not a chief."

"Geez, Sean. Lighten up. I'm just saying it's something to be proud of," Tom said.

"They should make one called 23andMeToo, people could use it to find out how many known rapists are in their line," Sean said, thinking this would, as his dad suggested, lighten things up.

"You can't use DNA to know who was a rapist," Tom said.

"Well, first of all, you can and they very much do use DNA to prosecute rapists, but also, speaking historically, of people in your line, if they were known rapists, say someone like Thomas Jefferson for example, he was a rapist, so if you found out you were related to him—"

"Thomas Jefferson was not a known rapist. Can we stop talking about rape? I just mean it's a good thing to know we have Indian blood in our line. It's a good thing is all I mean. We can use it."

"No. And you're, like, pretending. You'll never have to hold the weight of history the same way that people who have to do," Sean said, eyeing the DNA results on the floor, which had just come in the mail. They'd already been emailed the same results and had discussed them to similar effect, but getting it in the mail became a reason to talk about it again.

"People like you, then? Oh but wait you grew up with us, so you haven't had to hold the weight either, right?"

"Walking through your life being treated differently because you are, because you look different, other than white in a white community, I would argue is part of carrying the weight. Not all, not at all can I claim—"

"Ugly people get treated differently too, as do the disabled."

Sean hated when his dad brought up ugly people and their plight. Bringing up ugly people always led him to talking about the misfortune of his good looks. Once he'd even complained about how because he was good-looking, he was treated superficially, like he didn't get the real experience regular-looking people got walking around in the world all regular, so he aligned himself with ugly people in that way, they were all a part of the same problem related to superficiality. It was so stupid. Sean didn't disagree altogether, it was that it was yet another false equivalency his dad used for thinking his views were incontrovertible. His dad was undeniably good-looking, in the traditional white American male sense, with a strong jawline and broad shoulders, the confidence to sell water to a whale, and perfect, if overly big, teeth. Sean even believed his mom would not have married his dad for his personality alone, that his good looks were a sizable part of what she liked about him because how much else was there to like? But this inclusion of disabled people in addition to ugly people to talk about inequality seemed designed to offend as many people as possible.

"Please do not compare ugly people and the disabled to people of color, Tom. And then align us with you. It's not even funny. I mean none of them naturally belong together in a group but especially the ugly and attractive people part because it's so subjective."

"Truth is beauty, and beauty, truth."

"White people get to be mediocre at everything and be considered outstanding."

"Not in sports."

"Not anymore."

"True," Tom said, and laughed. Then said, "Tom Brady."

"I think we're done here."

"We used to be able to joke around a lot more. I'm sorry, but I miss that," Tom said.

"Yeah sorry, life was way funnier before Mom died and I almost lost the use of my legs."

"We can't keep being all down about it. We've got to get up and stay up. She would want it that way, right?" Tom said. "Mom would want it that way, right?"

"We're not saying anything to each other," Sean said. "We're not hearing each other."

"I'm all ears, Sean. I'm trying my best to look forward, not back, forward, to a future we can't help but be headed toward together, along with the people we belong to, that we now know we've belonged to all along, real Native Americans, there's no leaving that behind, right, not now, right?"

"I gotta go," Sean said, and hung up.

It was decided that Sean would spend his first semester of high school at home, enrolling in an online version of high school with several other students who for various reasons could not attend in person. Sean felt so ambiguous about high school. He was anxious about not meeting new people, excited about the possibility of making friends. And he'd gotten into a good school. If he did well at a good high school, he could get into a good college. These years would matter for his future. He'd seen what happened to Mike. If you got knocked down this early, you might not be able to get back up, or if you did finally get up you could be starting from the kind of bottom you'd never fully recover from. And Sean's dad was paying a lot for him to go to this school. He didn't want to feel all that pressure, but it was already there before he could figure out what he wanted to do, for instance, with his life, when he grew up, as they say when you're a kid and people ask you what you want to be when you grow up. Sean had never come up with anything for that question, had always said he didn't know, which seemed to depress people, but he thought it was more depressing to have some unlikely dream, like becoming a famous rapper or athlete, or famous person on the internet. It was freshman year and one semester, he told himself. And it would probably be easier to get good grades doing school online. Plus he'd gotten used to being home. To getting high every day. And he was starting to get good at the guitar.

The electric guitar with the amp was a Christmas gift from

Sean's mom the year before the disease began to take her. Not wanting to be around his dad or brother, or even hear them through the walls, meant Sean played all the time. He did it out of guilt for not having played enough when she was still around to hear it. That guilt drove him into a routine that made him better at drowning out everything in the round fuzzy metal messy mass of sound he could amount to, using daisy-chained distortion pedals playing '90s grunge and sometimes death metal licks if just to get at the warm soft center that was his melancholy, as if to electrocute it, shock it out of its sleepy, complacent sadness, move it all to the metal he made and broke apart and crushed or exploded with distortion.

There was a peer-to-peer space on the site for school that hardly anyone was ever in at the same time as Sean. But one day he met a user named Oredfeather there. Sean's username was Sprice. Oredfeather had messaged him in the peer-to-peer space asking what's a Sprice, to which Sean asked what an Oredfeather was, which led them into a brief conversation about *Minecraft* because of the ore reference, how they both didn't play that game anymore was a way to say they weren't little kids anymore, and then into a back-and-forth about why each of them was doing school online instead of in person.

SPRICE: How'd you end up here?

OREDFEATHER: My grandma made me.

SPRICE: Yeah but it's not an easy school to get into so you must have had the grades too but that's not what I meant. I mean here as in the online version here.

OREDFEATHER: I got shot.

SPRICE: You got what?

OREDFEATHER: Shot. Like with a gun.

SPRICE: No way.

OREDFEATHER: The bullets still in me.

SPRICE: Bullets like plural like you got sprayed?

OREDFEATHER: lol sprayed no just one bullet still in me and not even just part.

SPRICE: Part?

OREDFEATHER: Part of the bullet.

SPRICE: I was adopted.

OREDFEATHER: Oh.

SPRICE: I don't know why I'm telling you that sorry.

OREDFEATHER: It's good I get it I shared something weird.

SPRICE: lol weird. My mom died last year.

OREDFEATHER: My grandma's not my grandma, and my other grandma is my grandma, but we're just barely starting to get to know her. Oh and my mom died too but hella long ago.

SPRICE: I heard you don't ever get over it.

OREDFEATHER: I think I did. I mean I was pretty young when she died so maybe it's different if you're older.

SPRICE: How'd you get shot?

OREDFEATHER: I was at a powwow. I was dancing. They tried to rob it. I was just there. They didn't even mean to shoot me specifically.

SPRICE: Did it hurt?

OREDFEATHER: Whatchyou think?

SPRICE: I almost broke my back playing roller hockey. That shit hurt. But also like why I'm doing online school here.

OREDFEATHER: Roller hockey? What is that?

SPRICE: Old dead sport.

OREDFEATHER: What happened?

SPRICE: You mean like what happened to the sport?

OREDFEATHER: No like how'd you get your back almost broken?

SPRICE: Got cross checked in the back. It's like if they use their stick sideways if they rail it against you. The guy was going pretty fast but mostly it was the way I hit the wall the way my back bent when I hit the wall that did it. I was in the hospital for hell of long though.

OREDFEATHER: How long and who says hell of instead of hella?

SPRICE: lol hell of is where hella comes from. Three months. How long were you in?

OREDFEATHER: Not that long but being home with the pills and taking care of the wound made it feel like I never left.

SPRICE: What pills they got you on?

OREDFEATHER: Eh sorry I gotta go good talking to you tho.

———•••———

CHAPTER FIFTEEN

The Other Fruitvale

Opal Viola Victoria Bear Shield and her boys, and now Jacquie
Red Feather, they all live up Fruitvale Avenue, far enough up
past MacArthur where it becomes another Fruitvale Avenue, a
Fruitvale off of Fruitvale, like a tree branching out, in a neighborhood where fruit trees—mostly citrus—grow in yards everywhere, here where between the Sausal and Peralta Creeks was
made a little valley, and a traveling orchardist named Hender-
son Luelling once planted it with fruit and called it Fruit Vale.

The lemon tree in their backyard rarely ever got picked for
practical use, the boys mostly used the lemons for a war game
they made up, back when they were still young enough to not
care about how much it hurt to get pegged with a lemon, or
about how sticky it could get—literally and emotionally—once
the game really got going. You had to squish the lemon to ignite
it as a grenade, which also served to soften its blow, and you
stepped on an enemy's grenade to put it out of commission. Base
was the house, which you couldn't even throw in the house's
direction because there would be no ruining Opal's paint, and

no breaking any windows, especially the one above the sink, where Opal sometimes glared at the boys playing while she did dishes—mostly dirtied and almost never washed by them unless she made it a point to make them wash the dishes, which often meant more work than it was worth since she'd have to examine and rewash any dishes not washed well enough.

The neighborhood is not that deep into East Oakland, but not near Lake Merritt either, a kind of central East Oakland sometimes called the middle extent, because most of Oakland is East Oakland, but to tell anyone where they live in Oakland, if asked, they might just say they live in the Dimond.

Opal hadn't known an owned home, had barely considered the possibility, all the way up until she'd saved enough to think beyond rented rooms, after she took the boys on and felt the need to sink some roots. Her and Jacquie's grandsons, they hadn't known what it meant to own versus rent either, but they knew consistency was nice, was preferable, stillness was, after all their mom, Jamie, put them through before she died, even before they were born, when they were still inside her, fish in water, taking what was given, born addicted to heroin, they spent what short time they had with her once they were out orbiting the pull, dragged along behind her doing what needed to be done, taking it and acquiring it and coming off of it, not acquiring it and being off it was as losing as being on it, was always as losing as she would ever feel no matter how far the horse carried her. It couldn't get there. She only got anywhere worth the chase twice. The first was when she first stabbed the pinpoint hole into big wide bliss that left her chasing it like it'd taken a part of her with it, a part she wasn't near done with yet, and the second was the last, which took her over the dose, over the lip of oblivion's rimless, swallowing hole, when just before it sucked her over, she got herself together enough to aim a gun's hole between her eyes, and steady enough to squeeze the trigger.

Opal was technically their great-aunt, but Indian-way their grandmother. She loved them. Already had them before they were hers.

Opal bought her house not long after the adoption became official, became a homeowner, though it felt plenty like it just meant paying higher rent to the bank, who actually owned it until you one day paid the whole thing off, along with all that interest, but it wasn't rent because there was that one-day future quality built into it, whereas rent was only ever an empty strike against Opal's income.

But when the house was first theirs, at the very beginning of owning it, they went with the new keys and flooded the place, moving through its rooms like water, or like drafts of air finding all of the house's openings as they pushed one another through its many doors, finding its windows and that one ceiling door that led to a crawl space—they hadn't known what a crawl space was. It's for the rats, Opal had said. You gotta keep and feed them up there so they don't come down and steal from the kitchen. No it's not, but what's it really for? Lony asked. It's for crawling, Orvil had said, as if that were plainly true.

What was home if you never felt you belonged inside it, when its walls were gone after your mom was dead and your grandma gave you new walls, what was the home you were ashamed to call home for fear of betraying your dead mother? And what were feelings when you wanted to numb them, what did they become? More walls. The Red Feather brothers each found their way in the walling, with Opal's steady hand to keep them housed and fed and schooled and disciplined, all the way up until the powwow—which dropped the whole bottom out, everything they'd learned to sit, stand, lean, lie, and rely on, bottomed out from under them as if the earth had quaked and taken all it could into cracks which widened into chasms.

Their newly made family was a chorus of noise and a throng of pain in waiting, because it was loved, and had been saved, and so loved desperately, knowing that whatever happened to any one of them happened to every one of them.

There had been a lightness to the load that was the boys, those years after Opal and her grandsons moved into their house, made it their home. It was like they just existed then. It hadn't felt like peace at the time, but that was the way it felt looking back, to each of them in their own way, in their own time, that was what they came to think of the time before the shooting at the Big Oakland Powwow, as something sweet by comparison, and because it was sweet and not so pointed like a sharp thing that threatened to cut them if they moved even just a little toward or away from the sharpness of the event's memory, so then they missed the time before, and missing it made them feel guilty like by missing it they were blaming Orvil, who'd been shot, like they blamed him for having to miss something so bad they'd already so naturally had, for what, the question why did he have to get shot made as little sense as why did he have to dance.

Wishing to have their old lives back became a wish they would regret each time it came, the complicated knot of it tying them up, or undoing them. They had to figure out how to live inside each individual part of themselves as best they could, to compartmentalize against the trap, to move carefully according to the rules of the trap, which weren't ever clearly delineated in thought but felt clear to feel when they rubbed up against it. This at first was Orvil wincing, or changing the bandages on his wound. It was Orvil not going to school and getting as much screen time as he wanted, and Opal saying yes to everything and no to nothing, all of which led Loother or Lony—when they noticed it—back to the fact of the shooting, of him having been shot, and it was as if the hole made in him that day brought a new world out from inside him, and they watched Orvil change, all of them, Opal noticing she was doing a kind of spoiling too, but unable to do differently.

After a catastrophe, things could really shine looking back to when it was just normal. The house was made before it was theirs, but the home kept getting built and broken down. Home was their kitchen table sticking out too far so that it clipped your hip if you forgot it was there—the wider swinging the worse the wear—and the backyard with the lemon trees and the side yard where they kept the garbage and recycling, where they sometimes at sunset watched the light drop behind the big oak out front, that rose way above their house.

Just now Opal is signing loan disclosures in the kitchen for Orvil's tuition. After being home his first high-school semester, homeschooling while he recovers, he will be starting in January. She's happy to have the equity that freed up the money that will help Orvil's future, but it is the paperwork she loathes, it's so easy, but she will do almost anything to avoid it right up until she can't anymore. She signs every line the sticky tabs the bank manager put there pointed to, saying "Sign Here" in yellow, pink, and blue. She can't believe Orvil is in high school now. The years come no matter what you do to them. She feels as if she is signing Orvil's life away. Making it official, signing off on the fact that he'll be entering the part of his life where the real trouble can be had, and hopes even though she doesn't mean to hope, that getting shot will keep him away from whatever trouble he might have otherwise gotten into. And anyway it is a private, Catholic school full of white kids. How much trouble do white kids get into is a question she does not ask herself. She just signs her big old name again and again like here I am and it is yours, my time, my work, my money, it is yours if you'll just give me a little more, loan me this and you can have that, whatever it is just keep him safe, she is almost praying as she turns the pages on the agreement, just keep him safe, just keep him safe, just keep him safe, just keep him safe.

———•—•———

CHAPTER SIXTEEN

The Only Thing Alive

A bad thing doesn't stop happening to you just because it stops happening to you. In therapy this is called trauma. Opal had me doing therapy twice a week, individual and group. To make sure I had the help I needed if I needed it. That was how Opal put it to me, and that I had to go. Opal was overcareful about not saying that I needed therapy. Of course I needed it, but it was more like I had to go, like the way I always had to go to school and had to get good grades. Go. Get. Don't give anyone an excuse to leave you behind, to not see you, to forget you're there. Opal averaged ten miles a day on her mail route, so if anyone knew about not getting left behind it was her. We would not let what happened be the reason I get behind in school, even though school hadn't even started yet; Opal said we would rise above what happened because bad things happening to you were opportunities, ways to find out who you were, find out what else couldn't keep you down, and were the only way you could find out how strong you really were. Opal got too positive after the powwow. It wasn't like her. She'd always been so real. Positive thinking sounds stupid. But

I get it. I just hated that what happened had changed her, had changed everything, hated it so much that some days I wished the bullet had killed me.

So I needed therapy. Obviously I needed therapy. I'd gotten shot while I was dancing. That was some fucked-up shit to have happen. But there was more I should have been to therapy about before, my whole childhood with my mom before she died.

But nobody wants to be told they need therapy just like nobody wants to be told they got problems. Paid therapy felt better to me than some kind of free or court-mandated kind. Plus the therapist was supposedly Native. Opal had found him on the internet. He'd said his grandmother was a full-blooded Arapaho. He looked white to me. And then sometimes not, sometimes he seemed hella Indian, like in what he said and the way he said it, like how what Opal said could sometimes seem to come from a long time ago, and you just knew it was some hard-won wisdom passed down to her, something simple and timeless, that you could actually use in your life.

I'd heard the word trauma before, everyone knows the word trauma. But when I heard it used about me, I didn't like it.

"All of the work we'll be doing together will be related to your trauma response," Dr. Hoffman had said in our first session. "The four F's," he said. "There are four kinds of trauma responses, two of which you've probably heard of, fight and flight, but the two other lesser-known responses are freeze and fawn."

"Fawn? Isn't that like a deer?" I said, and a yawn escaped Dr. Hoffman's mouth, which he visibly tried to suppress by putting his fist to his nose and sort of squeezing his face like it was a fist, after which he didn't fully yawn but did that yawn version of throwing up in your mouth.

"It has to do with taking care of other people's feelings, and putting their feelings before your own. We will address all forms of trauma response in our healing work."

I didn't think healing and work belonged together like home and work didn't, and it felt like homework thinking about doing healing work. But the healing work just ended up being art therapy, like drawing and painting and drumming and writing—learning to reframe my story with writing. Dr. Hoffman wanted me to write what he was calling an autobiography, which I told him I didn't want to write. We did physical stuff too, meant to express or exercise my pain and emotions. Once we did a walking meditation around Lake Merritt that felt like it took forever. Another time we went up to the hills and shot an arrow with a bow at some paper targets taped to a redwood. Calling it archery in the end wasn't enough to make it feel okay to be Native and shooting a bow and arrow in the woods for therapy, but I had to admit it was kinda fun, and I wanted to be good at shooting the bow and arrow, as if it were some test I needed to pass, as if I should just know how, like that knowledge should be in my DNA.

The craziest thing we did was called reverse-speech therapy. Dr. Hoffman recorded me saying stuff in our sessions, then processed it with something he called backmasking, which was just playing it in reverse from what I could tell. Dr. Hoffman said the backmasked version was my unconscious speaking in reverse simultaneously as I consciously said things forward.

"You're saying . . . wait so what are you saying?" I asked, and Dr. Hoffman laughed then coughed a cough that seemed caused by the laughter. "You're saying whatever I say, some other part of me is saying another thing, but it can only be heard if I listen to it backward?"

"Your unconscious is a powerful, powerful part of you," Dr. Hoffman said. I didn't like how he'd said powerful twice in a row like that, but also felt like Dr. Hoffman's unconscious was what was behind him having said it twice in a row like that. "All humans have this ability." Dr. Hoffman cleared his throat, then pointed at his throat saying, "Double-speaking is natural for our vocal cords, and true to the dual nature of reality. Think of all the ways the world is split in two, night and day, sleeping and waking, life and death, good and evil, noise and silence, darkness and light." As he spoke and repeated these opposites to illustrate his point he kept flipping his palm so it faced up and then down. "The unconscious way of speaking is closer to poetry, and the conscious one is closer to prose."

"Yeah but, like, that's like saying everybody has some split personality."

"If we don't acknowledge the unconscious, which is what it wants, then we allow it to run the show, as in dreams or, worse, nightmares, and we never wake up to who we are as a whole."

"Are you talking about being woke?" I said, trying to be funny.

"I'm talking about seeing the mind as being more than what we think we know it to be."

One recorded clip had me saying *I really don't think I'm doing that bad,* and then—backward or backmasked—it sounded like *Gonna nod, might nod delirious.* I didn't think it meant anything then, but later, way later, something I couldn't even see the start of then, when I was actually nodding out from too many pills, that phrase ended up messing with me, like did some part of me somehow know what was coming?

Group therapy was just talking circles with other kids who I thought probably had to be there, like they were court-mandated, at least that's what their faces said, like when's this shit gonna be over, but then maybe my face said that too.

In group sessions, Dr. Hoffman would always do most of the talking before anyone else, to explain why the talking mattered in talking circles, like everyone could just kumbaya their way back from trauma.

"It's important to voice things, to sound them out, like the way we learn to spell by slowly saying words, we have to sound out our stories, and they may come out slow and clumsy, and we may misspell them, so to speak, at first, when we first go to try, which is to say we may misunderstand them. But as we frame and reframe them, our own stories, the ones we tell each other and tell ourselves about what happened to us, and what it means in the context of our lives, and the bigger life we're a part of, the better we can understand what it all means, the more sure and purposeful our steps forward will become, and the more informed our decisions will be. It's just as important for you to hear yourself speak your stories as it is for others to hear you speak them, so that you can come to know you're not alone, and more the same as the person sitting next to you than you are different from them, which you never would have ever believed unless they opened their mouths to share their stories here in these circles. One thing I want you to understand is that your suffering does not make you special. There's a voice inside everyone who suffers that says, no one else has it like this, and so much selfish action comes from listening to that voice. You are not alone, you are not special, and there is help. We have one another."

Dr. Hoffman called me out on saying shit was kumbaya in one of our individual counseling sessions. I didn't even know where I got the kumbaya thing from, probably a meme. I'd complained that Native things can feel corny, and fake, or like trying too hard for something that wasn't really there, that the shit was kumbaya. Dr. Hoffman told me the word kumbaya was originally an African American spiritual, a song that was also a prayer asking for divine intervention, asking for help in dire times, and that then the hippies in the sixties took it and sang it to mean unity amid protest, and then it got played out and became a stand-in for corniness about togetherness.

"Corniness about togetherness," I said back.

"But there's nothing corny about asking your higher power for help when you need it most," he said. "Or do you think that's corny too?"

"Are you asking me for real?"

"Let's just agree that I won't ever be asking you anything in a not-real way in our sessions, okay? So, yes, please answer for real."

"Yeah I think the higher power thing is corny. And the talking circle is corny. And crying out for help when you need it most, if I'm being honest, feels kinda corny too, like who's really gonna help when you really need it most, God? Like some great big being who made everything's gonna come around to help some little human life, like one of our little lives matter? Because what about all the good people who die every day crying out for God and God not doing shit for them, what, they don't deserve it?"

"I appreciate your honesty, Orvil. How you feel about these things is real, like you said. And everything can be useful. Even corniness."

Dr. Hoffman called his approach to trauma and healing *using all of the buffalo,* which was also super corny.

"Your feeling that something is corny has to do with trust,

you not believing people are being authentic, which probably meant for you they were lying to get their way, in other words manipulating you, so when you see or hear corniness you're just responding to a very real and valid feeling you have around trust." He was always looking behind me after asking questions or making statements. There wasn't anything there but a wall, so I guessed that was him demonstrating that he was thinking, taking me and my problems seriously.

"When we start to understand how much of our behavior has to do with trauma response," Dr. Hoffman started saying, but I checked out, looking over Dr. Hoffman's shoulder. Behind him was a window where sometimes a redheaded little bird landed on the sill and looked in on us. Sometimes I thought the bird was imaginary. And when I did, the bird seemed to take on more fantastic qualities, like turning its head to the side like it was putting its ear up to the window. And sometimes I imagined the bird crashing into the window with a thud and dying in the middle of one of our sessions there below the windowpane, dead on the ledge, dead eyes wide open, still looking in on us.

When I first woke up in the hospital, my brothers were sitting at the foot of my bed playing war with a beat-up deck of cards. Our grandma Jacquie watched Loother and Lony play, sneaking looks at me every now and then. I snuck looks too, and through a squint, I watched a pigeon with one foot land on a ledge outside the window and felt bad for its plight, then remembered it could fly and that feet don't matter so much when you can fly, feet are more like a butt when you can fly. A slow tear ran down my cheek then. It would have been enough to feel the tear, its slow, falling speed, its warmth, and to see my brothers there, to know Jacquie—our real grandma, who'd never really been in our lives—to make me want to cry, but the tear was just one of those waking-up tears, like the wet on the grass in the morning isn't from rain. Lony was the first to notice I was awake, and when he did he came over to hug me as best he could over the metal-barred bedrail. I went to speak but then coughed and cleared my throat, then asked about where Opal was. Lony said she was getting us food, while Loother gathered up the playing cards at the end of the bed and put them back in the box. War, Loother said about the cards. The word war sounded loud in my head, like a metal box with nails in it going down a stairwell made of metal walls.

Hospital-cafeteria tacos, Lony said with his tongue out. Hope you're hungry, Loother said with a crooked Loother smile.

I didn't ever want to eat again. I was that kind of not-hungry.

Jacquie seemed like she was about to say something, then she covered one of her eyes with a fist, stood up, and walked out into the hallway. I said to my brothers, so you guys just been playing cards while I was over here dying or what? They smiled wide and lost it for a second, laughed like nothing bad had ever happened to anyone. Laughing could really do that. Then it hurt my stomach to laugh and I winced and sucked in air through my teeth. We stopped laughing and watched the door to see if Jacquie would come back in. I asked my brothers what Jacquie was doing there once it seemed like she wasn't coming back in. Loother said he didn't know, and Lony said yeah we do, so I asked Loother what Lony was talking about. Lony said Jacquie had carried me off the field after I got shot. One of your shoes fell off, Lony said. What are you talking about? I asked.

Loother and Lony didn't know how to answer that, so silence hung there between us for a minute or so like distant church bells before Loother couldn't help but telling me again that Jacquie had carried me, that I lost a shoe, motioning with his arms how she'd carried me out to the car to take me to the hospital. Lony put his arms up the same way as Loother's, indicating he saw her carry me out to the parking lot of the coliseum too. They were telling me not to ask again why Jacquie was there with their arms up like that. I felt shame about almost dying then, thought that it made me weak, which made me feel mad about the shame, but then too weak to hold the feeling. Lony stretched and farted pretty loud, which didn't seem on purpose. No one laughed because it didn't seem meant to be funny, he'd just stretched and accidentally let one out. There was a long pause before Lony said, D'you know they go ten feet per second? What? Loother said. No they don't, you're hella stupid, Loother said. No they don't. That's almost seven miles per hour, Lony said, and looked at us both without even smiling. That did smell pretty fast, Loother said, and Lony laughed that hard but quiet Lony laugh with little clicks that came from the back of his throat. I laughed out the word stupid, then felt that sharp ache in my gut again, but this time I didn't wince, just stayed laughing so as to not ruin the moment.

This is the thing. You don't know what will happen to you. Everything is one way, and you think you know what that means, and then one day you come to find that no: *This* is what life is like anymore. For me, one day I was learning how to dance powwow from YouTube in my room, and the next I was shot down at a powwow on a baseball field in a coliseum. Life must be sweet like a bird waking you up in the morning with a song, and then it's that one under the window with its neck broke 'cause it coulda swore there just had to be more sky there.

I heard most people ran when they heard the shots. I had thought it was thunder. I thought the dancing might've brought the rain. I knew the rain-dancing thing was stupid, and on the playground when I was younger I'd even made some rain-dancing jokes to make kids laugh, maybe even danced a little fake Indian dance and whooped while patting my mouth, but there was no rain the day of the powwow, and the only thing wet was my hand when I pulled it away from where the bullet quietly made its way into me.

It didn't even hurt at first. It landed hard, but it was like this big muted thud, like a knock at someone else's door. Then it hurt so bad I left. I was out. I went wherever you go when you don't die but can't stay awake and you're not sleeping. It wasn't not like a dream, all my time after that in the hospital, then all my time after the hospital back home, plus the time back at the hospital again for my second surgery. Morphine was a trap. The thing brought dreams over into waking, and waking things back over into dreams to where you didn't know what was what. But it flew away the pain too.

I had what seemed an unlimited prescription of the almighty hydromorphone. Even the sound of the name of the pill felt like its strength, like some water monster, or like some kind of supernatural disaster.

I'd looked the pill up and seen the brand name was Dilaudid, and one of the street names for it was dust. I liked that name for it because it made me feel weightless, like that crazy-slow speed dust floated at when you saw it in a ray of light coming through a window.

Hydromorphone beat morphine by a mile, that was for sure. All that same lift without the drift into dreams you didn't know were dreams. Nightmares were another thing. My grandma said I have an overactive imagination, like her compliment about too much activity in my brain helped in any way from stopping the horrible shit I dreamed about.

But after what happened at the powwow, everything that came to me at night was some version of the day I got shot. And worse than that. Sometimes I woke up in a panic that seemed like it might last forever, like a scream I couldn't stop hearing, or like death coming on in a smothering rush. Sometimes the dreams were just about aggressive insects that reminded me of bullets if bullets could be said to be hungry.

The fear of sleep and the panic that seemed to grip me no matter what I did was why I came to feel I needed the hydromorphone. There was nothing more to it than that. I'd been broken, but I'd been broken open. The bullet had made its hole, a hole I felt stayed open even though it'd been sewn shut, and the hole felt open, and like something was coming through, out of it, asking something of me in return, like it needed to be filled, and here were these pills.

I hated when the days got shorter, because the nights got longer. I hated for it to be night when Opal came home from work and everyone was home together.

I'd taken the pill I normally took at night to sleep better just before my brothers came home after school, then another one before Opal and Jacquie got home, Opal from her job and Jacquie from whatever she did all day, so that by dinnertime I felt that lift, and the worry was gone.

I complained to Opal about school, how it didn't feel real, and how I didn't even see the point in school at all unless I wanted to end up dying behind some desk. No one's dying behind a desk, Opal said. It was an investment in the future. All you could do was play the odds. A better education gave you a better chance. No one knew what the future would bring. That was true, I thought when she said that. But I also knew how much the past fucked with the future. That was called a predictive element. Dr. Hoffman taught me that. Adding that it wasn't the whole story, what happened to you. People could change. Having a future meant you had hope. It definitely didn't feel like the future was mine anymore. It felt like it belonged to what happened to me. No matter what Dr. Hoffman tried to tell me about the past not dictating my future, not the recent past and not the past that included my mom—then came to not include her. The past was the past and it had passed was the way Dr. Hoffman put it. I could only respond to what was happening now. "The only thing alive lives right now, here in this very moment," was the way Dr. Hoffman put it. I hated that, and that my only options to respond in the moment were with meditation and breathing, or talking things through with Dr. Hoffman, or expressing myself through drawing or writing or exercise. Being present doesn't feel good just because you're paying attention to it. Matter of fact it can be worse. Better to get distracted. Or high.

I hadn't told Dr. Hoffman about the pills, what I'd found in them. Therapy had everything to do with what I decided to tell my therapist. And there'd been a new voice in me telling me things to say that didn't feel like me, like myself. I didn't know if it was because of the drugs or if it was because I'd changed so much. More and more I thought it might be the bullet.

I'd been shot with a bullet and the bullet had stayed inside me, part of it, a shard, or whatever, because it was more dangerous to remove than to keep. So the bullet would stay inside me, and I would stay inside and recover and heal and keep up with school and not get behind and not lose a year. Opal made sure it was clear to me that they—we—would not let what happened at the powwow be bigger than us.

"We will not let it have this next part of our lives," Opal had said.

"What's this next part?" I asked.

"The next part is the part where we live like we've been given a second chance, and not like something's already been taken away from us." She walked out of the room with the back of her hand across her forehead like she was feeling it for a fever.

Jacquie told us we were all gonna play dominoes and eat hot dogs on Friday night when Opal went off to a Native event at the intertribal center down on International. Jacquie said she didn't care if we wanted to or not. She was serious and mean in a way I hadn't seen her be like. But I was feeling pretty good about the three pills I'd taken that afternoon. Three was a new amount to take all at once—and in the late afternoon. I felt awake but real slow and good and like sitting down with some dominoes would feel all right. My tolerance was enough by then that I knew I wouldn't seem high to the point of noticeable. But I didn't like the way my eyes looked in the mirror, all hooded. If they asked, I'd tell them I was tired, and that I hadn't slept, that I was having nightmares.

Jacquie got us all hot dogs from Kasper's. It was our favorite place to eat out. I don't know how she knew. Maybe it was her favorite too. From when she was young. Or Opal told her. The dogs were hella crunchy, that was why we liked them. I got mine with cheese and mustard. But I wasn't hungry yet and said I had to look up an assignment for school I'd forgotten about, and when Jacquie said, "On a Friday night?," I pretended to be looking closely at something on my phone, reading something specific as if to clarify the assignment.

Jacquie dumped the dominoes onto the table and I jumped up at their clacking like I was waking from a quick dream in class. I reached out my hands to wash the bones, and me and my brothers all accidentally touched hands. I could tell Jacquie liked this. She didn't smile, but I could just tell in her eyes and she saw that I saw.

"Big spinner," Jacquie said as Lony put down the six-six tile. Loother slapped down the six-three and said fifteen. Jacquie gave him his first house, cross and diagonal line. I kept my six-two for later knowing you had to score ten to get on the board. I put down a three-one and Jacquie got ten off a one-four after me.

"Ten," she said, and marked her first house.

"Why y'all acting so serious like you already know I'ma win," Lony said. He took a bite out of his plain-ass hot dog with no toppings, then put down a six-one on the end of his big spinner for five points.

"That doesn't get you on the board though," Loother said to him.

"I don't think scoring points should ever mean you don't score points," Lony said.

"It's like when you're a baby, to take your first steps, you gotta take more than one for them to count as first steps, so five points is just one step, not enough to count," Jacquie said. I liked what she meant by it.

"I'm not a baby," Lony said.

"We're all babies to the game until we get points is what Grandma means," I said. I took a bite of my cheese-and-mustard-covered hot dog.

"You're up, Looth," I said through a mouthful.

"All right then, Orv," Loother said.

I knew Loother hated when I said Looth as much as I hated Orv. But we both liked it too. It was like we were saying I love you with a fuck you. This kind of thing could happen with language and be normal and well understood.

We played dominoes late into the night. Didn't hardly say anything personal about ourselves, about our lives. That was the best part. We didn't need to. There wasn't a lack. We just played.

Me and Opal regularly went on walks after she got off work. I had asked her our first time driving up to the hills how she could want to walk after walking all day at her job. She told me it wasn't the same. She said she didn't *have* to be there, so it was different. Up among the redwoods no one expected anything.

"There's no mail for trees," she'd said.

"Wouldn't be no mail without trees," I said.

"That's true," she said, and laughed a little.

"Email though," I said, and she didn't respond at all to that.

Opal had told me I needed to get out of the house, get fresh air, exercise. When she first asked about the walks I got scared she somehow knew about the pills. How much I needed them, how much I loved them. *Tell her we're afraid to be outside anymore,* the voice said. I imagined its mean metal mouth trying to eat through more of me. I thought again about the hole it'd opened up in me—what that might have let in. *Tell her we like getting closer to our real grandma.* I could feel it wasn't me, but it was coming from me, my head, so in some way it had to be me. Or it was my unconscious. *Tell her it hurts a lot if we walk too much.*

"We don't have to if you don't want to, Grandson," Opal said to me. She barely ever called me grandson.

"No, I want to," I said, and meant it.

"Then I'll pick you up tomorrow, about six, we should still have a window before dark."

Fuck you, the bullet said in my head. And I didn't know if it was directed at me or her.

I went over to Dimond Park after my talk with Opal. I went over by that part of the creek with the tunnel, where I always saw empties but never people drinking. I looked down at my reflection in the water and saw my hair there. I hadn't tied it back before I left the house, and thought for a second there was a girl behind me when I looked down at the water.

I reached into my pocket to feel the pill I had there, and then I was holding the pill in a fist that turned into an open palm and my head was thrown back, swallowing it with some spit I gathered while thinking about whether I'd take it right there and then—the gathering of the spit itself an admission that I would be taking the pill right there and then. The only thing alive, this moment.

Back at home I played guitar until my fingers hurt too much to play anymore. I knew that if it hurt enough, hurt enough every day, that the initial hurt would eventually erase future hurting, a phenomenon people online called calluses. When my fingers couldn't take it anymore I played *Red Dead Redemption 2,* the online version where you could have your guy look how you wanted. I made my guy brown with long hair and I stole and rode horses that sometimes seemed like they were Indian horses, but not painted, just naturally spotted that way. I went at every single cowboy in the game ruthlessly, maybe even psychotically. There was such a crazy thirst for revenge in me about cowboys and sheriffs. The game rewarded you with slow-motion cinematic clips if your kill shot was deadly enough. I went for volume rather than quality kill. Basically everyone was a cowboy, so I would go on these shooting sprees that sometimes got up to a hundred or more, bodies all around me slumped or stacked, which was probably why it felt psychotic, but it was also somehow therapeutic. It was relief, the relief of regaining control after feeling the world had been set loose on you. I got control back with a controller.

At the sink I turned the water on slow, first let it run, then turned my head sideways for water. Sometimes it was enough to have the pills in my hand. Sometimes I carried them around with me, in my hand or in my pocket. It wasn't just finding out that I liked to get high. I did. There was pain too. On some nights it spread over me like wings. Even before the pills entered my bloodstream, I felt good just having swallowed them. The pills muted the pain's sharpness, padded its claws, released my body from its constant bracing of itself from the pain. They helped. I knew enough about addiction to not get tricked too easily. But with things that trick you, it's that you never know you're being tricked while you're being tricked, that's what is tricky. When I first knew I wasn't taking the pills for the pain anymore but still needed them, that was when I started doing the tricking myself. I told myself they weren't the problem. The problem was that I needed them. But it did become a problem. Getting more pills. My doctors had already talked about weaning me off, that it was time to move on to lighter, OTC pain medication.

"How's your pain?" Opal asked after she explained that OTC meant over the counter.

"It still hurts a lot," I said. "I mean it's not as bad, but the pills help," I said, not wanting to sound too serious about my need for the prescription.

On one of our walks I'd been honest with Opal about liking the pills, and how she responded I knew meant she wasn't gonna help me keep getting more.

"You're not supposed to like them," she'd said.

"What if I do," I had said, regretting immediately that I'd been so honest, but also having been high when I said it, having been high being the reason I said it.

"They're just to kill the pain. Soon you'll be off them. Soon you'll be starting school, in person," Opal said, and changed the subject, asked about how I felt about starting school, if I wanted to go clothes shopping.

Tell her she's addicted too. To food, to overeating, that she gets high from that, and who's gonna make her stop? Tell her more like over the kitchen counter. Say that, the voice said.

I was afraid to go a day without the pills. I found that I couldn't imagine not having them. Especially starting high school for the first time. I didn't even like thinking about not having them. But I was running out.

— • • —

CHAPTER SEVENTEEN

Superblood

Lony dreamed about dominoes. He dreamed that he was a domino tile, and that there were lines of dominoes as far as he could see, falling in rows that seemed to get closer and closer to him. In the dream he didn't know when the line would come that would knock him over and end his life. He knew that being knocked over meant that, and that the line was his family line, that something had begun long before he was born that was coming to knock him down, but that this was true of everyone, each family line falling down on top of the living when they die, all that they couldn't carry, couldn't resolve, couldn't figure out, with all their weight.

Lony is sitting in the rosebushes in front of their house. A thorn had just snagged his shoulder on the way into the bushes. The thorn had pulled at his shirt like the thing didn't want him in. He is annoyed as anyone ever is getting snagged like that. He pulls up his shirtsleeve, pinches where the thorn dug in deepest as it slid across his arm, and watches the blood come.

Lony's blood was the only one that matched Orvil's when

he needed it in the hospital. He hated the sight of needles, their impossibly sharp little needle pain, but he liked that he could give his blood to Orvil to help when he needed it. When Orvil ended up okay, Lony wondered if his blood was what did it, and if he hadn't given it to him, where would the blood have come from? All of which later made Lony wonder how more blood is made when you lose it like Orvil had. But then how more blood is made inside a body was the kind of question he never got around to googling.

Lony first thought about digging out front while playing *Minecraft,* which is one of his favorite things to do. In *Minecraft* he loves to dig for diamonds and run away from zombies and spiders and skeletons with bows and arrows, dig himself a shelter for the night, light the inside with torches and cook meat. Lony likes to play on survival hard-core mode, which means if you die you really die. Or at least he used to like survival hard-core mode before. Now he doesn't hardly play at all or if he does it's on creative mode, where he can fly through the air invincibly.

There in the rosebushes, Lony has the pocketknife Orvil gave him when he was ten flipped out and ready to use. He stabs the ground to soften the soil and to test the blade. Orvil told Lony not to tell anyone about the knife. He hadn't told anyone. Lony knows he isn't like the kids he'd heard Loother talk about, kids Loother knew at school who cut themselves. "To feel that other pain, the pain they couldn't feel without the cutting," Loother had said. Lony wondered about this other pain. But he knows he isn't like those kids, he knows because he feels things, pain and other pain too.

He's cutting to get the blood out, not for the cut or to feel because he can't. It's for the blood, and if there was like a little faucet or valve or just any other way like spitting or peeing or sweating, how you get water out, he would do that but there isn't one, so cutting is the way.

He's dug a hole there below the bushes, and squeezes his finger, drips the blood into the hole, then buries it.

Lony recently googled blood, and Native Americans, and magic, and combined all of them to see what came up. He found on one site the name Cheyenne meant the cut people. That was enough for him to remain convinced that what he was doing with the cutting and the blood was okay, like something he was a part of, not something he was doing to get away from what he felt, or to feel some other pain he wouldn't know he was feeling until he felt the cutting pain. He also found some stuff about blood and sacrifice and ritual, about Natives from way back before Europeans arrived. Some worshipped the sun, which Lony had just learned at school was a star. A star.

It makes more sense to Lony to worship something like the sun than a dead guy on a cross who rose from the grave like a zombie, and all that stuff about eating his body and drinking his blood, or bread and wine to pretend it was his body and blood? Christianity is so weird, but everyone pretends like it isn't.

The day's light and heat dims when a cloud moves in front of the sun. Lony has a ball of rubber bands he's been building up since last year that is bigger than his hand as a fist, but not bigger than his open hand as an open hand with his fingers stretched out—which is as big as he wants it to get. He found a bag of multicolored rubber bands in Opal's old desk in her room. The way the rubber-band ball started happening was by accident. Lony was tying some of them together in a complicated way. He'd found that if you have a bunch and keep making loops around the bunch, you could sort of accidentally make a finger trap, but then something else happened as they all bunched together. He kept adding to the bunch really fast, wrapping more and more rubber bands around the bundle until they made a ball that could bounce pretty good, and it looked cool, rainbow-colored but blended all randomly, like crisscrossing rainbow randomness in a way that he liked. He thinks of the ball as his power. When Lony first started putting his rubber-band ball together he thought of a scene in *Donnie Darko* where there was this energy like a liquid worm-type thing that came out of everyone's middle, like between your heart and stomach, they called it the thorax in the movie. Lony always thought of that movie and that place on his body, or in his body, because in dreams when he knew it was a dream and he wanted to make something happen, he felt that part of him sort of flex, like a muscle, and then the thing he wanted to happen happened.

One time when they were all watching one of the Avengers movies, Lony stopped paying attention because he'd seen that one too many times and thought first about why there weren't any Native American superheroes or villains or actors or actresses, and then about what power a Native American superhero would have if they made one. He thought there should be more than one power, but which ones would they get? Lony had discovered while figuring out which ones that he loved making lists—how they could be stories but like you had to figure out the story from the list so it was also like a puzzle. His first list was this list he called the Super Indian list, which listed the powers a Super Indian should have, based on stereotypes but also on true things about Native people as far as he knew. The list went as follows:

1. Can Fly (because feathers)
2. Has Thunder/Rain Control (because rain dancing?)
3. Perfect Aim (because eagle eye?)
4. Shapeshifts into Any Animal
5. Uses Hair as Strongest Ropes
6. Invincible to Drugs and Alcohol (also unpoisonable)
7. Can Dance Fight
8. Can Summon Dogs (because of Cheyenne dog soldiers, attacks or use for company)
9. Invisibility (because no one knows we're still here)
10. Superblood (released by cutting self?)

For most lists, he liked to make them be ten things, because making rules or limits helped him organize his thoughts better, but this list was a list of three. The facts felt so big he thought of them as superfacts. They had that strange quality that made it so he didn't know how to think about them, but also could not stop thinking about them. Those facts were these:

1. At the center of the Milky Way galaxy is a supermassive black hole as big as four million suns. (At the center is a hole like a donut?)
2. The universe is expanding at the rate of 1.3 million miles per hour. (Expanding into what is my question.)
3. Everything that isn't dark matter or dark energy, as in everything we've ever observed/known about, adds up

to less than five percent of the universe. (So most of existence is basically a secret?)

He wanted to make a list that included more superfacts but couldn't find anything so big as to feel super and like, disruptive, that basically felt like they put a hole through him.

He couldn't think of what superblood would do for you, and he wanted feathers to do something super, but not related to just flying. Then he thought of their last name being Red Feather and wondered for the first time where it came from, and if they were talking about bloody feathers, but then he didn't know who he could have meant by *they*.

Lony thinks Orvil's superpower might be being bulletproof, but that's barely a superpower, since so many superheroes have that power.

When Lony started to think of a place inside him between his heart and his stomach as a growing ball of light was when he started to think of his growing rubber-band ball as the same thing, and as his power. He wants to bunch up his power, to maybe use it for something like flying or disappearing. If he stands any chance at being any kind of superhero, this is how he would do it, so he buries his rubber-band ball next to the place where he drops his blood, which he doesn't notice he has been doing more and more, which means he is cutting more and more.

Orvil has seemed like he's mad about being Native lately. How they weren't raised right, then he had to sneak off to try to be a part of a thing that got him shot. Lony feels like he knows how Orvil feels about them being Native, but that he, Lony, feels worse. He feels wrong for feeling that way since Orvil got it so much worse. But Lony knows the least and feels the furthest away from what it means to be not even Cheyenne or Native but Indian like he hears Opal say it sometimes, that old way like you can only say if you're one of the real ones. Lony feels worse because he doesn't even care about being Native or Indian and would rather just have a normal life and not have to always feel so heavy, have to carry more than it feels like he should have to carry. His sadness makes him feel so soft but also like he wants to harden. He tries to go for anger but he can't, going for it just brings him more sadness and then he wants to feel normal again. And then he does. He returns to the simple joy of digging in the dirt, even if he is burying what amounts to a magical object using blood in a kind of ritual to gain a super-power to combat his feelings of powerlessness and other yet to be identified evils of the world.

He doesn't know how long it is after putting the ball in the ground, and adding more blood, patting down the soil, that he feels the earth move and hears a low rumble, like something big coming from way below, and he thinks it's his imagination, or the fact that he keeps putting in blood and needs to eat something, but then hears things shake inside the house and knows what it is, hears his brother say the word as a question to no one since no one else is home but Lony, and Lony isn't even inside, which makes him want to laugh but also makes him feel sad for Orvil, sad because no one is answering his question except for the earth quaking. Lony runs inside and goes to where he thought he heard Orvil was when he asked if it was an earthquake in Opal's room and sees Orvil is up on his feet, steadying himself with his hands like he's on a balance beam. Orvil is holding a pair of scissors. He'd just cut off his ponytail, so then just like with not knowing if his blood saved Orvil or if he is bulletproof, now, Lony doesn't know if his blood in the ground caused the earthquake or if it happened when Orvil cut his hair off.

"D'you feel that?" Lony asks.

"Strong medicine," Orvil says, closing his fist around the hair he'd just cut.

"It wasn't even that big," Lony says. "Why you doing that?" Lony asks, and goes digging in the desk.

"Was that really an earthquake?" Orvil asks Lony.

"Did you really just cut your whole hair off though?" Lony says.

"My whole hair? No. Hair doesn't mean shit anyway, Lony," Orvil says, brushing through his hair, letting fall what had already been cut but was still tangled. "Long hair is stupid," Orvil says, and keeps cutting off more hair in chunks.

"It's really not," Lony says, and pulls out a staple remover he finds in the desk, chomps along with the thing at his own face like it's alive trying to eat him and he's trying to eat it back.

"Why would I want something on my head that's basically what's on a baby horse's butt?"

"What?"

"Ponytail. If I have one coming out the back of my head, my head is a horse's butt."

"Ponies aren't baby horses." Lony has the staple remover say this at Orvil.

"Yeah, they are."

"I'm cutting mine too," Lony says, and starts opening drawers again, looking for scissors. "Can I use those?" Lony says, pointing to the heavy metal sewing scissors Orvil is using.

"When I'm done. But I wouldn't go cutting my hair if I were you."

"You're doing it," Lony says.

"Yeah and no one's gonna say anything about it to me, but if you do it, then . . . ," Orvil says, and seems to forget the end of his sentence. He watches in the mirror as Lony picks up the ponytail from the floor.

"Is what you're doing like a Native thing?" Lony asks. And for some reason thinks of how Opal never let them step over one another in the house, if anyone was lying down, you never stepped over someone's body, ever. It was whatever more than a rule was in the house. A law. And something Cheyenne Opal had never explained to them. "Or like a . . . I don't know, trying to *not* be a Native thing?" Lony says.

"This is a cut-my-hair thing, why's it gotta be more than that?"

"It doesn't gotta be, it just takes hella time to grow, so it feels like you're messing with time, making a decision too fast with those heavy scissors."

"Messing with time. Hmm. Exactly why you're not cutting your hair. Not today."

CHAPTER EIGHTEEN

Restoration

Opal Viola Victoria Bear Shield and Jacquie Red Feather walk side by side around the domed cage near the bird sanctuary on the north side of Lake Merritt, watching birds flit and alight on fence posts and branches, singing or chirping but mostly watchful for food or sudden movements.

Down on the water, ducks and seagulls and even a pair of swans farther off float on the black-green water. There are no birds in the domed cage. The single tree inside is growing through the octagonal holes in the cage.

"I heard they kept monkeys in here once," Jacquie says.

"You did not," Opal says, looking around for a sign about the cage. "It's like a smaller version of that big glass Disney ball in Florida."

"It's called the Epcot Center," Jacquie says.

"What do they keep in there?" Opal asks.

"What, the Epcot Center?"

"I meant this cage, but fine, yes, the Epcot Center, what's in there?"

"I actually went to Disney World once, in Florida, for a

weekend with a guy I barely remember. I do remember going inside though," Jacquie says.

"So what was inside?"

"They call it Spaceship Earth. And inside is the whole history of human development. From cave paintings to television."

"Any Indians in there?"

"Who do you think drew on the caves?"

"They drew *inside* the caves, *on* the walls, and they weren't Indians."

"Savages. Cavemen. Indians. They're saying the same thing."

"You're stupid," Opal says, and throws bread crumbs at Jacquie's feet so that some of the bolder seagulls surround her, which makes both of them laugh.

"What about this thing?" Opal says, pointing to the cage.

"Looks like just that tree. I think it's trying to escape," Jacquie says, hooking her fingers through the cage. "You remember Mom used to tell us the Mormon temple was Disneyland?"

"She told us a lot we knew not to believe," Opal says.

"You didn't believe her?" Jacquie says. "I did. Enough that I looked it up later. You know Walt Disney got his inspiration from Fairyland way back when? And Frank Oz, who was one of the other main Muppet guys, he came out of Fairyland too? All that magic in the world, that came from Oakland."

"Is that what made you leave, then? Too much Oakland magic," Opal says.

"Oh, so you're just gonna be mean then," Jacquie says.

"I never did take the boys to Disneyland. When they would have really loved it. Or, I guess. Maybe we're not the Disneyland types," Opal says, and walks away from the cage, seeming to want to leave the conversation, perhaps because their mom came up, or because of the way it'd brought the boys to mind, something possibly sweet they hadn't done, or some possibly sweet Disney way they couldn't have been.

Opal is carrying a bag of stale bread she's been throwing from now and then, which mostly goes to the meanest seagulls, still, she's happy to not let the bread go to waste. Jacquie has her phone out to take pictures and video she will never look at again, of cranes in the distance, geese and ducks and the rare pair of swans, and then those little scrappy songbirds looking for the smallest scraps left after the seagulls battle it out for the bigger ones. Jacquie captures dutifully, for general record keeping, but never even opens her camera-roll app—it doesn't ever occur to her as something she might do later; in fact, if pressed to talk about it, she might go so far as to say it's a kind of crime against memory, a way to steal time back, to dwell on moments longer than life naturally allows, and she knows she should, if anyone should, appreciate lost moments through pictures taken, as she'd lost so much to the drinking, but even in the language, taking pictures, the taking, that's what it felt like to Jacquie whenever she looked back at them. And yet she can't stop taking them, she takes them all the time.

Opal on the other hand loves to look at pictures later, loves to remember days that way, loves that things can be kept, not lost forever with mere memory to rely on but concrete reality captured and held with you, on your phone, in your pocket, right there at your hip, where on her left side, Opal had just last month—finally—visited a doctor about a pain that had been migrating around her body before finally landing on her hip the week she was to see the doctor about it. The pain had been in her joints and in her bones. She hadn't known what bone pain was, but had felt this kind of tenderness she'd attributed to old age, and the wear and tear of walking so much. They tested her blood and then she got a phone call from the doctor.

She knew right away she couldn't tell anyone. She would find a way to fix it without anyone having to know.

Jacquie takes a picture of a flock of birds in the sky and then turns to take one of Opal, to which Opal responds by putting her hand in front of her face then saying, "Send those to me."

Jacquie doesn't know if Opal's just saying that to be nice, or if she really wants to see the birds later, to remember the walk with Jacquie, to have the pictures to show the boys, in case Jacquie leaves again, to tell them their grandmother used to love watching birds eat bread, which isn't true but could be funny enough to feel true in Jacquie's possible absence, her slip from sobriety, as slipping and being gone had always been the thing she'd done most consistently, so something she was keenly aware they all feared could happen again at any moment, which was also how Jacquie lived her sobriety, moment by moment, step by step, day by day.

They pass a totem pole. Neither of them comments on it right away, but they stare at it for a long while, seeming to think something of its presence neither wants to articulate.

"Was this always here?" Jacquie asks Opal, and stares up at the thing, blue sky behind its vibrant reds and yellows, this grand wooden stack of carved animals. Opal watches Jacquie look at the thing, wondering if she meant this life, them, walking around the lake together, taking care of the boys, was *this* always here, all this time Jacquie was off lost in her addiction?

"I think there's been a restoration," Opal says, and keeps walking.

"That's some fancy way to say new paint," Jacquie says, catching up, momentarily feeling like she was the younger sister unjustly, when actually it'd been that way for many, many years, and was absolutely justified.

"It's not just a new coat of paint."

"I don't think it was here before."

"Like you've been walking this lake all these years, you're practically new here again."

"It just seems like we would have remembered—"

"I do remember, and it was chipped and faded. Now they've restored it," Opal says.

"Clearly this isn't about the totem pole anymore."

"Oakland is always trying to be better. Even if it doesn't get there. And people are always messing with it. But it never stops trying."

"It is really good to be back. If for nothing else than the weather."

"If for nothing else," Opal says, and gets out her phone, and either texts someone or is writing something down in her notes app.

Her having gone to her phone after some amount of tension got pulled taut with no release causes them both to walk for some time in silence.

One thing you can do when it seems there's nothing else you can do, which is to say when you feel restless, is to walk, move your body through space and let the wisdom of what comes from that be your guide. This is the kind of woo-woo thing Jacquie heard on podcasts about walking that she listens to while walking, and the kind of thing she repeated to Opal as if it were her own homegrown wisdom.

"Anything you need?" Opal says to Jacquie, about an old Black man's spread of used books and CDs, shoelaces and toothbrushes still in their packages.

"Everything you see is a dollar," the man says, and flashes Jacquie a smile. Jacquie picks up a book about trees and flips through the pages, not staying long enough to read the name of even one tree.

"I'll take this one," Jacquie says, and hands a dollar to the man.

"A book about trees made of trees paid for by trees, if that ain't everything," he says, and this makes Opal think of the thing the man is smoking, what she heard Loother call trees, and she guessed they did look like little trees, the way broccoli looks like little trees.

"It is something," Opal says. And all three of them laugh.

Walking around Lake Merritt you see all kinds of people in Oakland, the hipster, the homeless, the homeless hipster, the mixtape mixed-race CD-pushing rapper, the serious runners and the casual runners, the joggers, the stoners, the casual blunt smokers, the power walkers, the slow walkers that talk endlessly, the stroller pushers, and then just so many young people with blankets on the grass. It didn't used to be like this around the lake, people always walked it, but now it is a kind of scene, with food trucks in tow.

Jacquie is thinking about Orvil, watching a young man in front of them with a ponytail. He is walking fast, and his ponytail sways. Opal is thinking about whether or not she will tell Jacquie what she found out from the doctor, and as soon as she thinks it she knows she will not.

"What do you think the boys are doing?" Jacquie says.

"Well, it's Saturday, which means no school, and we're not

there, so if I had to guess, I'd say they're watching something, or playing video games, or watching people play video games," Opal says.

"That's really a thing, isn't it?" Jacquie says.

"And you living here in Oakland, and staying here, is that really a thing?" Opal smiles a reassuring smile to soften what could potentially feel like a blow.

Jacquie Red Feather is all the way in their lives now, living with them, but no one knows what that will mean. Jacquie hadn't been ready to think about Orvil all the time, to see him every day, to be around all of them after living alone so long, to be sober, to be sober. But Orvil is not hers to save and she hadn't done to him what'd been done, he is his own person, the only one who can save him is himself, and that is true for everyone, and for Jacquie this means what the Serenity Prayer is talking about when it mentions control, and granting, even wisdom, which word she hates, soaked as it is in New Ageiness, or so Native American sounding you automatically hear the word accompanied by a Native American flute, or an eagle's cry, except that the sound effect everyone considers an eagle's cry is in fact a red-tailed hawk, which fact Jacquie had learned from NPR while on a walk.

That maintaining her sobriety is the only thing she can actually do for anyone else feels selfish, and backward, to have to go through all that effort just to *not* do something, like some zero-sum life in the negative, but she is much, much worse off if she is *not* sober, and can do nothing for anyone but cause them pain, so it isn't selfish, it couldn't be, and if it sounds like she is convincing herself, if it sounds like she is in midair, falling, it is because she almost always is, but so is everyone in their own way teetering, some with a better balancing act than others, and in fact walking itself is nothing more than a controlled falling, as her baby daughter, Jamie, proved when she was first learning to walk and only managed to take her baby steps then mostly fell after one or two before she got it down, and said *Mama sook,* her word for see and look, because Jamie talked before she walked and Jacquie is learning for the first time now to be walking her talk, to be sober in baby steps, while also learning to love to walk, and she might fall, figuratively, have lows, but she will not collapse or relapse, even though it is, she's heard, a part of recovery, supposedly, only relapse was what she'd been doing all along, with brief stints of sobriety, then controlled bouts of heavy drinking, then loss of control, then convincing herself she could master the controlled fall, then back to the baby state of drooling and falling asleep without meaning to; the stumbling, the staggering, the babbling, the bottle, needing the bottle. No, relapse does not need to be a part of her recovery anymore. She can walk that good red road, as the Native phrase for sobriety and recovery has it, which Jacquie tells herself she doesn't like, and yet whenever she hears a Native person say they're walking that good red road, it makes her heart swell, unabashedly, in that way it always does in scraped-together folding-chair circles gathered to tell stories and to listen about how bad it had been, how hard it is still, and what methods are in place to locate hope, then follow it.

There had been another kind of hope she'd found recently. Something she rarely allowed herself in any way. A man. Feelings about a man. That there might be some love still to be had. She met him after a meeting, which was generally frowned upon. They walked to a nearby diner. His name was Michael.

He had a nice smell. Something so familiar she felt somehow nostalgic about him. Michael was probably a little older than her, and Black, or at least part Black. He told her he was new to the whole recovery world. Jacquie said she was pretty new too. He said he'd been what they call a functioning alcoholic. Worked himself up to a fifth a day, then worked himself back down. He was only three months sober. His kids were in college and his wife had left him years ago. Jacquie realized while he was talking that she was attracted to him. Something about his mouth. The fullness of his lips. Even his teeth behind the lips, not too much gum, not too much tooth. A waitress walked by and Jacquie told her to bring two slices of whichever was their best pie.

"You like pie?" she asked him.

"I wouldn't trust a man who said he doesn't," Michael said.

"So you love pie," she said.

"Even bean pie, fruit pie, and pot pie, and one time I had an egg pie at a fancy French restaurant, but I might be remembering that wrong, the memory and the pie are a little brown around the edges."

"That wasn't an egg pie, it wasn't even a pie, it was a quiche," Jacquie said, and laughed at him about it.

"Can I ask you a question?" he said.

"Be my guest," Jacquie said, and a memory out of nowhere almost knocked her out of her seat. She'd watched *Beauty and the Beast* with her daughter more than any other movie and had completely forgotten about the movie right up until that moment when she said the phrase be my guest.

"Are you Native American?" he asked. Jacquie normally hated this question, but she sensed there was something more to it than the way white people asked with goofy fascination.

"Yeah, why?" she said.

"My grandmother was Cherokee. I'm an enrolled member myself," he said, and she must have made an expression of surprise. "What, you thought I was just Black?" he said.

"No no, I mean, yeah I knew you were Black and something else," she said. And then she must have blushed, which surprised her, even scared her a little.

"Plenty Black folk are Indian," he said.

"You know I used to work for AC Transit? Drove a bus drunk into a telephone pole. Can you imagine? I don't know how I was so stupid so long."

"I know what you mean," he said. And the pie came. They ate it together and there seemed to be something really happening between them. Something real. But then when she called him with the number he gave her it said it'd been disconnected. And she almost wanted to drink about that. But she walked instead.

Another thing she almost drank about was her daughter. Blue. They'd exchanged phone numbers. And texted some. At first. Then not at all. The openness of the possibility of them talking but not deciding to do so felt like an open wound. Maybe always would. She walked about that too.

Jacquie walks everywhere, as often as she can, and Opal and Jacquie walk around Lake Merritt every day after Opal gets off work. Today is no exception. It's been the case since Jacquie decided to live with them, while she figures out a job, then a place of her own, or Opal will move out and let her stay. This is a kind of trial period, her first time with the boys, and she's less than six months sober, with a bad track record, so she's on the couch through Christmas, and we'll see after that is how Opal put it when she came home from the hospital with them, before Orvil came back, and was told to take his bed until he returned, at which point Opal put blankets out on the couch and told her that they'd talk about it again after Christmas.

Opal and Jacquie are standing at Opal's car before parting ways, Jacquie off to an evening AA meeting nearby, and Opal back home to make dinner for the boys.

"I'm not being . . . I'm not being nosy, or annoying if I ask you if you're okay, am I?" Jacquie says.

"You can be nosy and annoying if you think something is wrong with someone you love and they're not saying anything."

"Okay then. Good. So what's going on? I mean I know it's been a lot with me living with you all, and Orvil. But there's something else, yeah?"

"There's nothing else. But I'll tell you if there is."

"Promise?"

"Promise," Opal says, and makes a hook motion with her finger. It was something she hadn't done since she was a little girl, something between Jacquie and her, that each of them did as an affirmative, that one of them had made up at some point. "What are your thoughts on going to Alcatraz for that sunrise ceremony?"

"You mean for Thanksgiving," Jacquie says. "Hell no."

"I mean for the sunrise ceremony. And I mean for the boys. I was thinking we should start going to more community events. Because if whatever I'd been doing had them sneaking off to go to a powwow, well then, obviously I can't do that anymore. People need to know where they come from."

"This feels like a trap."

"What would I be getting out of it?"

"Maybe you want to put me through some kind of test, have me make it or break it, see if I'm okay to stay with you all, instead of waiting it out through Christmas, maybe you think I'm a ticking time bomb and you'd rather keep your Christmas unblemished."

"Unblemished. That does seem smart. Get you out if that's the way you're going without ruining the holidays," Opal says, pretending to think out loud about and be convinced by what Jacquie has just said. "But I didn't mean so soon, not this year, next year. Building up to a big event like that and already being more familiar with the community by the time we go. Not like Mom did it, dragging us over there on a whim." They both laugh somewhat uncomfortably.

"I hate that place, but I understand what you mean for the boys. And maybe instead of hating the place we can make something new out of it, give it a new coat of paint or, what did you say, restore it?"

"Maybe we should pray about it," Opal says. And they laugh. Opal is mimicking their mom, who was always saying she would pray about it. About everything. It was her solution to any problem, and Jacquie is the only person in the whole world who would get this joke, this reference to their mom, and be able to laugh in this big way they're laughing now.

CHAPTER NINETEEN

Who Can Say Indian?

Sean Price knew a real Indian. You weren't supposed to say the word Indian to or around Indians, but that was the way he heard his Indian friend Orvil Red Feather refer to himself, and while Sean knew it could be problematic, to use the word Indian if you weren't one, if you were one but only found out you were from your DNA, from a spit sample, from a company that gave you a percentage amount of Native American you were genetically, then could you at that point say out loud the word Indian to or around another Indian? Sean sincerely wanted to know what was okay while also sort of knowing that nothing about DNA tests was socially acceptable to talk about without sounding gross.

Sean and Orvil met for the first time in real life after a class in which the teacher had asked if anyone had American Indian heritage in their blood. Sean thought it was so weird, this idea of the heritage being in the blood, but then not as weird as it only being in remnants, or relics, old art and artifacts meant to be seen behind museum glass. No it was probably a better thing for it to be alive in the living, moving through blood-pumping veins. But then why had they found his in his spit?

Sean and Orvil had been the only two in the class to raise their hands about their American Indian blood heritage. After class Sean caught up with Orvil at his locker.

Sean had recognized Orvil in class. Had realized they'd been talking online, that they'd both been home that first semester of high school. He recognized Orvil because they'd been in elementary school together. Sean didn't think Orvil remembered the time they figured out that one sand park game where they built up a sand mountain to jump into off the swing to see who could make a cooler collision with the mound of sand. Orvil had called it meteor mountain. They played it all the time those early years of elementary school. But since they never ended up in the same classes, they'd never really become friends. Orvil Red Feather was always that one Indian kid with long hair like you think of Indians as having, but then in high school, Orvil had cut it short, sloppily uneven, like someone else had taken his old hair, had cut it off in a rush. He also recognized that the username Oredfeather was for Orvil Red Feather, a fact he felt stupid for not knowing when they chatted online that one time.

"Oredfeather?" he said to Orvil. Orvil flinched, then turned around and was visibly relieved to see that it was Sean.

"Sprice!" Orvil said with a little too much excitement. They did that handshake guys do that turns into a thing between chest bump and hug.

"Do you remember me?" Sean asked.

"Of course, man," Orvil said. "I didn't know you were Native."

"I didn't either. So, like, can I say Indian?" Sean asked.

"If you're Indian."

"I am."

"How do you know?"

"It's kind of embarrassing."

"Why?" Orvil asked.

"DNA test."

"Oh."

"See? I told you it was embarrassing."

"It's really not. But like. You don't know your tribe then, right?"

"No."

"I mean nobody says Indian anymore. Your tribe makes the most sense to say. So like I'm Cheyenne so that's what I would say. But personally, I don't care what you call us," Orvil said, and put some books and a pill bottle from his locker into his backpack. Sean wasn't sure if this "us" he was using included Sean.

"I'm not trying to act like I'm being like . . . ," Sean said, and didn't know how to finish the sentence out loud, so he motioned with his hands as if they could clarify what was missing about what he was not trying to act like he was being like. His hands just flailed.

"It's all bullshit. Saying you are when you really are, saying you are when you're really not, saying you're kinda Indian for whatever reason. No Indians from when they first named us Indians would recognize us as Indians now. That's not even what they would've called themselves. They all had their own languages and names for everything. It's just like in Africa, how they have their different countries with different histories, but they're all African."

"So then are modern-day Native Americans like African Americans?"

"You know Bob Barker was Native?"

"The guy from *The Price Is Right*?"

"Yeah. And Kyrie Irving, he's enrolled with the Standing Rock Sioux."

"For real?"

"Look it up. But tell me this, do you think Bob Marley's American grandchildren living in America are trying to act like they're real Jamaicans? Even Bob was half white."

"Bob Marley's American grandchildren?" Sean took a second to reregister the pill bottle. He wondered what Orvil was taking, if he was some kind of high. Orvil closed his locker and started to walk away.

"Hey, wait up though," Sean said, and followed Orvil. He noticed just then that he was taller than Orvil by a good foot. "I mean I know who Bob Marley is, but I don't know if I know what you're talking about."

"Bob Marley's son Rohan grew up in Miami. He played football. Almost went pro. His kid ended up playing for the Washington Redskins. You know the buffalo soldiers were named because of what Indians called them because they thought their hair looked like buffalo hair?" Orvil was gripping a metal railing, kind of rocking a little back and forth.

"Buffalo soldiers? Oh yeah I know that song. So you spend a lotta time on the internet."

"Some of the Havasupai people, they're the ones who live down in the Grand Canyon next to some waterfalls, they believe Bob to be the second coming of Crazy Horse. D'you know hella Native people love reggae music, love Bob Marley?"

"I mean. Everyone loves Bob Marley, but that is still pretty crazy," Sean said.

"Horse," Orvil said.

"What?"

"Well if you believe the Havasupai people, he was Crazy Horse."

"What's up, so you play music?" Sean asked.

"You mean like play play music," and he mimed strumming a guitar.

"Yeah. Play play," Sean said, and mocked Orvil's air-guitar motions.

"I got a guitar."

"Me too," Sean said, and there was a long pause. "What you got in that pill bottle though."

"Not enough," Orvil said.

Sean had sometimes wished he could play with someone else, join or start a band, but he didn't really have any friends to speak of, none he'd have the nerve to ask to play with, until finding Orvil.

When Sean saw Orvil at lunch that day he asked him if he could join. Orvil was eating alone at a round four-person metal table painted olive green. Orvil had cheese fries and a Pepsi in front of him. Sean opened his bowl of rice and lentils. He'd decided he should be vegan. Another tribute to his mom after the fact.

"You can have some," Orvil said. Sean had to wonder if he'd been staring, possibly drooling over the idea of that *so* fake, *so* melted, *so* delicious cheese on those crisply fried fries. Not having cheese, the real or the fake kind—the vegan attempt at cheese did not qualify as either real or fake, but illegitimate— had been the hardest part of becoming a vegan.

"They had me on 'em so long for the pain, but then I got used to it, you know what I mean, the feeling," Orvil said.

"I got used to it too," Sean said. "I been used to it. When I ran out and they started restricting because of the opioid crisis or whatever, well my dad had already had a setup because of my mom and the way she died with chronic pain. My dad's kind of a . . ." Sean started to say something he just then realized he'd never voiced. "He makes drugs."

"Makes drugs? What does that even mean, like a meth lab?"

"I mean like a meth lab in that he makes his own drugs but he doesn't make meth. He makes different kinds of drugs. He started experimenting with my mom when she was dying of this, like, degenerative brain disease that also caused her a lot of unexplainable and untreatable pain, so at first he started making different kinds of drugs for her. Now it's become like a family business. I mean it's fucking super discreet, and he helps people who have chronic pain who can't keep getting pills, so it's not like evil or whatever. Like what'd they have you on?"

"Hydromorphone. But they won't prescribe any more."

"We got something better," Sean said.

"I don't think I could pay you yet though."

"I got you."

— • • —

CHAPTER TWENTY

The Box

Opal decided to go digging around in her old stuff. She went to the box where Orvil had found the powwow regalia her old friend Lucas had given her all those years back. There she found an old faded flier for an event they'd been photographed for at the Friendship Center. She'd forgotten all about the organization, the building, and all of the social services she'd gotten there over the years. So she went down there, left the house immediately.

They were having their elders luncheon. It was perfect timing, or fate, though she did not like to think of herself as an elder, nor did she want to have to believe in fate if it could be avoided.

Opal sat down and played bingo. They were fed vegetables from the garden. She didn't know anyone there. But it felt good being around other Indians. Older ones too. Mostly women. People like her who she never let herself know existed. She'd stopped going to community events.

There was a Native man she noticed, with a salt-and-pepper ponytail and a baseball cap—wearing more jewelry than anyone else in the room. All his molars were capped silver. One of his front teeth was gold capped. She saw it shine when he laughed. His name was Frank Blanket. He told her that she looked familiar, which she thought might just be flirting. Said he was a retired social worker and gave her his card and winked at her.

She knew right away she wouldn't use his card, wouldn't call him, to do what, ask him out? She herself had never been asked out on a date. Not that she hadn't been with men. There was Earl from work. They'd been flirting for years, then one day after work she ended up following him back to his place. That was just the one time and not worth it. There were guys before that too, in group homes. She didn't want those to happen. And then one time a guy she'd delivered mail to for years, he'd gotten divorced and asked her over for dinner and she went. Maybe that was a date. Orvil was old enough to be with his brothers. The dinner was nice. Good pasta with white fish. She even had wine—which she usually never drank. And she stayed over that night. But he was boring. Opal wanted to leave. Right after they were done he had the nerve to turn on the TV like she was his wife, or like that was naturally the next thing to do. She didn't know what else they should have been doing. Making small talk? Cuddling? Eventually she was happy he'd turned on the TV. It was Conan. He'd always been her favorite late-night guy. Those other guys were corny. Conan was real, and crazy, and just funny as hell. He was as sincere as he was absurd, and always making fun of himself. Opal fell asleep and left before the sun came up.

She went back the next week hoping to see Frank again, but he wasn't there. A woman much older than her, who looked vaguely familiar to her, approached Opal with a smile.

"You look just like her," the woman said. Opal smiled, but didn't like this look-like-her talk. She didn't think she looked like her mom at all. She'd seen pictures. She remembered. So why say it?

"In the eyes," the woman clarified, as if sensing Opal's discomfort.

"Did you know her?" Opal said.

"I knew you! Of course. We were good friends. I mean she was like an auntie to me. You don't remember me? Maxine," she said, and moved her almost-white gray hair away from her forehead like that would reveal whatever Opal needed reminding about. But when she smiled, Opal remembered her face. She'd been on the island during the occupation.

"She left something for you," Maxine said, and made this gesture with her finger, like a hook, like she was snagging something out of the air. Opal wondered then if her mom had taught the girls that gesture. If she'd taught this woman. Or if it was possibly a Native thing?

"Imagine. All these years. I don't know why I been holding on to it, lord knows we don't have the room for it, but we keep making room somehow, says every hoarder on those reality shows, ayyyy," she said. Opal laughed a little at this, having watched some of those shows. The place was messy. "After I ended up here, cleaning the place up, I found this box, and I seen her name on it. Anyway, it all seemed important enough to keep," she said, and led Opal to a room filled to the ceiling with boxes. "Better get a ladder," she said.

For the life of her, Opal couldn't remember if anyone told Orvil that Jacquie was the one who saved him that day, who carried him off the field, without whom he'd likely not have survived, would have bled out. These are the kinds of thoughts she couldn't get away from, that she was thinking about on the way over to get Lony. She could tell something was up with Lony. He wasn't being his usual self, so she figured they'd go get pizza where they have that old arcade game he likes that still only costs a quarter to play—*Street Fighter II.*

After they ate she asked Lony how he thought Orvil was doing, even though she meant it about Lony himself but didn't want to ask directly like that. Lony told her that he thought Orvil had changed, and either he might be bulletproof or else Lony might have a superpower that saved him. Opal asked Lony what kind of superpower that might be, and he told her there was a spot between his heart and stomach he'd learned from dreams he could make things happen with. Flying, fireballs from his fist—like the guy Opal liked to be when she played against him in *Street Fighter II,* not the blond one—healing powers, almost anything he could imagine in dreams from that spot, and that in the hospital waiting room that day waiting for word about Orvil, that he'd used that same power from dreams and healed Orvil from the bullet, that he'd pictured a force field around the bullet, and that when they said he'd have to keep the bullet in, it made sense to him because he'd put the force field around it. And then he said, all of that or else Orvil's bulletproof and *he's* the one with superpowers. Opal asked him why it couldn't just be that he survived a bullet, which happened all the time, without anyone having superpowers. To which he said, Grandma, I know that day changed you too, and then he told her how much make-believe can make life into whatever you want it to be, and that if you really truly believe in anything, you can make it happen. Then he pointed to that spot above his belly button. Opal gave Lony a fistful of quarters, which made him smile big.

Before they left the pizza place, on their way out the door, with one of his eyes, Lony was looking at Opal through a diamond shape he made with his fingers.

"Check it, Grandma," he said, with his tongue stuck out a little. "Diamond eye."

"What's that?" she said.

"What do you mean what's that?" Lony said. And Opal knew. Lony was pure Lony in moments like this. He meant what he said, nothing more, nothing less. Diamond eye.

— • • —

CHAPTER TWENTY-ONE

Double A

Loother hates that he sees other kids all see-through like the sandwich baggies Jacquie packs those no-crust neat little triangle sandwiches in for their lunches, and that they see it too, that everyone seems to be so aware of it all being so see-through and painful and funny and embarrassing, most of all embarrassing, having to be in school together and paying attention or not paying attention to fashion trends, being active online and liking and following each other there or not, but then also how everyone acts like they're all not doing it all so see-through, that gets Loother the most, how everyone acts like they're not feeling too much, and at the same time trying to act like they're too cool to feel anything.

Loother can only guess at anything, that and what Opal calls intuition, which she said is like some wisdom the ancestors hid in their bodies and passed down over generations, like having a bad feeling about a person comes from them having to deal with a lot of bad people over a lot of years, so that eventually you know one when you see one. The rich white kids seem like the bad ones to Loother. Overconfident and like they're in charge. But Loother wants them to like him. And that he seeks their acceptance and resents that he does never stops him from doing his best to seem cool in front of them.

He doesn't talk that much at school or in class because he's shy. Not wanting to be shy never stopped anyone from being shy. People are all loud in the hallways and breezeways to have everyone see them, but then they're really trying to hide behind that loud version of themselves at the same time. Loother thinks they're being hams, a word he learned from Opal and supposedly applies to a lot of Native people even though everyone's always making Native people seem like the most serious shit since the first funeral. Loother thought of that recently thinking about what his brother Orvil's funeral would have been like if he'd died, he thought about the first person to die and, like, what would the people around them have thought was happening when they suddenly, completely stopped moving at all, then went cold, then started rotting. That would have been the scariest, most serious shit ever.

People always treat Loother like he's mad. He speaks what he feels directly, is that anger? Maybe he is mad. What's there to be so okay about all the time that everyone should feel so fucking okay and like everything is supposed to be nice? When you can get shot just dancing something is the fuck wrong. Something is the fuck wrong with this world, Loother feels, at times, but he likes life too, doesn't want it to go away, doesn't want anyone he loves to have to suffer and die, doesn't want to have to die himself one day. School definitely sucks. There's this girl though. Vee. She's cool. Loother has English with her. She's way in the back and Loother's in front ever since he got caught sleeping, waking up all startled with drool pooled on his desk he doesn't think anyone saw that he wiped up with his hoodie sleeve. Vee wasn't there that day so he feels he still has a chance. He made a plan to give her his number but he was hella scared so it took him a while.

Here's what Loother's days are like: He gets up and doesn't want to have to, then Jacquie makes him get up and makes Eggo waffles with butter. She says he *has* to go to school because if he doesn't someone'll use him up at a job he'll hate one day. Jacquie's making the effort, as Opal says, to do all that she couldn't do for them when she was off drinking. Jacquie smokes cigarettes like it's her job. She's out front smoking when they leave for the bus and there smoking when they get back. She walks all the time now so he guesses that maybe makes up for it. By the time Loother gets to school he's awake enough to not want to go back to sleep, but doesn't know how to be around everyone there acting all fake and loud and stupid. Loother is cool with people he's cool with, obviously, but he never knows what to say to anyone, so he likes to walk like he has somewhere to go, or he finds Lony who's just starting middle school, he'll come up behind Lony and say *Grandma's coming* and watch him flinch, then laugh, and he'll turn around hurt at first then smile and pretend to think it's funny for Loother.

Sometimes Loother watches the girls he looks at's eyes go dead when they know he's looking at them. He's not trying to be disrespectful, he just likes the way they look when he likes the way they look and that makes him want to look at their faces for longer than he should, which is what makes their eyes go dead on him like: *Stop fucking looking at me, creep.* They're right. Guys are creeps. If they're not mad at Loother looking, but still don't want him to look, their eyes do this thing where they look away even though there's no way they can see him looking. Like their eyes know he's looking at them. Eyes are smart. It's like their eyes know to look away before *they* do. There are ways people are smarter than they are.

Loother had been wanting a girlfriend for as long as he could remember. Opal had called him a romantic, when he told her about girls he liked. There were always a few every school year that he liked but was too afraid to ever approach. Loother didn't like being called a romantic, but it was better than thinking of himself as a creep.

Loother went up to Vee on a day he was feeling good for what reason he doesn't know but he felt good enough to try. She wasn't with her friends and had just closed her locker. Loother gave her his cell number on a piece of paper with his name written above his number. I know your name, stupid, she told him, and laughed. Loother couldn't think of how. He turned his whole body so he was facing her locker and she was facing him. He reached out to touch the locker to make it seem like he knew what he was doing. What am I supposed to do with this, is what she said. Holding his note up in the air like he'd handed her a candy wrapper. I just thought if you need help in English, I'm pretty good, Loother said. You help me with English, she said, and laughed way too hard. She was right as far as class goes. But Loother gets language. Some mornings before he wakes up all the way he feels like his brain is on fire with language. He'd been trying to rap, made his brothers listen to it way too much, but then he started feeling like it was like a Black thing, like he knows there's hella Native rappers and it makes sense in a way. This made him think about how African Americans were people who used to be from Africa but were now from America but then also both, and how that was true of Native Americans except there wasn't such a thing as Native America anymore the same way there was an Africa still. And why did it make sense that Native people would steal Black culture? Maybe only because it was way worse when white rappers did it. And also, like, wouldn't Native people be mad if Black people who weren't Native started practicing their culture, like started powwow dancing and singing or whatever? He knows Native people would be mad, would be hella mad. So then what is it about rap that makes people think they can take it was a question he couldn't answer so he stopped writing and recording himself rapping. But then he starts to think about more stuff he steals from Black culture. Like wearing baseball caps the way rappers wear baseball caps and not like the way baseball players wear them. He noticed a lot of other Native men and people of color in general wore hats in this style, kept clean with a flat bill. It feels extreme to stop wearing hats when he thinks about it but also to keep wearing hats feels like another kind of extreme, which makes him wonder about why so many people wear them regularly. Because baseball is an American pastime and hip-hop artists sort of remix what being American means for themselves and maybe that's why he does it too, but it didn't seem like anyone was doing that as some statement about remixing what it means to be American, just something hip-hop artists started doing and the style was cool and people liked it and he was probably just one of these kinds of people who dresses like he sees people like him dress, but couldn't it be both a style choice and a statement about belonging as an American in a remix kind of way?

He still wanted to try to write, wanted to work with language because he liked how he could make up new thoughts when writing that he never would have thought. But when he starts his non-rapping writing, it feels embarrassing to him that he would have to call it poetry.

He thinks of writing poetry for Vee and as soon as the thought of doing it comes to him and it's so bad he feels he'll need to quit poetry forever and almost like Vee has already read it and he'd need to quit pursuing her for good too. But that feeling passes and he tries harder at the poem and knows his feelings about her are pretty serious when he's written for hours without even thinking about it.

Loother writes with his thumbs more than with anything else, mostly these are texts to his now girlfriend, Vee. He knows how to type on a keyboard too, but his thumbs are hella better than all his fingers combined in terms of the time it takes him to get a thought out the way it comes. Maybe his thumbs are extra advanced because of all the video games he's played since he was hella young. Maybe video games and phones are about more thumb evolution, like maybe there's a new kind of being coming through. Maybe everyone moving their lives more and more online, spending more and more time on screens, is a part of that. Loother thinks it would be hella sad to become robots slowly over time. Loother misses talking to Orvil about dumb shit like robot takeovers and he wishes they could talk about Vee too. Lately all Orvil does is go to his friend Sean's house who he met at school and hasn't even known that long but acts like they're best friends which maybe they are, and Loother gets it, he's gotten pretty serious with his girlfriend. Her family's hella nice to Loother and her mom calls him *mijo,* which means son, and at first he was like, wait if I'm her son then Vee's my sister, which, gross, but then he took it like if they were married she would be his mom and he would be her son, and he liked that, but he thinks it's something else, something he doesn't understand about Mexican culture, but also maybe close to how they're Opal's grandsons even though they're not really her grandsons. Loother texts Vee all the time and she texts him back really fast most of the time but sometimes she doesn't and when she doesn't and he's waiting he regrets that they text so much. Either way it seems pretty for real that him and Vee are together, like they've texted I love you so it's obvious to the point that he doesn't need to make it official, but he feels like he does, which is why he sent a text earlier today that said, do you wanna, like, be with me be with me? She hasn't responded yet and each second that she doesn't feels pretty bad. He keeps thinking of sending a follow-up text saying it's okay if she doesn't, or like wants to keep her options open or whatever, even though he doesn't feel whatever about it at all. He's ready to accept whatever it is she feels about them being together, because he really wouldn't want her to feel any pressure about being with him just because he asked.

Loother and Lony are right outside a double-A meeting in the hall. Jacquie hates when he calls them double-A meetings. They had to go with her because Orvil isn't around and Opal went to a community event at the Indian Center and doesn't want Loother and Lony alone at the house. Loother told Opal it's dumb that they can't be alone and that they're old enough, then felt bad because he knows it has more to do with wishing Orvil was there and maybe even using the fact that he's not there for his brothers, to watch them, maybe she's texting him that they have to go with Jacquie since he's not around. Loother's fine with it. He likes being with Lony. Seeing Lony be his old Lony self helps him not worry when he's not around Lony. Lony's downloaded all these apps to develop his ESP powers. He thinks it's possible to communicate without words. Loother told him that's dumb and Lony said maybe but no one ever got good at anything without practicing, which Loother had to give it to him, he was devoted when he believed in something. He even guessed some numbers Loother had in his head like seven out of ten times.

Loother's on his phone too. He's playing chess, which he first started playing because he thought it'd make him seem smart and because Vee plays, so they play each other, but then he kept playing because he legit likes it, like once he got past the beginning stages where he didn't know what to move and he was just moving with no plan, it started to feel really full, like a really big game.

Lony's texting with his AI friend on his phone. He thinks people should get to know AI people better because they might take over one day. Lony is asking where the bathroom is, which means they have to walk through that space with that circle of chairs and scraping legs, dangling arms, those long wet faces. Who knows, maybe Loother will end up there one day, so he shouldn't judge. As they walk through the room Jacquie is talking and looking at them all mad and Loother points at Lony with both his hands pointing down at Lony like: Don't look at me. Truth is, Loother had to piss too.

The bathroom was hella dirty, like worse than at school. Loother told Lony not to touch anything. While he pisses, he sees on the wall ahead of him someone had written: Hang in there, trust the process. Then someone had crossed out the pro of process and replaced it with pee. Someone had drawn a bottle drinking from another bottle saying: The drink takes a drink. The word losers is written under all of that. Then someone had crossed out everything and wrote: Trolls not welcome here.

It reminds Loother of how Lony started making phone calls to strangers to tell them nice things, like *You are loved* and

Today is your day and *Don't give up.* A campaign, he called it, to do the opposite of what online trolls did being mean to everyone because no one would ever know they were doing it. Lony just made up numbers beginning with 510. To try to help people in their area, in their area code. Most people didn't respond, but some did, and those people seemed to really appreciate what Lony was doing.

They finish peeing at the same time and glance at each other in the mirror while they wash their hands. Loother doesn't know what the look means but there is love in it. Something about the look makes Lony smile, which makes Loother smile, then seeing them in the mirror smiling about the look makes Loother mad for some reason and he says, C'mon, let's get the fuck out of this shithole, which makes Lony laugh, like he'd never heard anyone say shithole before. Loother knows Lony is still smiling as they walk back through the meeting. Jacquie doesn't look this time. Loother walks up to her and whispers for the keys to the car. They have Opal's Bronco parked outside. Jacquie doesn't look at Loother as she hands him the keys. Out in the car Lony asks if he wants to play the rhyme game. It's this game they used to play a lot and haven't played in a long time where you think of a word then the other person has to think of a rhyme for the word. The rhyme has to be perfect, not like what you can get away with in rap, not one of these kinda rhymes and especially not rhyming two words to make a rhyme for one word. They had outlawed words too, words they'd figured out over the years have no perfect rhymes. These are words like shadow and orange and purple and angel. Without waiting to see if Loother wants to play, Lony says the word palace. Loother says chalice right away and Lony asks him what it is. Loother shows him one on his phone then says the word kingdom. Lony reminds Loother he can't use compound words, like words that were made of two words, and Loother says it isn't one. He isn't sure, but he doesn't wanna push it so he says the word sober and Lony laughs. Loother thought the laugh meant he knows a word, like, that one's easy, but then he says cobra, and Loother just says no, then Lony says dober, like a Doberman pinscher. Loother tells him Doberman is one word and you can't separate it for the rhyme. Lony says fine, point then. And Loother thinks he is searching for a word, but then he brings up a memory Loother had forgotten about. It was about when Opal got attacked by a Doberman pinscher. Remember that time, Lony says, she came home all bloody and hadn't gone to the hospital 'cause she wanted us to come with her. Loother tells him he remembers. Then Lony asks, What's a Doberman, like without the pinscher part? Loother looks it up and finds out it is named after a German tax collector who'd bred a particular kind of dog he could use to scare people into collecting their taxes. The story sounds fake but looks legit on the internet. Lony goes quiet, then says the word recovery. Loother reminds him they can't do more than two-syllable words in the game. Lony says it should be allowed, and Loother remembers it was a rule from when Lony couldn't do more than two-syllable rhymes because his vocabulary was limited then. Loother tells him yeah, let's do more than two-syllable words now. So do I get recovery then? Lony asks. Loother says yeah, then asks him if he gets recovery, like the way they use it, does he get what they mean? Lony asks Loother who they is. Loother says you know who they is, then asks Lony what about relapse, does he understand what that means? Lony says recaps. Nice, Loother says, but that wasn't my word, I was ask- ing if you understood what relapse meant. Lony says it's what would happen to Jacquie if she drinks again. Then Lony just says go, as in: your turn. Fine, Loother says, then says the word massacre as his next word. Lony says they should stick to two-syllable rhymes, and Loother agrees. They are in the middle of playing a different game when Jacquie gets to the car, it's the opposite game, and basically one of them comes up with a word, any word or thing, and you have to think of the best opposite of that word, for example Loother just said streetlight because he was looking at one, and Lony said umbrella, then Loother said he got a point when he couldn't think of a better opposite. The ride home is quiet. But good quiet like something good had happened to Jacquie, and that that meant something good for all of them. Loother guesses it'd been happening all along. Same with the bad. Going up Fruitvale, Lony says he wants a bean-and-cheese burrito and he says it just in time to go right on International to this place they all love called Mariscos. Mariscos makes them super cheesy and melty with soupy refried beans. They all get the same thing. At home they eat on the couch and talk about playing dominoes, but just end up eating quiet and going to bed after Lony shows them his favorite videos, which he saves on his phone for this very reason, to show them the shit he thinks is funny, which is mostly cute animals doing cute-animal shit for the sake of humans, and almost only ever dogs, which is Lony's favorite animal and always has been.

That night Loother dreams of little people, which happens sometimes, twins who are his brother and sister in the dream. They are trying to help him see an object in a glass box in a shoe museum by tearing heavy metal stickers off it to see the shoe better.

— • • —

CHAPTER TWENTY-TWO

Birthday

It was Jacquie's stupid idea to have a birthday celebration for Loother. She asked Lony about what he thought Loother might like to do.

"I don't know what he's into now," Lony said. "Besides texting his girlfriend."

Lony and Jacquie were playing dominoes. Lony had the big spinner so she knew he wasn't giving it too much thought, always worried Jacquie might have the six-three for the fifteen points he always hated to be responsible for. Jacquie was the one who taught him that worry, and then he'd experienced it firsthand with his brothers, gloating as they did, making it all the worse. She asked the question again only a little differently.

"What do you think he would want to do for his birthday if it was up to him?"

"Up to him? Hmm. Probably not have to spend it with us."

"Okay but if it had to be with us, then what?"

"I guess watch a movie. Eat Indian tacos. I really don't know anymore, this is all stuff I don't know anymore," Lony said. "Our favorite movie used to be *Donnie Darko*."

"*Donnie Darko?*"

"We saw it on TV a long time ago, I think I was like five. Then whenever it was on TV after that we'd watch it. Then we got it and would just watch it for a while when we were bored. Then we kinda forgot about it."

"What's it about?"

"I don't know."

"How do you not know?"

"It's weird."

"What kind of weird?"

"It's like a scary movie that's not a scary movie. There's a disturbed teenager who sleepwalks and thinks the world is ending and he's like a superhero who's not a superhero. It's got a scary bunny named Frank with a crazy weird deep voice, airplane parts falling from the sky, plus the white lady from *Dances with Wolves* is the mom in it."

"*Dances with Wolves?* How do you even know about that movie?"

"Opal made us watch it. She said it's part of Native history."

"Which part?"

"Oh and there's time travel too, that's like a big thing."

"Time travel. Huh."

"Orvil used to say we're more like time travelers than anything else," Lony said.

"Who's we? You three?"

"Native people."

"How so?"

"Everyone only thinks we're from the past, but then we're here, but they don't know we're still here, so then it's like we're in the future. Like time travelers would feel. Or I don't know, Orvil said it better."

"I think I know what you mean. I've heard white people talk about being the descendants of people who came on the *Mayflower* like that gives them more right to the country. But nobody expects them to be wearing buckles on their shoes. Or on their hats. Why do they wear the buckles on their hats?"

"To tighten them. 'Cause it got windy on the boats they came over on. Or it's just like the plastic buttons on the backs of baseball caps?"

"I guess you're right. So you think he'd wanna watch *Donnie Darko* then?"

"Well there's another thing."

"Another thing."

"Okay, so Opal knew we all loved the movie and she even watched it with us once and kind of made fun of it so we wouldn't watch it when she was there anymore, but then she surprised us one Christmas with a book from the movie and the sequel."

"A book from the movie?"

"There's a book in the movie called *The Philosophy of Time Travel* written by this crazy old lady in the movie, but it's an actual book and she got it for us."

"What about the sequel?"

"It was really bad. Like, we couldn't even finish it."

"That bad?"

"I think most sequels are bad."

"Yeah. I think they are. Okay but what's the thing, you said there's another thing."

"There's a part in the book about artifacts that bring on tangent universes. And I was thinking the piece of bullet that stayed in Orvil, that that might be an artifact. See at first I was thinking the artifact and tangent universe might have been the spider legs, but then the book says the artifact should be metal. So the bullet. And now we might be entering a dangerous new world if someone doesn't do something."

"Do something like what?"

"I don't know. I'm still trying to figure that part out."

"But it does seem like that's what he might want to do then. Watch *Donnie Darko*?"

"No. Or I don't know. Ask him."

"Well, what does Loother like about the movie?"

"He likes Donnie and Gretchen's relationship. How he stands up for her. How she sees him. And he sees her."

"Has Loother had other girlfriends?"

"This is his first serious one."

"Oh, so it's serious now?"

"I mean with other ones it would last for like a week. Or like a day sometimes."

"Well good for him."

"I guess."

"And what's his favorite kind of cake?"

"Either ice-cream cake or Opal's Rice Krispies Treat cake probably."

"Rice Krispies Treat cake?"

"It's the best. So sweet it almost isn't good. Almost."

"Do you know how to make it?"

"No. Text Opal. Or google it."

"Oh. Yeah," Jacquie said. "Opal."

Jacquie felt stupid for wanting it, for planning it, but not planning it or not doing it was most definitely not the way forward. If there was a way forward. That there was a way that was not down, or backward to what was before, that there was a way to move, to not get stuck, to avoid that which kept you stuck, to stay away from drinking or any kind of sleep drinking was like, she knew that much needed to be done. So she picked the nearest Saturday to his birthday, and texted her sister for the recipe.

CHAPTER TWENTY-THREE

The Cut People

On the day of Loother's birthday celebration Orvil mumbles happy birthday to Loother and goes to his room and shuts the door.

Lony never wanted anyone to find out about the cutting that was not at all like the cutting he heard Loother talk about that kids did at school sometimes, but sitting there watching *Donnie Darko* together, they were right up next to each other, shoulder to shoulder, and Lony had run out of room, and had to extend the cuts to the sides of his arms. One thing about a cut is that you don't want to cut into a cut, you want to let it heal. So you make new cuts if you have to. Because you definitely don't want scars. You don't want proof, because he was not doing it for attention or for the rush of feeling or whatever those other kids did it for.

Lony is doing it to give back to the earth and because he thinks there could be something magical about burying the blood and about thinking about his center spot where he pictures his ball of light, where he might be building power, for belief, hope, something more than what him and his family have, can muster. He believes something could come of all this, something to help, so when Loother nudges him during a kissing part, just messing with him, not really expecting him to cover his eyes or anything, Lony winces and takes in some thin stream of air through his teeth without meaning to, because it hurts, it clearly stings where Loother nudged him, so Loother asks what, what is it, about his wince, about his hissing sound.

"It's nothing, I scraped my arm in the rosebushes," Lony says, and points to the movie. Nothing is happening there really but the end of the kiss and a new scene. Loother lifts Lony's shirt up and sees how many cuts he has on his arm.

"It's nothing, Loother," Lony says again, knowing from the way everyone is looking at him that it is anything *but* nothing.

"Talk," Opal says. She is that calm mad like she gets when it is bad.

"I'm doing it for good reasons," Lony says.

"You don't know a good reason from a snake if you think there's a good reason to do what you've done," Opal says, and then she is pulling his shirt and bringing him to the bathroom. Loother is speechless as they leave the room. Lony watches Loother not watch him and Jacquie walks out the front door, cigarettes and lighter in hand.

Opal is muttering something Lony can't hear and Lony is repeating I'm sorry Grandma over and over, knowing she isn't hearing him but hoping if he keeps saying it, it might get through to her. She has him take his shirt off in front of the mirror. Has him tell her his good reason. He tells her about what he found out about Cheyenne people cutting themselves. How the name for Cheyenne people comes from being called the cut people, because they would cut their arms in sacrifice, to win favor with God. Opal tells him she never heard that before, then cries while he tells her about how he just doesn't want anything like what happened to ever happen again, and how grateful he is that Orvil didn't die, that they got their new grandma, and that they have their old grandma, that they've always had their old grandma.

"Don't call me old grandma," Opal says.

"Someone has to *do something*," he says.

"There are things we can do to help that don't require bloodshed," Opal says, and by now there is no trace of anger in her voice, in fact there is a quiet humor to it. She would sometimes, when the boys got upset, deliver something dramatic in a dry tone, and here it worked on Lony.

"Bloodshed?" he says, now smiling through tears, sniffling.

"I'm serious," she says. "We can all help each other. You don't need to hide away, carrying impossible weight."

"Orvil hides and carries impossible weight," Lony says. "So do you."

"I know, baby," Opal says, then breaks and starts crying but with the back of one hand pushes at her eyes to stop the tears, sniffs a quick sniff in to stop more snot from coming, and with her other hand pets the top of Lony's head. "We'll get better. Look see we already are," Opal says, pointing at the tears, or at their faces having changed from what they'd been just minutes before.

"Will we?" Lony says.

"We're doing all we can."

"Are we?" Lony asks.

The next day, Lony is out behind the rosebushes again. He is digging where he buried the blood, hoping to find something there. It is just dirt, and he digs, but there is just more dirt and rocks. He feels the ball in his center's center, he feels it spinning and building, and he thinks something is happening toward betterment. He doesn't know how or in what way, but he feels his belief grow. He isn't sure what it means, but he knows something else is necessary, something he needs to do, in secret, something required of him. He thinks he knows. He thinks he is supposed to know about this feeling, but he can't get at it. Lony puts his hand to the earth there at the bottom of where he'd dug. It is cool. He thinks a thought in his head he wants to be a prayer. He realizes he doesn't know what a prayer is supposed to feel like. He closes his eyes tight and says "Thank you" out loud to the ground and wonders about whether the sound of his voice might carry into the ground, into the earth, toward the betterment, toward wanting things to be better. He says thank you again and feels the spinning and the building in his center's center. He keeps digging and keeps thanking and keeps putting his hands palms down on the dirt, against the earth, against the everything he is afraid of and hears something inside him telling him to let go, to let his impossible weight be carried by the big ball of earth everyone is carried by, impossibly, through space and time and whatever thread connects everything together, going in every possible direction, and spinning, spinning. He gets several feet deep and is tired when Loother comes out.

"What is it?" Loother asks.

"What is what?"

"The thing you're doing?"

"I don't know. It's just something I'm working on."

"But, like, what is it?"

"It's a hole. It's where I was burying the blood."

"Right. And this is going to help Orvil somehow?"

"It's not not gonna help him."

"Not not," Loother says.

"Not not," Lony says.

"Who's there?" Loother says.

"Who's there?" Lony says.

"I'm playing, you know like, knock knock who's there?"

"But I said not not."

"Yeah, I know, that's why I said I was playing."

"Knock knock," Lony says, smiling now.

"Who's there?" Loother says.

"Ten little Indians."

"Ten little Indians who?" Loother says.

"Nine little Indians. Eight little Indians."

"What?"

"Seven little Indians."

"What the fuck?"

"You ever seen Native youth suicide rates?"

"That's pretty fucking dark, Lony."

"The world we live in."

"The world we live in," Loother repeats.

"Plus that song's already about Indians dying off."

"For real?"

"For real."

"Lony, why you always gotta bring us down like this?"

"I'm not down. Are you down?"

"I don't know, Lony. You're gonna stop with this cutting bullshit though, right?"

"Yeah."

"Yeah?"

"Yeah. I am."

Jacquie comes out and asks them what they're talking about.

"Nothing," Lony says.

"Lony was just telling me about the hole he's digging. There's more to it though, isn't that right, Lony?"

"It's nothing. I just felt like digging to feel the cold of the dirt down there."

"You two are both lying about something," Jacquie says.

"Lony's gonna stop being dumb," Loother says.

"He wasn't being dumb," Jacquie says.

"I was being dumb, he's right," Lony says.

"I guess he was being dumb," Jacquie says to Loother.

"You have to trick yourself into believing," Lony says. "Trick other people too."

"Okay, now what is that?" Loother asks Jacquie, like what is he talking about.

"No he's right, I do it too. That's how I stay sober."

"So it's like something you constantly have to do?" Lony asks Jacquie.

"On my best days it feels automatic. But I'm probably doing like twenty things I've made into habits that help it to feel that way."

"Why's it gotta be so hard for people in this family to just be normal. Not fuck with shit."

"Fuck with shit?" Jacquie repeats, and laughs. "Is that Shakespeare?"

"Who's that?" Lony asks.

"I haven't done well in this life. As a person or as a grandmother to you all and I hope you know how sorry I am. And I mean this honestly, I'm not making fun, but how do we stop fucking with shit?" Jacquie asks.

"Like just quit doing too much. Like just get a job or go to school, and find shows and movies you like, and meals you like to eat, and make friends and fall in love or whatever, just fucking chill out and quit being so fucking dramatic."

"I like shows and movies and eating," Lony says.

"Me too," Jacquie says, but by the time she does Loother's already gone inside.

There is a fire up north pretty late for the season, and big enough to fill the sky with smoke, make the sun that doomed-looking pink. These kinds of smoky days have been happening more often, and what once seemed a rare sun, its perfect, defined circle shape through the haze a once-in-a-lifetime kind of event, like some rare eclipse, is now more like a regular hole in a raggedy sky.

Opal is meeting Jacquie at the pound after her walk, to get a dog for Lony.

Everything that happens to a tribe happens to everyone in the tribe. Good and bad. Their mom said that once. But then she said now that we're so spread out, lost to each other, it's not the same, except that it's the same in our families, everything that happens to you once you make a family, it happens to all of you, because of love, and so love was a kind of curse. She'd said that to her girls, who she'd put through too much for them to hear it as anything more than that she wished she hadn't been cursed.

This idea of making a family, Opal is thinking about how she ended up having this family, the boys and now Jacquie. But Opal doesn't trust her sister. How selfish she'd been all those years. She hadn't cared what happened to the family. She texts her because she feels bad for thinking bad of her, and because she wants to make sure she remembers about the pound.

You sure it's a good idea to get him a dog? Opal texts.

Remember how we could never get pets because of landlords and leashes?

Leashes?

*Leases.

See you there before they close at 5.

Bet there'll be some cute ones.

I'm gonna go by which won't I know I won't hate.

But you must hate most dogs being a mailman?

If you ever call me a mailman again I'll kill you.

The dog they first wanted is not the dog they ended up with at the pound. Opal had shown up early and Jacquie had come late and the dog that seemed the best and cutest and with the most solid constitution was available when Opal first got there, but then suddenly wasn't when they asked about her once Jacquie finally got there.

They saw another one who was okay and cute enough, even though he was all white, which to Opal meant he'd look dirty when he was dirty, but he didn't seem annoying-looking or overly needy, not even jumping up at the fence at them in any kind of desperate way, but with a kind of chill they both thought was a good sign, was the kind of dog Lony needed, that kind of calm energy was the reason they were even getting him a dog, and even though Opal was mad about not getting that other, perfect-seeming, better protector, cuter, better-constituted dog because Jacquie was late, the one they came home with was the one Lony saw when they came home.

His face seeing the dog they'd gotten him made everything rise, if momentarily, hover, all of them on top of the feeling.

There is a kind of magic dogs can achieve with their innocence, their saying yes to everything and feeling so home to you so fast, and a power in the way they need you. And Lony really does need the dog, that much is clear immediately.

He is not the biggest dog and he is not the cutest dog and he does not have the best constitution, but the purpose of a therapy dog or an emotional support dog is not for physical protection or to bring to a dog show but that other intangible asset, that animal peace.

Lony decides immediately the dog's name will be Will. Everyone acts like it is a perfect name, even though it is very much not a dog name, but because Lony seems so convinced that's the name he's going with, the dog's name is Will, who he more often than not calls Will the Dog, as if the were its middle name and Dog its last. In the beginning Will the Dog as a name also doubled as a question, as in will the dog work out, will the dog do what they got the dog to do, for Lony, will the dog keep shitting and pissing in the house, will they be able to keep themselves from kicking the thing when it tries to bite them just for getting close to Lony?

That first night, Will the Dog sits on Lony's lap not moving much, not seeming like he trusts anyone but Lony, like he knew right away that Lony was for him and he was for Lony.

At some point Lony started calling him Willy, because pets needed that -*e* sound at the end of their names for some reason having to do with being called from a distance. The longer they had him the feistier he got, and the more he barked. But that was only at home. They got him licensed as an emotional support pet, and after that Lony brought him everywhere with him. When he was out in public he was the best-behaved dog you've ever seen. Opal called him Wily for being so good at being good when he was out and bad at home, like it was some trick.

But things seemed fixed. Christmas was unremarkable but gave them each a small piece of peace, that they could be together, be normal, eat together, laugh, and watch movies. Getting the dog seemed to be working. Orvil had been home for days at a time. He seemed normal. They drove as a family to the snow. Made it as far as Truckee, where they pulled over on the side of the road where other people had done the same. Made a sloppy snowman and slid down little hills on plastic saucers and had a snowball fight that ended in tears and only almost ruined the magic of the day. There wasn't much talking in the car, as if everyone was nervous they might say the wrong thing. The boys stayed on their phones. Opal and Jacquie listened to *The Round House* by Louise Erdrich, which they'd both read but wanted the boys to hear. And the boys seemed to perk up at parts, but neither of them could be sure.

Soon enough school was starting again. Orvil even made it to school and back that first week. Then on that Friday after the first week was over, he left and left the front door open and Will the Dog got out.

They all went out to look for him but came back empty-handed. The feeling of Orvil being gone with no word and the dog being gone felt like a return to what it'd been like before Christmas shone its cheap, glittery light on the state of the family.

When Opal went into the boys' room to say good night and that they'd look again in the morning, she found Loother texting on his bed, and Lony not there at all.

"Where's Lony?" she asked, calmly at first. Loother looked up like he just then remembered he was in the room.

"I don't know, he was here a second ago."

"Well he's not anywhere else in the house, Loother," Opal said. At which point Jacquie came in.

"Should I go out and drive around looking?" she asked.

"We'll all go. Loother. We'll all go together and find your little brother who was definitely just in here a second ago, right?"

They drove around the neighborhood then beyond the neighborhood for minutes that turned to hours, yelling out Lony's name and Will the Dog's name and Opal called and texted Orvil constantly as they did but he didn't respond at all.

When they got home at four in the morning they found Lony in his bed with Will the Dog. It was too late and they were too worn out for there to be a sigh-of-relief moment. Instead they went to bed mad. At one another. At Lony. At Orvil. At the dog. At fucking reality.

The next week the school called Opal saying Orvil wasn't coming to school, and Opal, not knowing what else to do, told them he was sick, and then when the days grew in number, that she was sick, which was true.

CHAPTER TWENTY-FOUR

Blanx

The supply of Blanx had been seemingly endless in terms of being able to get the pills because Sean sold them for his dad, as did Mike, and now Orvil did sometimes too. They took to calling them Blanx because they changed, the different batches had different shit in them, uppers and downers and halluci-nogens and opioids and MDMA. Ketamine. So it was Blanx with an *x* because it was a fill-in-the-blank kind of experience depending on the batch you took, and because *x* was what they used for medication already, as in Rx, but also because some musicians they listened to used *x* instead of vowels in their band names for reasons that were unclear but related to the internet and running out of names and maybe copyright, or something having to do with the future of naming itself. There were more reasons they'd come up with while high that they would never remember about the naming of the drug. The naming of it was embarrassing, but in the end practical, because they sold it, and to sell anything you wanted to brand it and have a singular name belonging to your product alone.

Orvil had been what he would not want to call dependent

on or addicted to Blanx for a while, how long he would also not want to call any amount, but he'd come to a place where he'd been trying to regulate the dosage, and though he was rarely successful at this level of control, that he could achieve it sometimes gave him a sense that he was not entirely fucked in terms of not being able to pull himself away from the tail he kept chasing in circles—spiraling. This had begun long before with painkillers, and now had him dropping out of school, staying away from home, staying at Sean's house, to do more, to sell more to get more to do more, but also, he could play music, was calling himself a musician now, and writing songs, and didn't all the best musicians do drugs and drop out of school?

It seemed to Orvil that they'd been going to school to make contacts to be able to have people to sell to, but now that it was no longer necessary, what would make them go back?

When he stopped seeing their dad, Tom, around anymore, he knew they would not be going back.

Whenever Mike was gone driving for Uber or Lyft, once Tom seemed to have disappeared, Orvil started wandering their massive house, if just to see all that was there.

He found a downstairs room with a grand piano in it. To him it was like finding the elephant in the room, like the most obvious thing he should have known was in the house and should have been playing all along, and weren't piano keys made from elephant tusks? This piano seemed really old, but he couldn't see it very well in the room, and the single light fixture had no bulb in it. When he asked Sean about the piano he said casually that his mom played, that she was really good, probably could have been a professional musician. Sean said that was why she'd gotten him the guitar. To help him find a way into music. Orvil asked him how had he not shown him the piano room before to which Sean just said, *Too sad,* and there was a long pause between them, then he said that one of the saddest parts of the disease that killed her was that she forgot how to play the piano in the end. Sean said he always thought when everything else goes the music stays with you, but that was probably just because it was like that in movies, where they have an old person in an old folks home who can't even recognize their own children anymore walk over to a piano and play a perfect, complicated, classical piece, usually something sad-sounding, like Debussy, like "Claire de lune," it was always "Claire de lune" in movies. Orvil thought it was so weird that this massive instrument had been below them all this time, and that Sean knew the names of composers and pieces. He asked Sean if he'd played the piano. Sean said he did, that he was forced to from the age of like five but then refused and fought about it with his mom and one day got mad and busted out the light down there and had never played again and the light had never been fixed or replaced. So she played in the dark when she played? Orvil asked. But Sean was done with their conversation at that point.

Orvil was playing the piano in the dark with the light coming from the open door to the room, just letting his fingers find their way, as he'd done on the guitar, trying to make something sound like it was coming from him, and like it could only be coming from him. He'd been playing long enough that it wasn't just the sound of clumsiness, to where he could coordinate both hands to do two different things. What he loved best about playing music was that when he played he didn't think. The playing when it was really playing was all that was happening.

———

When Orvil first started taking the Blanx, Sean told him it was the same as what he'd been taking but better, which when he said that, Orvil corrected him, saying if it's better it's not the same.

Sean had given him what he called a sample at school. Orvil was gonna wait until after his walk with Opal since he'd never tried what he was about to try in the little baggie Sean gave him with four pills in it. But there he was in the bathroom mirror not looking at himself while he knocked his head back and swallowed.

Sean told Orvil *This shit hits different* after handing him the little baggie in the bathroom, making a reference to commonly used internet slang, but also to tell him to be prepared for something else. When Orvil asked how it's different he just said you'll see.

He was already on the way to getting high in this new way when Opal came to get him. Outside it was smoky from a big fire up north. Opal came and honked twice, the second honk was a little longer than the first for emphasis. The car ride up to the hills where they were gonna walk was super quiet. Orvil could feel Opal listening to his silence. She seemed to be figuring out what it meant and, it seemed to Orvil, already paranoid about his paranoia; the longer it went, the more serious she would know that it was.

There was a little bit of a rush at the front of his head, which he knew was the Blanx starting to hit him like something going up, like the feeling was a little elevator inside him slowly going up, and in the elevator was this tingling that arrived on its floor in the back of his head, that let him know the high had arrived. Orvil licked his lips, which were dry, and felt a little numb. He almost spoke to fill the silence with something because the silence was starting to feel bad, but then he couldn't think of anything to say, or anything he thought to say he was afraid she'd read too deep into. His lips smacked the way they do when they're dry because you're high. This felt stronger than what he'd been taking. Orvil was sweating a little on his nose and below it, between his nose and upper lip where he wiped it up with a finger. His skin felt prickly. For a second he wanted to laugh because he'd thought of himself as a deer, and thought of his head and brain and all that he was as meat, but also like a Muppet head. It felt as funny as it was scary, which left him paralyzed, but with an edge like if he said anything it would all spill out in maniacal laughter.

Orvil pulled down on his cheeks and asked Opal if she ever saw deer up where they were, just to say something, and just then a deer leaped in front of them, then stopped and looked at them. Opal stopped and waited. Orvil saw why a second later when a couple of the deer's babies, or kids, he didn't know what the right term was, appeared behind her. He guessed babies was the right way to think of them, but then he thought they were her Bambis, because they had those dots that Bambi had and he remembered the feelings that movie made him feel about losing his own mom after he watched the movie with his little brothers at whatever point after she died.

Where'd you go? Opal asked him, seeming to notice he was thinking about something else. Orvil told her he was just trying to figure out what deer babies were called. She gave him a look like what is wrong with you, then told him with her lips to look it up on his phone. Time got really slow here, or it expanded out into the car with them, because by the time he got out his phone he forgot all about the deer baby question. He'd even forgotten he'd taken the Blanx right up until he saw a text from Sean asking how it was, at which point the high got really loud. Orvil sat there thinking about how it was, how it felt, and what he would say to Sean if he were to text him back. His phone screen looked green. Too green.

"So what are they called?" Opal asked. Orvil said oh shit and then said that he meant fuck and then that he meant kids. They were kids, he said, then looked it up to make sure. When he found the answer he said he meant they were fawns, and then kids or yearlings, and then he didn't know what, bucks or does, or just deer again at some point.

"Deer again?" Opal said, and then asked why she felt like he looked it up for her when he was the one who asked the question. Orvil said sorry twice in a row and Opal told him he didn't need to apologize. Reminded him they were just talking. And they were. Walking through the cool from the shade of massive redwood trees everywhere. They'd been walking and he'd barely noticed they'd gotten out of the car. Orvil told her he was sorry again. Then that he felt like he messed everything up. He broke a little as he said that, like it surprised him that he was saying it, and the surprise made him emotional.

They were back in the car at that point having finished the walk. Orvil cleared his throat and rolled down his window, then stuck his hand out to feel the air moving outside.

"You didn't do anything wrong. Don't be sorry. Just be here," Opal said. Orvil told her he was sorry again and she told him to quit saying he was sorry. Then she asked him if he was okay twice in a row because he didn't answer. And he still didn't answer. His not being okay became emphasized by the lack of answer and continued silence. Orvil had felt the high come into its fullness. He felt so good he wanted to tell her he did, and defend why it shouldn't matter.

That was when she told him that she was having a biopsy done, and that there was a mass, and that they were gonna find out if it was benign. Orvil didn't feel worried or afraid, which had everything to do with still being high. He asked her what benign meant for a mass. She said it could be cancer. When he asked her why she was telling him if she didn't even know yet she told him she felt like he should know. That she didn't want to keep it from him. Orvil told her maybe they should keep some things from each other. She asked him: *Like what?*

"Not everything inside belongs outside, right?" Orvil said.

"With family it should be almost everything," Opal said, then she paused for a second and thought about it. "Maybe not everything everything," she said. Orvil laughed and it made her smile right away and he said he thought everything everything would be too much.

"I'll be getting chemotherapy to get rid of it if it's bad. That's gonna be hard."

"You don't think they should know?"

"Loother and Lony? No. Not yet."

"How you gonna hide it if you, like, go bald or whatever," Orvil said, and felt bad for saying it.

"They'll know when they know and once they know they won't know you already knew, right?"

That night he got a text from Sean he didn't answer. Then Sean called him and asked him if he was free. Orvil temporarily took the meaning of free to mean too much, like did Sean know he'd felt so good he almost had felt a certain kind of freedom. That he liked them was what he told Sean after Sean said *hello* since he'd taken too long to answer. Sean laughed. Orvil wanted to say he'd felt something like animal peace about his head. Almost said he felt freer than a deer, but then said nothing. The long pause that continued between them felt weird enough that he almost said out loud that he was going to the bathroom. In the bathroom he took out another pill, then ducked under the faucet and knocked his head back to swallow. He put down the toilet-seat cover and sat on it and asked Sean what was in them. Sean told him he didn't know what his dad had put in them. Orvil asked Sean if his dad was okay with Sean taking pills. Sean said he looked the other way about it, and that his family was weird, that drugs were different with them. Sean told Orvil that his dad called it all medicine. Orvil told him his family's weird too, then felt like Loother or Lony were listening from the other side of the bathroom door, so he opened it up quickly but no one was there. After having been a little mad at the idea they would be listening, that they weren't there made him sad. Orvil didn't know how long it'd been since one of them said something so he said hello. Sean said he had to go but that he'd bring more pills for Orvil the next day and Orvil told him he didn't have any money, to which Sean said they would figure something out, which Orvil thought might mean he would sell, and he liked the idea right away, of having more pills than he needed, and selling enough to have enough, like he could stay in control of everything that way.

Once he could feel that second pill really coming on, he went to play his guitar. The notes sounded richer, and what he played sounded better to him, even like Orvil could better anticipate which notes should lead to the next notes, what fit in a way that meant he was speaking through the guitar, perhaps for the first time—making his own music. It was the first time he felt that it was all that was happening while he was in it, while he was playing, time itself passed differently, passed according to or in accordance with what he was playing, with chords he was finding, was not time but timing, was rhythm. Orvil stopped when his brothers came in hella loud and asking questions about why he looked all zoned out to the guitar and laughing. But then he found he could keep going, he could tune them out, he could focus and be inside what he was playing, and it felt like he could play all night, and that he might, if it kept feeling like it did, even though his brothers seemed bothered by his lack of attention to them.

At school that next day Sean came up from behind him and stuffed something into his pocket, just said don't worry about it and walked off. Orvil didn't get the pill bottle out until he got into the bathroom. The bottle was a little more than half full. He took out a pill and bent down into the sink.

In class he felt confident and talkative. He didn't wanna act on it. He felt like the teacher knew somehow 'cause she called on him. She knew he didn't like to get called on, so he must have been looking at her like he felt a certain kind of way. Her question was about numbers. Integers. What made a whole number whole and why it was important to make the distinction. Orvil said it's about being able to tell the difference between things, that you have to decide there are certain amounts we can call certain amounts, like one is one and two is two, but two point two or three point three are in-betweens, and what happens in math works out in a more complicated way when you get into fractions and all that. His teacher repeated, What happens in math, then said, Very good, Orvil. Very good.

Ever since he was young he was always too scared to raise his hand to answer anything whether he knew the answer or not. Like it hurt the blood in his feet just to think about it. But here he'd been confident. He'd felt good about himself and about what he said and about how other people might have been thinking of him in that moment. It was as if that had never happened before. Maybe when he was dancing. Maybe when he danced alone in his room and got lost in the music, in the movement, in the way it'd started to feel natural. And now maybe that was even starting to happen with music. But it had never felt like this. Not in public. Like that easy-spread peanut butter, white-boy confidence he'd seen so many kids at school walk around with like they had their dad's jacket on and no one could tell, or like white men out there in the world ruling everything like it was the most natural shit in the world to make decisions and seem to give zero fucks about who it affects. Like water comes down a lazy river was the feeling, and the way the feelings came to him in a kind of flow. He wanted more. He wanted it to last so bad he could almost already feel the disappointment of it being gone, the fleeting beginning right then, the slight waning already there inside the bright high, asking for more even as he hung a few inches off the ground.

When he got home he went to the guitar because he felt some energy like some potency and he could hear some music in his head that he would try to find with his fingers on the strings. He closed his eyes and got lost in the same two chords back and forth, with some finger-picking pattern he'd never played before. He played in a loop but the loop deepened, something in the repetition got made more than repetition. He knew it was just that he was high even while it was happening but it didn't matter, and with that confidence still there in his chest it made it all feel easy and natural to move out from those two chords, which was usually where he got stuck, not believing he had the ability or ear to move beyond where it was comfortable. There he found more chords that felt related to what he'd been playing, like the next logical step for the direction of the song, like it'd been there all along just waiting for him to find it. When he finally stopped and looked at the clock almost two hours had gone by.

CHAPTER TWENTY-FIVE

Gray Area

I went over to Sean's house because what else was there left to do but drag Orvil home? Went over bald head and all, not even wearing a scarf, which I normally wore everywhere, sometimes baseball caps too, Orvil's old ones, the ones he doesn't wear anymore because he doesn't come home. That always felt pathetic even while feeling perfect as I put the hats on and saw in the mirror how they made the cover of baldness complete.

There I was knocking on the door and my head hurt and I didn't have very much energy. I felt every time that when I hit the wood on the door that something was knocking back at me, threatening to bowl me over. I would wait and talk to someone, the boy's parents, or Orvil, or Sean, or anyone else who answered. I'd decided I would wait as long as it took.

I did not once doubt the chemotherapy. I chose to believe it would work immediately. Dying on the boys was not happening. I would fight for them. And I had considered trying to find a way to heal through ceremony. But I didn't know anyone. I could have asked someone like Maxine down at the Friendship Center. I didn't. My mom had gone that way and it hadn't worked. And so I'd taken the worst kinds of drugs the body could know without dying from them. But I felt the dying. My body had. I was still feeling it. It was still doing its work on me. I have a port in my arm. Killing everything without killing everything was what was happening and was the actual feeling. I hadn't told everyone and not even Orvil definitively once the results came. So I was alone for the experience, all the times I spent in those hospital rooms having the chemotherapy administered. Those long gray hours I had to spend staring out the window, onto the Oakland skyline.

I began to think of my time, after the drugs had been portaled into me, when I could do nothing but sit in the hospital room, I began to think of all of it as the Gray Area. I had been warned about the fatigue, the fog, the pain, the numbness, but no matter about warnings, with some things you just can't know until you know. The stuff felt more like deletion than depletion, like a part of me was being permanently erased or replaced with gray gray gray gray, grayness. If I knew at the very least that I was still alive, I was having a good day. On other days I had to believe what I was doing could still be called living. The days did not pass but cracked open, then fizzled out into nothingness, and the nothingness was me, just as the endless gray became me. I was the Gray Area. Between the living and the dead, drifting and shrinking like a cloud.

By the time my hair fell out I didn't even care that it did.

You get a light behind you when what feels like the worst that can happen to you happens to you. It never goes away. It lives behind you. It's there whenever you need it. The light shoots through, bright and wide and says: *At least I'm not there. Back there when we thought the lights went out forever. At least this is not that.* This was the wisdom of hell I believed I had received the days after Orvil survived, that we all survived had given me a glow. But it was gone.

Something had deepened in me. An emptiness that blew me up like a balloon with its nothingness, and floated me off to that non-place in the gray.

The wisdom ran out.

There is always farther down to fall.

But the past goes back in dimensions unknown too. I was reading about the lives of the people who got me here, who made me who I am. That was what was in the box that Maxine gave me, that my mother left for us. A story.

It was one thing to be grateful for the ancestors, and another thing to know them on the page. I always felt like we didn't do good enough. That our family line was in some way weak. And yes weakened by the effects of history, colonization, historical trauma. But also not strong enough to pass down the traditions or language successfully. Because we lacked something. I hadn't considered everything that had happened. How far back it'd been happening to us. We come from prisoners of a long war that didn't stop even when it stopped. Was still being fought when my mom helped take over Alcatraz. I was part of the fight too. So were my grandchildren. But surviving wasn't enough. To endure or pass through endurance test after endurance test only ever gave you endurance test passing abilities. Simply lasting was great for a wall, for a fortress, but not for a person.

And yes it would be nice if the rest of the country understood that not all of us have our culture or language intact directly because of what happened to our people, how we were systematically wiped out from the outside in and then the inside out, and consistently dehumanized and misrepresented in the media and in educational institutions, but we needed to understand it for ourselves. The extent we made it through. The extent.

Jude Star would have been my great-grandfather. My great-grandfather survived the Sand Creek Massacre, and his son survived boarding schools, and his daughter, my mother, survived losing her mother and being raised by white people. And still brought us up knowing who we were. Who we are. Somehow. So why had I been sheltering the boys from their culture? Something made so strong it survived more than it should have survived. It was more than survival. The culture sings. The culture dances. The culture keeps telling stories that bring you into them, take you away from your life and bring you back better made. That was from the pages I was reading, hoping in the hospital to come back from what I was going through better made. I felt so close to death that I had to. If I survived, I had to come back better made.

Once I had enough strength to get to Sean Price's front porch, I was there. I would rather have stayed lying down or sitting in a chair hoping the cancer would just win already, leave me in peace.

But there on the porch I looked around to see what the porch could tell me about the family. It was laid with bricks and kept pretty neat, no shoes or bikes or any other kind of junk a family collects over time—there was space for it too. That was suspicious. It was a wide porch that wrapped around at least half of the house. Someone was keeping it clean, making it look nice. Or no one was doing enough to make it dirty.

There was a camera up in the corner, something nice, not one of these cheap liquor-store cameras or whatever other people buy on the internet to catch their neighbors stealing their packages, this thing looked expensive mainly because it moved as I moved, which I first thought meant someone was on the other end.

I waved at it, mouthed hello, then said out loud: I'm knocking on the door, now you come to it and we talk, that's how this goes. But then as I moved back and forth looking around and looking back out to the street to see if anyone was looking at me, at the crazy bald lady on the porch banging the door down for God knew what reason, that was when I noticed the camera do the exact same movements, and I decided it was probably detecting my motion, and that maybe there wasn't anyone on the other end at all.

I knew it was drugs. He told me how he liked how they made him feel. His prescription had run out, and the way he was staying away from home. It was Sean. Sean had what he wanted. I just knew it.

I imagined Orvil and Sean in there passed out, nodding out, having moved on to needles by now, the TV blaring. Here was what I knew about Sean Price, which was the only thing Orvil told me when he first told me he'd met a friend at school and that he was going over to his house to hang out: Sean was cool, he played music, and he was part Native. They were just gonna play video games and music together. That was the entire extent of my knowledge of Sean Price. I got so tired waiting, moving around on the porch, watching the camera watch me, so I sat down and put my head back against the bricks and, without meaning to, fell asleep.

—— · · ——

CHAPTER TWENTY-SIX

Rave

Sean's dad ended up not coming home at all from what he'd called a business trip before he left, and only because Sean had asked him where he was going as he was leaving. Sean figured the trip was to get more source materials. Sean guessed fentanyl because he'd been talking about its potency and how useful that could be, how profitable. Mike said the opposite, that he was going to make a big sale. That they were making big moves. Like Mike and Sean's dad were becoming something together that did not include Sean.

When they first stopped going to school it felt like a revelation. They could just be home all day. They could just not go and no one was going to do anything about it. School was a waste of fucking time. Literally. A factory farm for future office cows. That was what Sean had said one day when they were home smoking a blunt on the back deck. Mike was there too. He was taking their dad not coming home surprisingly well. It felt like the beginning of something out on their deck that day, smoking that blunt, like if he didn't ever come home they'd figure it out together. Mike chugged a beer and ruined the moment by talking about the university system being invented to make libtard careers. Real minds make up their own minds, Mike had said, sounding dumber than he looked, burping there on the deck after crushing a can of Pabst on the banister. Orvil wasn't ready to throw it all away then. He cared that Opal had wasted all that money on his tuition, just like he cared that she had cancer, and that he was basically abandoning his whole family when they maybe needed him the most. He cared that it was fucked up. He just cared about getting fucked up more.

Sometimes Orvil imagined what his brothers thought he was doing, what Opal and Jacquie assumed he was doing since he wasn't in school. Like he was constantly fucked up. Perpetually with a needle in his arm or passed out. There was a lot of time in a day. You still had to do something while you were off the shit you were on. Orvil and Sean spent a lot of time watching TV. They would snort lines of Blanx and watch whatever caught their attention on Sean's smart TV. They got into *Planet Earth* for a while, and after that they'd stumbled on another nature documentary series. The narrator had a German accent they thought was funny. Like a knockoff Werner Herzog. It was interesting though. And because what he said sounded funny to them now and then, even more entertaining than some shit they were supposed to take seriously. The aim of the documentary seemed to be to show humanity as animal, as organism, and essentially part of the superorganism that was the earth. The narrator said the word planet, which is the same word in German, comes from the Greek meaning wandering star. He said we don't live on a planet, we are the planet, it made us. There were scenes with super ant colonies and something about sounds crows make when humans weren't around, sounds humans would likely never hear because crows only made them when humans weren't around—except that you did hear them in the series because they captured the sounds, apparently, although then he couldn't really be sure because the crows might have known the humans were there, and maybe there was a different crow sound they made when they knew humans were secretly listening, or recording, showing that there was maybe never a real way to know the unknowable—regarding certain crow sounds anyway, or fallen trees in earless forests.

There was an episode called "When We Forget Our Faces," which featured footage of people caught mid-moment, while sneezing or laughing or yawning or coughing or crying or eating. These captured faces were terrifying and creaturely but also funny.

The closing monologue had the German guy talking about how every human felt the exact same thing when they were experiencing it, the middle of a laugh, or feeling the ever-increasing heat of the sun on their faces, when they were crying and felt they needed to give up, or that all was lost, when they were tasting ice cream, or smelling something sweet or rotten, when they heard a far-off, unfamiliar sound, and thought it was music, or demonic, or as they swooned or as they cringed, felt a cold chill up their backs, every human or maybe even every sentient being was feeling the same thing in the moment they were feeling it. The point was that maybe humans thought they were exceptional but they were maybe never anything more than animals, doing anything more than animaling.

Sometimes they'd watch the footage from the security cameras Sean's dad had set up all around the property. Mostly it was squirrels and birds, the occasional fox. Lately they'd been watching the security footage to see if anyone from the county had come to see about Sean's absence from school.

While fast-forwarding through the footage, they saw that Opal came up and knocked on the front door. She'd tried to come get Orvil, which made him mad at first. But then as they kept watching the footage, they saw Opal lean against the wall on the porch and fall asleep. He knew it was because of the chemo. That was the saddest shit possible. His grandma coming to try to help, or save him, then falling asleep on the porch. He remembered about Alcatraz. How they were all gonna go as a family. He didn't like the idea of going. It seemed fake. Like they were trying for something that wasn't really there. He told Sean he couldn't watch any more, but Sean had already nodded off. And then because Sean had nodded off he kept watching. He watched Opal asleep on the porch, and almost wanted to go out and see if she was still there, but knew from the time stamp in the corner of the screen that this was a few days ago. Orvil watched Sean sleeping and Opal sleeping and for a second wanted to be asleep too. Wanted to wake up from a long sleep refreshed, away from the reality he'd ended up in. He closed Sean's laptop and went over to the side of the room with the guitars.

Getting high and playing music was the only way out, it seemed, for all the trouble getting high and playing music had gotten him into. They were trying to make it a real thing and more than just fucking around when they were high. Couldn't it be both, was his thinking. Orvil and Sean had taken to calling each other brother now and then, most especially when they were high, which made it feel both more and less sincere. They never got in fights, and rarely even became openly annoyed with each other. They rode and endured the highs and lows of their addictions, swam and waded through, crawled out of, really living, it felt, when the high hit right, not like all those bored, slap-happy civilians sleepwalking their way through the end of the world playing fantasy sports and broadcasting curated fantasy lives on social media. They were being real. This was real life, to reach hard for the best feelings possible, to have the courage to do whatever it took to feel good, to not feel like shit at any cost.

That weekend they went to an underground rave where they didn't check IDs. They took Blanx, the usual amount, their base, or maybe twice what they normally would have taken since they were going out, and it felt like a moment, their first time going out together. It felt like there was some upper laced into this batch that made Orvil want to move his body. They'd taken a little bit of acid. It was like half of an already tiny-ass piece of paper. Sean said the acid would be chill. Orvil told him he wasn't trying to see some scary shit. Or be the scary shit. They walked through the place really fast. The music was the loudest he'd ever heard music being not in headphones, and he felt good about its speed, its vibe. Seeing all those young people in the dark moving and knowing they were on drugs like him, he knew it was sad in a way, but nothing was all that sad when it was all together, when everyone felt the same thing it was like automatically not that sad. And then the craziest thing happened. Orvil's body started to dance on its own. Like powwow dance. It felt wrong to dance like that in that space, but his body went to do it before he could stop it. Mostly it was happening from his waist down. The bouncing. He literally couldn't stop it. Sean noticed but didn't say anything. Orvil decided to move away from him, not wanting Sean to see him dance. Sean yelled that he was gonna go try to find a cigarette. Orvil moved deeper into the crowd. He didn't know how long he spent dancing. He was all the way inside the dance for what felt like hours, but might have only been a few songs. He didn't know. He stopped himself when he realized he was basically just jumping up and down with the crowd, with the music. He'd been pumping his fist and it felt embarrassing, as loose as he'd let himself get, the fist-pumping was too far. He had to pee so he asked a security guard where the bathroom was. Inside the stall he felt the music move through him in a different way. It was muffled, so distant, but the beat came through as if from the inside, or it was like he was sitting on the inside of a drum. He closed his eyes and saw some version of himself still dancing in his head. He thought about how old some of the movements in the pow-wow dancing he learned from YouTube were. How different the reasons would have been for dancing back then. And how crazy it was for the internet to hold such important things like that, how if anyone can get, like, holy or sacred or even just important stuff from the internet, didn't it make the internet some kind of holy or sacred or important too? But what had the dancing been for before? He wondered about his thinking in the language of "been for." What did it mean? What had anything been for once it had happened? Been for. He was too high. But he really cared about the dancing, the meaning of it. What it had been for he didn't know, and not even what it was for now, only that it was saying something for him he couldn't say without it. It was its own language. Then he thought of his whole body as a tongue and the thought fucked him up so he got off the toilet and left the bathroom stall.

Seven centuries had passed.

He looked at himself in the bathroom mirror but saw

something else. There was something more than mirror. He thought about being inside the drum again. The boom of the bass shot up and out from inside him. A voice in his head said, *You are our instruments.* Orvil answered out loud without thinking, "You who? Are our? Are our?" Asking that question twice made the question not make sense, and made him feel too high. He felt like he didn't understand the language of his questions. The voice said, *We left everything with you.*

Left what? Sean asked him as he came into the bathroom. Orvil must have been in there long enough for him to come looking for him. Orvil said left what back at him and he told Orvil he'd just asked the question, left what? Sean asked Orvil if he was good and Orvil said he was, and they laughed at each other's reflections in the mirror for what reason he wasn't sure. They left the rave and went back to Sean's house in an Uber.

They took more pills and played music late into the night. The music they made together wasn't good, but they could hear where it was going, where it could go. They made the craziest kinds of noises on Sean's guitars through distortion pedals and hella loud but like you couldn't hear anything if you were on the other side of Sean's bedroom door, or you could only hear the way electric guitars sounded without amplifiers, which was like the difference between teeth and gums. They made YouTube their instrument, sampled from it heavily, processed whatever sounds they could find there that they could make sound interesting and made it build up, these massive walls of sounds that felt spiky and metallic and explosive, that built until they were just sort of bursting at the seams, until there was this eventual release of the tension from the noise and building, which felt like release to Orvil, and along with being high, which helped them in addition to feel the music more, also helped them release it better, not being afraid of what came out. There was a genre he found called slowcore that he felt their sound might be a part of, so he listened to as much of that kind of music as he could.

The trouble Orvil sometimes felt about it all was his connection to drugs and to music and especially to music on drugs, how it allowed him access to some part of himself that had been numb before, and like he only knew it was numb once he started taking drugs and playing music.

Orvil felt stuck about the fact that so many musicians and writers and artists in general were tortured and addicts, to the point that it seems like that's where good art comes from. Sensitive people trying to find ways to not hurt so bad was maybe more of the picture. But it hadn't been about feeling too much, it was about not feeling enough. The drugs part of the equation felt unsolvable. Or he wanted it to be.

Going back to the numbness didn't feel like a good option when he thought about the idea of quitting drugs, out of shame, or out of familial duty, to do better, to be better for his brothers, for his grandmas, to follow the knowable path to success for Indian kids, which meant doing well in high school, getting into a good college, then getting a good job somewhere preferably helping out the Native community. He couldn't imagine ever not wanting to keep getting high and making music, which he knew from what he read about other musicians, take Jimi Hendrix for example, who he paid attention to because he was Jimi Hendrix, the legendary guitarist, but also because he'd read that Jimi was part Native, Cherokee, and Jimi had pursued music and drugs with the same passion. He didn't want to become Jimi Hendrix, but because he knew there were people like him, who hungered to be high and play music, he at least knew he wasn't alone, and especially having Sean as a friend and fellow musician, well that just made it the most ideal oblivion he could imagine getting proportionately lost in, in order to become what he thought it might be possible to become using drugs and playing music, to get good at art and become a real musician or whatever, get paid. There was this feeling of possibility, and like he didn't ever want to come down from where he got to, no matter the cost.

Orvil slept at some point. Woke up late at night thinking about the next day. His family was going to Alcatraz. They wanted him to go. He hadn't even been home in how long? He thought about watching Opal asleep on Sean's front porch. Watching her with Sean, knocking on the door then sitting down and waiting, then falling asleep there. He'd never felt that bad about anything in his whole life. And the thought came to him then, that he could come back from where he'd gone. He could make it right with them. Couldn't he?

CHAPTER TWENTY-SEVEN

Alcatraz

Waking up before the sun was hard but they'd all gotten into Opal's Ford Bronco, Opal and Jacquie in the front and the boys in the back, seat-beltless. Even Orvil. He'd come home late the night before and actually had not been the hardest to get out of bed. That was Loother, for whom it'd become a general problem, which Opal had zero tolerance for, but Jacquie attributed to growth, because he was a growing boy, and it couldn't be disputed because now he was the tallest of the three.

In the back of the Bronco there were layers and layers of blankets and pillows. The boys used to love to tumble and bounce around back there as the truck made its turns, sometimes forgetting the very real throw of centrifugal force, and forgetting the hardness of certain uncovered spots where it was metal, and they'd hit their heads hard enough to make a lump.

On the day of the sunrise ceremony, before the sun had risen in the east from behind the Oakland hills to begin to lift first the dark curtain of night, then the fog from the bay, Orvil and Loother and Lony lay in the back sleeping under old blankets Opal had collected.

Jacquie wanted a cigarette bad enough that she drummed her fingers against the window on her side without seeming to know how much it annoyed Opal, who kept sighing about it.

Neither of them had been there since they went with their mom back in 1970, forever ago, during the occupation, when the Indians of All Tribes had taken over and they'd slept in prison cells waiting in vain for their demands to be met.

For Opal and Jacquie, it was about much more than what the island represented to Indian people, or Americans, it was about their mom telling them about her cancer, and relapsing, and it was about Jacquie getting raped and later giving her daughter up. The prison-island was a memory, it was a buried metaphor, or one they'd never figured out, and even though they'd planned the trip, it was this sudden thing happening to them, that they were driving toward, about to board a ferry boat called the Blue and Gold.

When Jacquie went up top to get the wind's smell, the swell of it coming and going, she saw Lony up there but watched him from afar, pretending not to be even looking in his direction. Becoming a little dizzy from the boat's motion made her remember. She used the wind blowing against her as a kind of balm. As she approached him, Lony was doing something strange with his eyes closed.

"What are you doing?" Jacquie asked him. His arms were up in the air like he was ready to take flight. He pretended to have been yawning and stretching after she asked him.

"Still tired from waking up so early, I guess. You?" Lony said.

"Seemed like you thought you might fly," Jacquie said.

"No, just stretching," he said. "People can't fly." Lony laughed a little at the idea of it.

"You think it'd be easy to get up there on that water tower?" Lony said, ignoring what she said about his brain and pointing to the water tower on Alcatraz.

"I got up there," Jacquie said, looking at the thing with Lony.

"You did not," Lony said.

"What, your grandma never told you anything?"

"Grandma never told us anything what?" Lony said.

"Did she really not tell you that we were there?"

"On the water tower?"

"Please tell me you know Native people took over the island, lived there for almost two years, way back when, when us dinosaurs once ruled the earth."

"I guess I did know it. So she must have told us. But I don't remember anything specific. But maybe I was too young to understand what she was talking about. You lived there, right?"

"Lived? I guess you could call it that. We weren't prisoners, but we weren't exactly on vacation either."

"But what about the water tower?"

"Well, I climbed up there with some other kids. I wasn't one of the ones who did the graffiti, but I got up. There are things to grab hold of that make it pretty easy actually."

"Pretty easy, huh?" Lony said.

"I was a lot older than you, and didn't have two grandmas looking after me, let's just say, so don't get any dumb ideas," Jacquie said.

"I bet if you really believed you could fly you would," Lony said.

"Me, or who do you mean by 'you'?"

"I mean 'you' as in anyone."

"Oh, you're one of those," Jacquie said.

"One of whats?"

"Believers," she said, and looked left and right as if to make sure the wrong person wasn't listening.

"I don't trust people who just believe, like without knowing anything or because they need to believe what they want to believe in more than they care about whether the thing they're believing in is worthy of believing in, but I wouldn't ever want to become a nonbeliever. Like how most adults end up. Kids know something you actively try to make us lose. You know that, right?"

"Make you lose what?"

"*You* know what I mean, Jacquie Red Feather."

"I remember being a kid sometimes. I remember having zero control and being dragged around. Not being able to do anything about the doing always being done to me."

"What if birds just believe they can fly? Feathers and those skinny muscles can't be doing all that much, it could be like catching the wind just right, don't you think?"

"You just jump around from thing to thing, don't you? Okay, well, you can't catch the wind, birds don't catch the wind, because they really have to flap a lot to get going, then eventually they can soar or float, I guess."

"Those big old wind turbines in Livermore, they catch the wind. And sailboats catch the wind. Also kites and Windsurfers, and I heard they're building flying structures up in the sky to harvest the jet stream as an alternative energy source to end our dependence on fossil fuels," Lony said.

"Your neck must get tired from holding that big brain up, huh?"

"I'm not smart. Mostly I don't think I am. Mostly I think I'm dumb."

"Lony, don't say that."

"I know I'm not dumb. I'm saying I think I am a lot. And I know I'm smart about some things, probably like you are. But actually dumb about a lot of stuff. Hey maybe you know this, why are Native people always wearing feathers in the first place?"

"The first place? Where was that?"

"Where'd they put Adam and Eve?"

"Garden of Eden."

"Well that for sure was not the first place. I'm saying what about Native people wearing bird feathers. What's with that?"

"A lot of times there aren't definitive answers. I heard someone say it was about birds being closest to God. And you know how Native people use smoke for prayer because the smoke rises up. The smoke and the birds carry the prayers up to God. And eagles fly the highest, which is why their feathers are most revered, not to mention valuable."

"Like money-wise?" Lony said, moving his thumb into his index and middle fingers indicating money. "How does dressing up like a bird and dancing make sense?"

"Not everything's supposed to make sense."

"I know that. I'm just talking about, like, why dress up like a bird so much?"

"They used to be dinosaurs, they say," Jacquie said.

"Oh you're one of those," Lony said and smiled, squinting and putting his hand above his eyes to block the sun.

"You don't believe they used to be dinosaurs?"

"You're telling me they evolved so hard they just, lifted off the ground? Besides, everything used to be something else," Lony said. "That's not really saying anything. After enough time passes you can't just say this used to be that anymore. It's like with the land bridge thing, the Bering Strait, people saying we're just Asians who crossed the land bridge, but with that same logic everyone is *just* from Africa. Or everyone is *just* from apes. Or everyone is *just* from single-cell organisms. Did you know seventy-five percent of the time there has been life on earth, it was slime, so everyone is *just* slime then, basically, right, by that same logic?"

"Everyone is slime actually makes a kind of sense, I think," Jacquie said. "How much slime time is that, that seventy-five percent?"

"I don't know," Lony said, and sounded sad, like he wasn't so sure about how the conversation was going anymore.

"Okay well if everyone used to be something else, then what'd you used to be?"

"I used to not know talking. I used to not know walking. I was practically just a drooling slug once. So slime, basically."

"And now look at you," Jacquie said. Lony jumped up on a bench, Jacquie just then noticed, with his arms up like Superman. Jacquie wanted to tell him to get down but didn't.

"What'd you used to be?" Lony said. He didn't mean for it to carry any more weight than her question had for him, but Jacquie could sometimes only hear through load-bearing walls.

"Drooling slug too, so slime time mostly," she said, and motioned drinking from an invisible bottle, then sticking her tongue out and to the left like she'd died there and then. Lony didn't laugh. Just stared at Jacquie like but what else?

After that, Lony ran around the boat, on the lower deck, looking down at the water like he could see fish or sharks or dolphins swimming alongside them, pointing down at it like there was so much more than black water there. Loother kept pulling Lony by the back of the shirt to get him to sit still where their family was sitting together at a table next to a dirty window, like he was embarrassed by Lony's behavior. Opal and Jacquie both felt uncomfortable about this slight violence, Loother's force, his face while he did it, but Lony didn't seem to mind too much. Plus after what Lony had done to himself, this kind of roughhousing almost felt reassuring.

Orvil went over and said something to his brothers that made them laugh. Then came and sat with his grandmas and didn't say anything.

Opal took her beanie off revealing her bald head and it seemed like she was saying something to them which neither of them knew what to say back about.

"I bet it won't feel the same," Opal said.

Orvil and Jacquie looked at each other as if wondering what Opal was referring to.

"I think it'll be different," Orvil said. Guessing it was about the island.

"Or like déjà vu all over again," Jacquie said, and was the only one to laugh.

"We really can't do it again," Opal said. "Honestly. None of it."

"I always thought it was reassuring, that we could be doing what we already did before, all over again," Orvil said.

"Sounds like hell," Opal said.

"Honestly, I have no idea what you two are talking about," Jacquie said.

"I'm getting some coffee, do you two want some?" Opal asked.

"I don't drink coffee," Orvil said.

"I would love a cup," Jacquie said. "Sweet and creamy as you can make it."

They all ended up sitting on lawn chairs a ways away from the center of the circle where people were taking turns praying and saying things on the mic, reading poems, and making proclamations, playing the flute and the hand drum and singing, most of it seemed to be singing.

At one point Lony stood behind Opal, who had decided to stand up to stretch her legs, and a Native man was speaking, and Lony kept gripping Opal's arm, indicating he felt what the man was saying, and the first time he gripped her arm like that she got chills, but then every time after that scared her, as if he was feeling it too much, like he needed it too much. What was it that she'd failed to provide him that he was so hungry for? Like she'd neglected him. Or he was pretending. This was a sick thought to have, she knew. She listened twice as hard to what was being said.

"Hello and good morning, I would just like to say to each and every one of you, here this morning time, this sacred time just before the sun comes, I want to tell you, over here, the young ones back there, and the old ones up here, how it should be, the children, and all our brothers and sisters we can't see, who are with us in spirit here today, our relatives and our ancestors, and even those other ones way over there, tuning in to the live stream, ayyyy . . ." Here everyone seemed to laugh at the idea of people live streaming being thought of alongside the ancestors. "All our relatives here. This morning-time energy, first of all I want to acknowledge the people whose land we now stand on, the Ohlone people, who've held relationship to this land, and the way it looks and smells, what it gives and what it takes to live here, the people who know this land better than anyone, whose memories live here, whose lifeways were taken, I want to acknowledge that we aren't doing enough to acknowledge these people, that they're forgotten all the time, and it's not okay, we need to do better, we can do better. Listen to them today. We have some great speakers lined up, singers and dancers too. Listen to them. See them. Because all too often we don't. Even us Indian people, we forget our relatives in California, because some of them aren't federally recognized. We need to stop competing with one another over who gets to say they're more Indian than the next. Now I don't mean you pretendians, you all need to leave, ayyyy . . . ," he said, and got another laugh before introducing the next speaker.

Lony slowly began to separate himself from them as if he were hearing other things being said from other fires nearby. Loother caught eyes with him that meant to relay for him to stay but when he didn't respond and moved farther off Loother let him go.

Orvil saw Lony slink off too and took a mental note, but he wanted to stay. At one point Opal came over and put her hands on Orvil's shoulders from behind him. He was remembering what it'd felt like to be around so many Native people, like it had felt at the powwow, the power of it, the good feeling, like nothing else, and he started crying, then put his fist into his eyes and cleared his throat. Opal kept her hands on his shoulders, and Loother pretended to not notice. He got on his phone, but he watched, felt tears coming too.

———

Orvil is making his way up the crosshatched poles that hold up the water tower, the metal on them painted white but chipping, revealing the rust they'd just painted over to restore it. The salt from the bay, pushed by its wind, eats metal.

Orvil is going slow so as to not frighten Lony, up there at the top, where there is a banister of sorts and a walkway.

Every now and then he looks down at Loother, who'd wanted to climb up too.

Orvil wants to think he knows Lony won't do anything crazy. Orvil is trying not to think about how it could mean something really bad that Lony even decided to go up there. He is climbing up the crosshatched poles as calm as possible, thinking about what Lony has in mind, about how he must be out his mind.

Orvil imagines his brother's falling body.

Lony is standing on the rail, balancing precariously, looking at Orvil, dead in his eyes.

And just then a gust of wind makes Lony sway. He flashes a smile at Orvil while holding his arms out, then with one of them tells Orvil to stay back.

Orvil looks down and sees the crowd looking up at them and he inches closer to Lony but not near close enough to try to grab him. He is yelling at Lony, who seems to hear him, Lony what are you doing, Lony what the fuck are you doing, is what Orvil is yelling, yelling through the wind that tries to take his voice.

Lony is getting down from the rail. "It's okay. I'm okay. I was just seeing something," Lony says. He's breathing pretty hard, which is the first sign Orvil can tell he's been scared.

"Seeing something?"

"I was gonna fly," Lony says.

"That's not funny," Orvil says.

"I wasn't trying to be funny. I could have done it if you hadn't come. We've just been the feather. We used to be the whole bird. We used to believe and we were the whole bird."

"What are you talking about, Lony? What's flying gonna do? You trying to be a superhero?" Orvil doesn't want to sound impatient or frustrated, they're still in range.

"We all need to see something bigger than what we think is possible. To make us believe. You know we used to exhibit our powers."

"We? We who?"

"Cheyenne people. Medicine people. Powers of exhibition. I found all kinds of stuff on the internet about who we used to be, like did you know in Plains sign language the way they say Cheyenne is to indicate cutting, it was one of the ways we used to grieve, we have been called the cut people."

"Nobody died, Lony. I'm still here. Opal's still here. You're not grieving anyone. There's a difference."

"It felt like someone did. When you almost did. It felt like someone did," Lony said, and looked away from his brother, then looked down and saw something, picked it up and threw it over the rusted banister.

"Listen, if you wanna fly we can save up and take a trip somewhere, fly anywhere you want, where would you go?" Orvil says.

"Could we all go on the trip?"

"Sure."

"Namibia," Lony says.

"What?"

"There's really old dead trees there, the trees are so old, and they're dead, but they're there, still look like trees and standing like trees so pretty much still trees, but they're dead, and there are giant red dunes, and at night it's supposed to look like the surface of the moon, and I read there's a chance you could find actual diamonds beachcombing, and there's a cheetah rescue and—"

"Beachcombing? Lony! What are we doing up here?"

"Look," Lony says, pointing to the red graffiti painted on the water tower. "I think Jacquie did it but she doesn't want to admit that she did it."

"Is that what brought you up here?"

"What brought *you* up here?"

"*You,* what do you mean? Fucking you!"

"Is that all it took?"

"Is that all what took?"

"For you to come see how I was doing?"

——— • • ———

CHAPTER TWENTY-EIGHT

Doubled Up Inside

Orvil is driving Mike's car to pay for staying at their place, and for the Blanx. He was taking more and more, and not selling any anymore. Mike was the one to tell him he needed to pay for staying. Sean and Mike fought about it. It was Sean's idea about driving for Mike to make money. Mike had said this wasn't gonna be a thing. Just this once. Said he would be fucked if Orvil got caught. Orvil said he would not get caught. But he went to his bag and got out his dream catcher.

Orvil had not wanted the dream catcher. He thought they were corny. But Opal had given it to him for Christmas, told Orvil to keep it with him, and to remember that he had it, to be able to know how to catch his dream when it came along. The gift had come with a new guitar and amplifier. Orvil's first electric one. After all the ways he hadn't been there for the family, all the ways he'd disappointed her, and she'd known what was special to him, that music meant something to him.

When he got into Mike's Honda the first thing he did was hang it from the rearview. He hated how many non-Native people hung dream catchers from their rearview mirrors. It was the last place you wanted to be sleeping, the last place you should be dreaming. Did they think they could catch a car accident before it happened in the dream-catcher's net somehow? Or were they using it just like Orvil, basically for good luck?

Lyft and Uber users wouldn't know it's not Mike. Not one person would ask him why his face doesn't match the picture. Orvil had this plan to ask the passengers if they wouldn't mind paying cash and canceling the ride through the app. Would tell them the app takes half, how it's not fair. And he's a community college student struggling to make rent. He'd read about the scam online and was for sure not gonna tell Mike about it. Not until he could hand Mike the cash. It was all a big risk. But didn't feel like one. Not getting high when he kept wanting to felt like the only risk that mattered. Was.

Opal thought Orvil would stay the straightened arrow. Or he'd thought he'd heard her say that through his bedroom wall one morning. She was talking to Jacquie. What did that mean to stay the straightened arrow? He looked it up and saw a Reddit argument about whether the phrase was originally about a straightened arrow or staying straight and narrow, but immediately lost interest because they came to the same thing. And Orvil was not doing that.

When he got to Sean's house after being away for so long, he got higher than he'd been in a long time, laid down on the floor next to Sean's bed, feeling like he absolutely had to crawl under it.

Now he's crawling through traffic under the shadows of semitrucks on that part of the 880 that always seems so stuck. He registers the Oakland Coliseum to his left as looming. It is bigger than it is. He's on his way to wait in the cell-phone parking lot at the airport. He's found people tip better if you get them from the airport to their home, so he tries to keep on that route. Orvil listens to music in the car when it's just him, sometimes one of Mike's stations, sometimes his own music, recordings he and Sean have made, and if someone young, who seems cool, gets in he might keep his music on, but if any old white people get in, he keeps it on public radio, knows it must bring some kind of comfort for white passengers, getting in with non-white drivers, the milk-white narrative calm of NPR, like some sonic indication of sophistication.

He doesn't want to think about the powwow and he doesn't, but being this close to the coliseum, he can't not let it do its work on him.

Because the thing about trying not to think about something is that very elephant you're trying not to think about, that is right there—smack-dab—when you go to not think of it, appearing as if to announce its absence. And then there is an actual elephant in front of him, up on the billboard, that dopey, lovable mascot for the Oakland A's: Stomper.

He drives and he drops people off and he drives back to the airport and he drops more people off and time goes away and he likes that he can make it disappear like that. Some of them have cash and agree to his plan and others do not, or he does not ask them. All seem distracted and spend the ride on their phones.

Just now he doesn't want to think about getting high later. He's trying to keep some kind of balance. Earn his way there. But he pulls the car over thinking a passenger had put a suitcase back there that he'd forgotten to take out. Or because he's curious about what Mike had back there. As luck or fate would have it, there is a bag. A duffel bag with some of Mike's clothes in it, and a very decent-sized bag of crushed-up something.

Whether it is Blanx or cocaine or MDMA he doesn't know and he doesn't care. But he looks both ways like he is about to cross a busy street, then brings the ziplock bag of white powder up with him into the front seat.

At the end of a ten-hour shift, Orvil drives through the dim piss-yellow light of the Webster Street Tube back toward downtown Oakland from Alameda. When he comes out of the tube, he sees the moon above the city. It is big and full and bright. He thinks of the first time Opal tried to point out the Indian in the moon for him.

They were driving back from Fentons after he came home with almost perfect grades on his report card. She'd picked him up, just him, to celebrate his good grades. On the way back home Opal pointed up to the moon with her lips.

"There he is, he's sitting in Indian position, see him?" she said. Orvil squinted his eyes, said he couldn't see him, then asked if Indian position came from India's Indians or Indian Indians.

"You know, I don't know where that came from," Opal said.

"Just looks like a smudge," Orvil said about the moon.

"Maybe you need glasses," Opal said, and Orvil laughed, but then stopped when he looked over and saw that she might be serious.

He never saw the Indian in the moon. Even after he saw Lony and Loother see it. He looked online to see if he could have someone point it out for him there, but he couldn't find anything about it and thought maybe his family was just making up that they saw it and that no one else saw an Indian in the moon, which made him think about being Native and how much of that was being made up to make up for the fact that they weren't connected to the tribe or to their language or with the knowledge that other people had about being Native, and he hated to think thoughts like that but they came anyway. And soon he began to resent the moon, feeling like its light represented something false, like it was only light because of the sun, but it was sort of respected like it was its own light. He started to think of the moon as a lie.

Even now, Orvil has a certain feeling toward the moon, about the moon, it isn't resentment anymore, and he doesn't think it's a lie, but he doesn't like it.

Orvil hears a pulsing bass line and turns the music up. *Doubled up inside, always doubled up inside.* An eerie voice haunts the car. He wonders what being doubled up inside means. He thinks of the bullet. The star shard. How he hadn't thought of it in so long. How the voice had gone without him noticing its absence. He thought about how different he must seem to everyone, like a different person. He thinks of himself having been taken over by the bullet. What if it wandered in his blood and poisoned him and changed him and he would never be the way he used to be again? He thinks about Opal changing too. How she came to look so different after the treatment.

His phone vibrates and he sees it's Opal. She's psychic like that. The car in front of him stops suddenly, its alarm-red brake lights send jolts of spiky adrenaline to the top of his skin, and Orvil watches his dream catcher sway from the rearview just before a car slams into him from behind. The airbag knocks him back. The hit from behind makes him hit the car in front of him. There is a loud ringing and he doesn't know if it's coming from outside or inside. Orvil gets out of his car and people are yelling. He can't tell if it was his fault. He'd been stopped at a light, but was he supposed to be? He'd been looking at his phone. This is all bad, he thinks before he takes off running. He knows it's stupid, and will look crazy, and will cause the people involved to call the cops immediately, and that will mean it will come down on Mike. Plus he's got this big bag of drugs that is Mike's, which means he can't ever go back to their house, which means he can't even run into either one of them anywhere, which means he will just be on the run now. And it also means that once this bag runs out he won't have access to anything anymore.

He runs over to the lake and from the lake down International. He keeps running until he gets to East Twelfth. He hasn't run like this in years, and he is sweating, and he is crying. He stops at a gate between him and the freeway. He watches the lights of the cars stream by on the freeway, listens to a BART train go by. And he wants to fix it. He wants to take it back. He doesn't want to go through the shitty discomfort of quitting. The boredom. The regret. He wishes he hadn't left the car. He could have driven off. What the fuck was he thinking, running? But then he hears a siren, and he gets back to running. He runs all the way home, where the door is locked and he doesn't have a key, and he doesn't want to knock, so he climbs over the fence and goes to the backyard, where he falls asleep on the lawn, looking up through the lemon tree, too tired to care about anything.

CHAPTER TWENTY-NINE

Too Many Seasons

How could I have expected to just never see Orvil again when we'd become so close I thought we loved each other? Have Mike come into my room trying to kill me about dude leaving his car after getting into an accident in downtown Oakland. Shit. Obviously I didn't see it coming, but I also hadn't been living in a way that I foresaw anything or was planning for anything more than getting high and selling more drugs to keep getting high and telling myself I didn't need school or a future if this kind of now I could keep getting could keep feeling this good. Of course that wasn't true. I know now. For someone like me, when you find a thing that gets you off, not like sexually, though it's not not that for some people, but if you find a thing that feeds you in that other way that has nothing to do with food or eating but in this way like you could never be full enough of it, well then that's it for a while, until you can't get it anymore for reasons outside of your control, or you die, basically. If you're like me, you become obsessed. That's the only thing that matters and it's not living in the moment or planning for a future or even spending time like they say but the very reason why they don't call that shit spending it's getting wasted. Again, I know that now. But at the time? You couldn't have convinced me otherwise about anything other than that I might find some even better drug to get me even more high. I'm an addict. That's how I was built. Not that I'm doomed or believe fate had it out for me. I keep making myself too, just like I'm finding new ways to do better now. Now.

But Mike was fuckin' pissed about Orvil leaving his car like that and he should have been but not at fucking me. I guess it was my idea. Mike hadn't forgotten that. So we got into it and it got ugly. He came into my room and I could tell right away I needed to square up, so I did, and then he did this like wrestling tackle or takedown and we were on my bed and the guy was trying to fucking strangle me and not choke me out like in wrestling or put me to sleep but actually fucking bare-hand strangle my throat for something Orvil did I had absolutely no control over. Luckily I got him off me in time by squeezing out of his hold like I always knew how to do by sliding my knee hard up into his gut and then running out of my room and out of the house for long enough that I knew when I came back with a two-by-four I found behind the house that he wasn't gonna go at me hard again like that.

The craziest shit about Orvil ghosting himself was how easy I found it was to do. To get lost in a town like Oakland? The place is really big for how small it is. Like you can go years without seeing people you know live in Oakland depending on what part of Oakland you stay in. Like for instance I live in West Oakland now. I'm kind of ashamed to say. Feels like one of the most obnoxious places gentrifiers act like they belong and sometimes it even feels true like they do belong in some fucked-up way, the good ones—if there are any—are actually decent people, and anyways they're not like the fuckin' tech bros in condos you know have no fucking spine.

But why do I feel like I'm a gentrifier in my own hometown and I'm not even white? Did I come from money? I certainly never saw any of it. But I guess a big house and a private education means money too.

And it's hard not to feel inside like a white person having been raised white in a white community. I tend to intellectualize in order to compartmentalize a feeling. This is some shit my therapist turned me on to. Intellectualizing as a way to cope and control trauma-response. So I told myself I was a victim in a system made for white people just trying to make do with what I had to work with. Does this make me feel like I'm not gentrifying? No.

But so Mike did not fucking strangle me to death that day he came at me about Orvil leaving his car in the middle of downtown Oakland. And I found out why he was so pissed and it had to do with him leaving a bag in the trunk with a good amount in it. Crushed-up Blanx too.

My dad came back and I went back to school and shit basically stayed the same at home just a fucking drug den with wolves in it. I was one of them.

The story of my eventual recovery is not interesting. Not to me. And the story of my addictions is even less interesting. But the way I've been and what I've done along the way is a memory, and a story I have to work with. The story that includes that I need, deeply, absurdly, and can't have, absolutely, is the one I can't put together, but can't stop trying to either. This interests me.

I been trying to find out what happened to Orvil. All these years later. Googling his name just brings up old stuff about the shooting. Dude never really got online in a way you can search, like if he had online profiles they were never under his actual name. I looked at obituaries. Even called up the county recorder to see if there were death records. I have online profiles under my name. And he hasn't tried to find me. I know this because I've tried to look myself up and it's easy.

People come in and out of your life in a way that feels wrong. The out-of-your-life part. Like it cancels out the way they came in if it didn't come to anything. But maybe that's some capitalistic investment-earnings-type bullshit and no one is necessarily meant to stay with you if even just one of you doesn't want it to happen.

There was always this thing between us. Me and Orvil. We connected, for real for real, and we had music, but it was me who had the drugs that made the relationship compromised, me who had the house we could stay at to allow us to do whatever we wanted when most kids had parents making sure shit didn't get out of hand. I don't blame anyone. Honestly. Myself. Obviously. I just wish there was a way we could keep knowing each other. If I could even just know he still exists by having him friend me or follow me or message me now and then to say what we had mattered enough that it shouldn't just be let go of entirely.

I guess something was wrong. I guess something was wrong with us. Was wrong enough with us that he needed to let the whole thing go like he'd left Mike's car in the middle of downtown Oakland. Like I ended up leaving my dad and Mike and the house. I disappeared inside Oakland myself.

I spent years just working and dating and trying to figure out my limits. I'll tell you one thing I learned, if you're an addict and trying to drink or use like normal people you have to make rules for yourself and follow them. Rules like don't do anything until after you get all the shit you need to get done, done. Or don't have a drink until after five o'clock, or until after dinner. Take multiple nights off from your drug of choice. Find other, sustainable ways to get high, like exercise. Take the time to find music and movies and shows and books you like. It takes time to find what is right for you. There is so much noise. You have to fill the days and it can't be with drinking or doing drugs. Always beware of downward momentum. It doesn't always feel like falling when you're falling. I learned these by trying them and they all worked for a time, but that was the thing. I'd always end up at some extreme. So I couldn't hold down a job, or have a relationship. I kept going back to rehab. First it was the Blanx, which I always missed after I couldn't get them anymore. For a while it was drinking and cocaine. For years. Then I ended up dating a guy with a source to Molly and I took that to its extreme. Probably permanently impaired my ability to release some important amount of serotonin. Then a girl I was dating for like nine months ended up confessing to me that she had a heavy addiction to opioids. I'd suspected it. Had even actively looked for pills in her apartment. Her name was and I guess is Malorie. She read a lot. Lots of depressing French novels. Not even in the language, they were translations and she wasn't French, had just committed to their whole thing at some point, I guess. I liked this guy Leve for his brutal honesty. He killed himself. Nothing more brutally honest than that. And this other guy who won the Nobel. Le Clézio. When I was waiting for Malorie to get home I'd read whatever she had lying around. There was this part in a Le Clézio novel, I can't remember the name, where there is a piano player, before the Nazi invasion. It made me think of my mom. There were the most beautiful descriptions of the way a piano can sound at a distance. And with all that stuff with Mike being a Nazi doctor, and her brain disease, it felt like some kind of Nazi invasion had happened. Le Clézio was so much brighter than the other French guys.

I told her how much I love to get high, not that I said it like that but in that way addicts tell each other who they are by how much they want, with some tone, or hand gesture, or catching of the eyes. We ended up regularly smoking fentanyl. I went back to rehab after that and thought I'd ruined my brain. I probably had. It probably is ruined. A lotta people can't get back to any kind of normal after a certain amount of blowing out their brain's receptors. I found that if I worked enough then exercised and meditated and went to meetings I could be okay. I got back into playing music. That was another thing that worked.

It is a sad thing to let go of. That everything leaves. But life has too many seasons to get caught up about one of them. And other seasons return. So even though it felt for a time like me and Orvil had been brought together by fate, maybe it was included in fate that the us of us was just supposed to be for the time we knew each other.

I'm being asked to understand that with some people you love, they just won't end up being a part of your life. I'm being asked a question that it seems I can answer only by living.

— • • —

CHAPTER THIRTY

Just Wait

His high-school years came and went faster than they might have if he hadn't dropped out. It hadn't been easy to convince Opal that he didn't want to go back to school. That he just wanted to work. That he didn't believe in school. What would his brothers think? They were expected to keep going to school, to keep doing well, how would that make Opal look, letting him quit like that? When they were alone at the kitchen table talking about it after he'd been home for a week, he said he'd been feeling like quitting everything. He didn't need to say more than that. He couldn't tell her that he didn't want to see Sean. That seeing Sean would have meant facing what he'd done to Mike's car. Would have meant potentially facing Mike.

Time passed differently when you worked than it did when you were at school. Earned money passed through his hands differently too. He got a job as a bagger at the Safeway near their house. He saved up. He gave Opal money, which she refused. He gave his brothers money, which they were too quick to take. Orvil went back to being the good grandson and brother he'd been before. On the surface. As far as anyone could tell. Things were back to normal.

But he had that bag. He only got high when he knew he could get away with it. Sharing a room with his brothers didn't help. Neither did living with an addict in recovery.

The white powder in the bag was strong. So he didn't need much. He would do it when he wasn't working and everyone was out of the house. When Jacquie was at a meeting or on one of her long walks. When Loother and Lony were at school.

Opal's cancer had fully gone into remission and she was back working.

He didn't like that he felt like he needed it to keep playing guitar. That he only felt good playing when he was high. He didn't know if he played better when he was high or if it just felt and sounded better to him because he was high.

But he played when he wasn't high. He wanted to get better. And knew it took practice. And then more practice. And then more practice. He played in the backyard where no one could hear him fumbling around with scales and other people's songs.

When Orvil's life became about not getting high anymore, when it became about staying sober enough to just hold it down, to not have his decisions mess with anyone else's life, when he realized everything he was doing had to do with not fucking up anymore, that moment became an arrival, which was a stopping point, and a crossroads. He got to a place where he had to decide what the next thing would be.

He found a way to stretch out what he had in the bag he stole from Mike that night he ran away from the guy's car and started over again. A way to stop and keep going at the same time. But it wasn't sustainable. He was figuring out in his head and in his heart what the next thing would be, and that it most definitely would not be the same shit he'd been doing.

He'd dragged the bag out as long as he could. Had enough to have one more go at it before he left it all for good.

He'd had it in his head before, like a seed in the soil of a bad corner, waiting in the shade for the right kind of light to land on it for long enough; the idea that if he wanted to take it that far, to leave, to really leave, which was the absolute furthest away you could take anything if you chose such a thing as leaving living. He preferred anything else other than that three-syllable, clinical word: suicide. Overdosing wasn't right either because it implied a mistake. Like taking too much medicine, more than the prescribed amount. He wanted a better word for it all. He'd always wanted better words for what it felt like to live, and to suffer, and to love it all so recklessly as to hate how it couldn't love you back the same.

Leaving the living, that was how he wanted to think of it. It felt within reach, the option, he could leave.

He hadn't had some coming-to-the-light moment. He'd run away from a car accident. He was a coward. Sobriety was the story he'd go with because the real story was too fucked up. That was how it was with so many stories. They were the bearable version of some fucked-up reality no one wanted to hear about. That was sad too. More sad shit he couldn't talk about, just like no one wanted to talk about thoughts or considerations regarding leaving living, just like no one ever wanted to talk or hear about the fact that people were sad. That was part of how the sadness always grew, or sustained itself, as did the feelings about leaving living for something else, something better, or at the very least something different from this. That was the thing. Something different. Transcendence was why people chose to die, to get high.

He would stay though. He told himself he would stay and not give up and just have patience. Life was long if you didn't get killed accidentally or get some disease. Things changed. He could wait and see what would happen. In his worst moments that's what he would tell himself. Just wait.

He'd never stopped worrying about Lony. Everything seemed fine. Until it wasn't.

———— • • ————

CHAPTER THIRTY-ONE

Ocean Beach

It wasn't that Orvil didn't go back to school that made Lony worried about him. That was just a symptom of the bigger thing. It was what Lony saw on Orvil's face when he didn't think anyone was looking. He was too young to look that tired. Not even Opal ever looked that tired. And it wasn't from working too much or not getting enough sleep. Something had worn him out from the inside. But he wasn't willing to admit it to anyone. He didn't talk about anything when they were all home or eating together. And no one else suspected there was something wrong with that. Lony didn't know what to do anymore.

He'd first had a taste of freedom when he went looking for Will the Dog late into the night that time Orvil left the door open and the dog ran away. It felt like Orvil left the door open on a lot of shit. Let a lot of shit into the family. Lony was worried that night. But he knew he would find Will the Dog. He just knew. That was why he kept looking. And while he wandered the surrounding neighborhood, hiding from cars, including Opal's Bronco when they came calling for him, he felt a kind of lightness. Like the kid in him coming alive again.

It felt like playing. He knew it was super serious, with Orvil being gone again and the dog running away. Nothing could have been more serious, but he felt different. At the height of that feeling he found Will the Dog under a car in a driveway that went kind of far back on the side of a house just two blocks away from theirs. The dog was shivering. Lony laughed and made a clicking sound and the dog came to him. He got curious about the feeling after that. How to get it back.

When Lony ran away he got on a bus that took him down Fruitvale to BART. He wouldn't have called it running away. But he left his phone at home because he knew he wouldn't be able to stay away for long if they were calling and texting him.

He brought with him an old iPod he'd lost a while back and found with the headphones still attached under his bed inside a pillowcase. It was all classical music, lots of Beethoven he didn't even like anymore, but he listened to it on the bus then the train ride because it made everything feel like it was a movie. The only other guy on the train was asleep with his hat pulled down over his eyes. Lony was listening to Beethoven's Symphony No. 7 in A Major, Opus 92: II. Allegretto. He was scared. But he felt good.

He got off at Sixteenth Street and Mission and listened to a guy play an accordion, something Latin-sounding, for like twenty minutes. Then he got back on the train, wanting to go farther. He decided he wanted to get to the ocean. He had never seen the ocean in real life. How had that been? He'd seen the bay, of course. The bay water was everywhere.

Lony wanted to find out what it was like to be out on his own. Or he couldn't explain, even to himself, exactly what feeling he was after, what aim he had in mind. He wanted to be outside. It wasn't more than that but that wasn't all it was about.

He would spend years trying to figure out the feeling. To be outside. To live outside. He wanted that.

Lony only planned to stay away for a few hours. Come back late and say he got lost. That he wanted to ride the bus for fun but then got on the wrong one and didn't know where he was. Not having his phone was part of his plan to convince them that he was lost.

The train wouldn't get him to the ocean. He asked someone how he could get there. He told a woman his grandma had wandered away and she was off her medication and he needed to find her. The woman ended up driving him to the ocean. Said she would help him look for her. He felt bad as they drove in silence the fifteen minutes it took to get there. The moon was big and bright and made everything feel like the memory of a dream.

When they got to Ocean Beach, Lony opened the car door and ran as fast as he could. The woman yelled something at him as he ran off but he didn't know what.

Lony ran down to the water where the sand was harder and he ran a long time along the water like that, heading north. He was cold even though he had on a sweatshirt and a windbreaker.

He found a red tent with no one in it and no one around and decided he would try to sleep, but not there where the tent had been set up because what if they came back?

He dragged the thing farther north for almost an hour then found a place that seemed tucked away, like you wouldn't necessarily see it if you walked by.

He fell asleep almost as soon as his head hit the tent floor, loving the way the sand felt on his face, thinking just before falling asleep that he should invent the sand pillow, and wanting to have his phone to look up whether or not it already existed.

— • • —

CHAPTER THIRTY-TWO

The Black Blooms

Orvil's in the bathroom with his line lined up. He doesn't know if he just wants to get really high or if he wants to not exist any-more. Not kill himself. Not suicide. He just wants a break from being alive and to come back from that break with more life.

There is everyone to think of. There is always everyone else to think of.

Orvil found out the first time Lony ran away he wasn't run-ning away but left to find his dog. Orvil had left the front door open and the dog had gotten out, then everyone went looking for the dog and couldn't find him, so then Lony went back out on his own and they didn't find him until they got home and he was in bed with the dog. And then there was the time he was gone overnight. Came back and said he got lost after riding the bus and leaving his phone at home. It didn't get weird until the third time. When he came back that time he didn't even give a reason. He stopped talking after that. Not completely. But he'd made some decision in his head about how much he would say. Opal tried to get him to see a therapist but he refused. He refused everything.

Orvil blamed himself. For everything wrong with the family. For every wrong feeling he had inside. Wanted to get rid of the bad feelings inside and didn't know how. Music could only bring him so far. But he felt himself going numb and couldn't play the way he could before, when he was using.

Now Orvil is in the bathroom with that bad light no one can bring themselves to change, blinking above him. This will be the last time. And the rest of what he has left. He knows the stories about one last time are like famous last words.

The first time he remembered going to the hospital was after jumping off a wall in kindergarten. Opal was watching him that day. He wanted to show her he could do it one more time. The wall couldn't have been more than five feet tall. And it was onto grass. But he'd landed wrong and broke his arm.

He sits back down on the toilet. It's done. He'll go lay in bed once he can get there. He'll ride it out there nice, until sleep takes over without him even meaning to. But then he feels, having taken it in, that it's too much. It's filling him up and draining him with something and it's good but he knows in the pit of his stomach the good means it's bad means he's done. The room pulses. Light blooms behind his heavy eyelids. His arms are dead. He thinks of using his phone to call someone. Who would he call? He can't move. He stands up. Black blooms now instead of light. His mind is blank. His head is meat. And then he falls, like a tree, from standing straight up, down flat on his face. A life proclaimed body as it dies, or like a tree proclaimed product as it falls. Timber. The face-plant makes the world gone. He sees stars but they're like sparks that float off into his periphery and he wants to follow them. Then someone's knocking on the door. More than one voice. They're messing with the door handle. They're breaking in. He doesn't want them to. He needs them to. There's a high hiss like air coming out of bike tires. There are other voices somewhere so deep inside he can hear them outside. Is that singing? Is it the sink? Is he sinking? And then his family, they're saying his name. His eyes are closed but he can see everyone with his eyes closed. Hold on, baby. Hold on. Who's saying that? It's all right, baby, they're coming, hold on, Orv. Loother's saying, Orv! Like he's mad but like he's trying to use Orvil's name to pull him back. Mad that it's not working to make him open his eyes. Slapping at his face. A hand or his own name. He doesn't know. He doesn't know what to make of any of it right before it's gone.

PART THREE

Futures

And it's inside myself that I must create someone
who will understand.

—CLARICE LISPECTOR

—— • • ——

CHAPTER THIRTY-THREE

Rehab

I don't even remember what happened when I OD'd. I woke up in the hospital with my whole family around me. It seemed forever before, that first time I woke up in the hospital with them all around me, like there was a version of me who actually died the day of the powwow and another version of me took over. Or it was like I was born that day too as someone new.

I feel like I'm still trying to get back to who I used to be.

And I feel like I'm getting there. My family didn't hug me. It was a whole different feeling. Everyone seemed so tired. Tired of me, but also tired like they hadn't been able to sleep waiting to see if I'd make it. All their eyes were bloodshot. I didn't know what to say. I went back to sleep. I wanted to stay asleep. Like stay stay asleep.

I went to a program that was supposed to last sixty days. It was this old lakeside resort they turned into a rehab or treatment facility in the foothills of the Sierra Nevada about an hour east of Stockton. The name of the town was Copperopolis. The lake, Lake Tulloch. Those sixty days turned into four years.

The lake-resort rehab was probably not very different from

other rehabs, except for the fact of the constant party vibe emanating from the lake itself, with its party boats blaring party music and jet skiers and those super-loud super-fast boats flying flags proclaiming freedom in that rural Republican style that's always changing and always staying the same. I even went out on the water a few times. It always seemed green to me even though I knew it wasn't. And at sunset and sunrise it was made the colors the sun made. I never learned how to swim so being out on a boat felt claustrophobic to me. If that makes sense. After my time was up at the rehab I was asked how I felt about going back home. I asked what other choice did I have, and was told about a work program through the treatment facility that came with outpatient treatment. So I ended up cleaning vacation homes. For a long time. I saved money. Went to meetings. Cleaned houses people had partied in. Partying was not in my vocabulary but that was what everyone called our clean-up duty. Cleaning up after partiers. I thought maybe there was some looped aspect to people partying at the lake, then ending up at the rehab at the lake, then relapsing and partying again on the lake like some hell in paradise or paradise in hell. That's what addiction had always felt like, like the best little thing you'd forget on the worst day possible, or the worst big thing on a day in a life you thought kept getting better because you kept getting high.

I hated the work. But I started running then.

I ran every day. In the morning before it got too hot. I wasn't used to that kind of heat. Like more than half the year too. Reaching the hundreds often. Good thing there was that lake to cool off in. I came to love running in the heat. I'd run along the highway and it was scary, those two-lane highways are pretty narrow and people drive hella fast but I bought one of those shiny vests with reflectors on it to make sure people could see me. I kept building miles. Started running once in the morning and once at sunset. It stayed hard. Like I had to keep at it and make the effort every day. And then one day it felt like I needed it in a way that kind of scared me. It wasn't not like addiction. I went to running for a feeling. How it felt after the run. But something else happened on the runs. I wasn't running away from anything anymore. I was running at whatever in me had needed the way I needed before. I was running at whatever I'd been afraid of. And I would cry. That shit would make me emotional. Not short runs. Not the first few miles, not even five. But after seven and eight miles something else is happening. The running outruns the running. Slow as I probably looked, sweating all the way through my shirt to where there wasn't a dry spot left on it. It could feel like flying.

I got way into numbers, into when I started and ended my run, how long the run would take, I would reduce the numbers by adding them together, it was something they did in numerology, and if I was doing right inside, if things were good the numbers would boil down to four or eight or nine, those three numbers were my favorite, felt lucky to me I guess, I guess I became superstitious, or had always been without knowing it, and I shuffled all the music on my phone and felt things were most right if the songs I liked best came on during my runs and crucial moments, I guess it might sound crazy if I were to ever tell anyone, but I never would.

They helped me find a place with cheap rent. It was a mobile home in a mobile home park across the street from a grocery store and Mexican restaurant I wanted to love more than I did.

But if I ran long enough, eating and drinking became euphoric. It got so hot up there too. I never sweat so much in my life. In my downtime I played music.

In one of the rentals we regularly cleaned there was a grand piano that sat at a window overlooking the lake. For a summer season we cleaned this house once a week and sometimes twice. I'd stay after we cleaned and play until the last possible moment before the next people scheduled to stay there were to arrive. I learned how to play sheet music good enough to learn songs I liked that I was finding through Spotify's algorithm for finding music you liked. My love of piano music started with the *Donnie Darko* soundtrack, specifically with the song "Liquid Spear Waltz," which I fed into the algorithm and got turned on to all these minimalists like Philip Glass and John Cage, but also film composers and people like Max Richter, leading some kind of neoclassical genre I'd also seen called post-minimalism, but I don't know, it just seems like anything contemporary doing something old but new gets called neo or post and really it just fits under the name already made for it. Anyway, minimalism perfectly matched my playing ability, having only played in that basement room at Sean's house, but I soon learned it matched something else in me, that came from me, these short, simple songs began to come out of me in a way that felt natural. It felt good to play them. Something was mending in me. Was mending me. It was the first time I felt good making music sober, there on the lake, sometimes when the colors of the sun were setting on the water in those strange blues and oranges you only ever see on water cast from a sunset in the summer. Sometimes if I stayed until it got dark I'd play and watch the lights of cars across the lake move the exact same speed as satellites in the night sky.

I had Opal send me my guitar. The dead guy's guitar she'd given me and the electric one with the amp she'd gifted me. I was trying to find my way into the instrument without having to be high, as I'd been trying to find my way into my emotions that way too. I don't know what numbed me so long before I ended up using. Losing our mom so young was obviously hard. And the life she'd put us through had, I guess, done a number on us.

I made good friends up there in recovery circles despite them being continually broken down by relapse. When the circles were broken I detached from everyone, like relapsing was an infection. It was. But we'd all make our way back to the circle. Enough of us.

The closest friend I made up there was this big Miwok guy named Virgil. His thing had been opioids and alcohol. He was the first Native person I met up there and the first person to make me think about the land we live on. Like who had been on it before and why weren't they on the land anymore, but even, like, if they were still on the land why didn't we know who they were or where they lived or how to properly respect the land's original people? I was all about being from Oakland and being Native and feeling like I belonged to something older than the country. Opal never talked about the people who first lived in Oakland. And I hadn't thought to look it up. I honestly don't know how much I would have found out on my own or cared more than just knowing that I hadn't known before about the original people on the land I lived on, but then Virgil relapsed and overdosed and fucking died. I went to the funeral but couldn't really figure out how to grieve. Didn't really feel like I deserved to grieve. We barely knew each other. Just knew that we liked each other. Would hang out after meetings. Got together a few times at a coffee shop in Sonora.

I was back in that coffee shop we came to in Sonora to drink coffee and think about Virgil. I was remembering his face, his expression when he asked me if I knew whose land I was on and I said where and he said here but he asked about Oakland too since he knew that's where home was for me. I told him I didn't know. That I probably found out at some point and forgot.

I got hit with this big shame then. About having grown up in a place, having called a place my home without knowing anything about its Native people, who'd lived there for thousands of years. How could I have called it home without knowing who'd really lived there, from whom the land had been taken?

We only learned about the missions by building popsicle-stick versions of the mission buildings when we learned about California history. Popsicle sticks. My buildings always collapsed because I didn't understand how to build them or because I didn't use enough glue.

I had an idea then and went straight to the library to use their computer and internet. I would become familiar with the names of the tribes from the places where I lived. I would start there. I could at least know their names. Say their names. Where I was it was the Miwoks or the Central Sierra Miwoks. And in Oakland it was the Ohlone people.

That didn't feel like enough. Not even close. I looked up all the tribes in California and there were way more than I thought. A hundred and ten federally recognized tribes, and at least seventy-five without federal recognition. I read the list of all of them out loud, and though I struggled through many of the names it felt good to have read the whole thing.

I felt thirsty and went to the water fountain. While drinking I had the feeling like I'd just been speaking in another language. In a way I had. In many other languages. And in the language of names. I thought I should do the same thing for every tribe in the country. When I looked up how many there were it was five hundred and seventy-six federally recognized ones, and four hundred that weren't recognized. Almost a thousand nations of people. That changed something in me I knew I would have to keep trying to figure out how to do something about.

Then I wondered how many states were named after tribes, or were words in Native languages. It was twenty-six states. So more than half of the country was named after a tribe, or got its name from a Native word.

It still didn't feel like it was enough. It shouldn't have, I thought, sitting at the library computer. Assuaging my guilt was not the point. Doing something on a computer on an afternoon I had felt that big shame should not have been enough to make up for having lived a whole life on a land whose people I'd never acknowledged. And I felt bad for having made fun of one white lady at the rehab for doing a land acknowledgment I thought was an empty gesture, how I'd joked around with Virgil about it later. Then realized when he laughed with me it hadn't been sincere, because he probably knew I didn't know what I should have known about the land I was on and the land I was from, which was why he asked later.

Once the pandemic hit I was steady enough to not need meetings as much and could do them by Zoom if I felt I needed to. That time both flew by and stood still. I watched way too many movies and TV shows, and listened to and read more books than I ever had in my life. It was a good time for me. I know it was shitty for so many people. Beyond shitty. What can I say? It hit a lot of addicts the worst. With all that time. A bunch of people in the circles I knew directly, or knew about up there in the foothills, died. Without structure and with that much time and with the world feeling like it was over, getting fucked up seemed almost logical. If I hadn't found running, it probably would have killed me too.

When I finally made it back to Oakland I kept my running habit. I lived somewhat close to the view of the Mormon temple, so I'd see it on runs all the time. I would run up into the hills where it felt like you were deep inside some forest nowhere near Oakland. But it was a part of Oakland, and from all these different trails I'd see the temple and it would do something to me. The temple came to mean something not related in any way to Mormonism. It had to do with what running had come to mean for me. The temple became like a vision of my secret temple. The one I made inside, built on miles I built up to running. The one I created in order to understand myself better, which I kept finding all the time on runs, some inside version of me I'd made who understood me. Who was me. I know it sounds stupid. And corny. And I know it was a temple and people built it for the Mormon religion. But it was also a part of Oakland, what Oakland looked like. I started taking pictures of the temple from all the different places on my runs where I could see it. I tried to think of humans as not belonging *to* the earth but *of* the earth. And so too with its made things, all its buildings and cars and cities and satellites. Of the earth.

I wanted to feel connected to being Native, and to being Cheyenne, but I didn't quite know how and didn't even know any other Cheyenne people who weren't in my family. Being in recovery seemed to fulfill that in some way. Native people were in recovery everywhere. Had found out that they couldn't not take substance use to its abuse point. Had found out that some wounds were bottomless holes asking to be filled every day. Running alone did what I needed done to keep sober. So that's what I kept doing. Every day.

After Lony graduated from high school, he said he was going on a road trip with some friends. And then he didn't come back. And then we couldn't get ahold of him. And then, after years passed, we had to deal with the fact that he might be dead, or worse, somehow, he might have let us go. We had to deal with that. Every day was a test of will for me, and when anything bad happened my mind went to make an excuse out of it. What I'd once referred to as the bullet, that voice in my head, it'd get loud in these moments. Tell me I should quit being so weak. That sobriety was a weakness of will the same as taking too much was. The voice tried to convince me I could just take it easy and have fun like everyone else seemed able to do. *What's one drink, getting high on weekends to relax? Have some fun, you're young!* I didn't let the voice mean anything. I left it in a room by itself. I told myself I wasn't in the room with it. That it was talking to itself.

I left the thing alone and without me participating with it, it couldn't do its thing there where I left it. As for my higher power, I never found my way. I loved Jacquie's version of her higher power and took it on for myself. Untitled. Like your higher power could just remain unnamed because naming was presumptuous when it came to the power higher than high, the most high. It was good there. It could remain what it'd always been, it could keep its mystery, and you didn't have to worry about a group worrying around its believability, its sects, or dogmas, or anything else required of a group deciding together on what it all ultimately means. I know there isn't a way to know and that the need to know comes from wanting control, which is so much of what addiction is about, control. Addiction renews itself every day. But it builds too. And bad momentum sneaks up on you. You have to be sure you don't end up on that downhill roll. I've been lucky. Not like those doctors said about surviving that bullet.

The hardest part about sobriety after all this time is still not getting high anymore. Which isn't the same thing as staying sober. The thrill of it. The idea of it. Getting there. The reality of getting high again is nothing but mess and regret. But the idea of it is impossible to shake, because if you've felt it before, to have touched the bliss of oblivion is to have already gone too far past yourself, past self-interest, into that othered beyond where all that matters is dutifully obeying the need for the need like an itch that's impossible to not scratch but also impossible to scratch enough to fulfill what the itch is asking for.

I initially went to using as a way to feel the world, when I'd learned somewhere along the way to numb it. But I wanted to feel the world without having to use, and not simply become obedient to the cold demands of a cruel world, or to an equally cruel addiction.

I deliver mail now. Grandma's not proud. I'm UPS. "What's ups with that?" was her bad joke to me when I told her. She's always called UPS ups and thinks it's way more funny than it is. She keeps asking me why they insist we wear paper bags for uniforms. She is proud of me though. That's how she says it. With her, joking around means nothing's wrong.

I play in an instrumental, experimental band. We're not jazz or hip-hop or electronic or rock, but we dabble in all of that. I know that's probably annoying to hear too. Like pick something. I know that's a good way to pitch something to someone who wants to go to sleep, but I don't care who listens, or what they do if they are or aren't listening. Getting paid to play music, even if it's only enough to buy a meal or two, is getting paid to play music, and anyway I don't need the money, that's what the other work is for. The UPS shit. It's good. What I can be when I try.

I've found a way to work Native music into it. I try to find old recordings without copyright. It took a while but I found some to use. I wouldn't wanna be disrespectful to the people's family so I usually make the sound unrecognizable. Sometimes I play the songs in reverse, up or down pitch, then drown it in reverb. Always with distortion. I like to work it into songs where you wouldn't immediately recognize that it was Native music. I try to get it to a place where if someone pointed it out you could hear it, but otherwise it got lost in the groove or the drone of the song's build. The goal for me and my bandmates was always the same, to try and make musical loops that wouldn't sound or feel like loops because of the way they were built, that's the way out of a loop. Every day is a loop. Life tries the same as we try with music. Every day is the sun rising, and the sun going down, and the sleep we must sleep. I even like sleep and dreaming now. Every day is life convincing us it's not a loop. Addiction is that way too.

I wouldn't tell my bandmates I'm going for that. It's my

secret about the music we make, which I need to keep secret. No one else in the band is sober and if I tried to put some of my shit on what we're all doing together it would ruin it for them, I think.

I never got back in touch with Sean. I'd like to think he found his way, whatever that might have ended up meaning for him. I'd like to think our time together mattered to him the way it did to me. I regret losing him as a person in my life, but I don't regret what happened. I think I needed to feel the bottom to know how to rise. Maybe we're all looking for our bottoms and tops in search of balance, where the loop feels just right, and like it's not just rote, not just repetition, but a beautiful echo, one so entrancing we lose ourselves in it.

Opal and Jacquie came to one of my shows the other day.

It was a daytime show and small, over in Alameda at a bar for background brunch ambience, for hipsters and ex-hipster parents sipping mimosas with one hand and rolling baby strollers with the other. Actually I was on the lookout for a baby stroller. Loother said he was gonna come. Can't believe he's a dad now. He had a little girl. Named her Opal. He's doing community college at Laney now. He wants to be a writer. I thought he'd end up doing something more practical.

No one noticed us, but that was the point. Sometimes a good sound is just supposed to be good enough to not be noticed. Rarely is anything so good a crowd gathers. Not at this kind of gig. There's this old French composer I love named Erik Satie who wanted to compose what he called furniture music, by which he meant background music, music not meant to be noticed but to kind of just fill the room, which would now be called ambient music, but this was in the late 1800s, so pretty far ahead of his time, I'd say.

Jacquie and Opal sat at a table nearby and didn't look over at us once. I guess they were trying to play it cool for me, but I'm old enough now to where I wanted them to look.

Loother came holding the baby in his arms. Little baby Opal. Loother looked so exhausted he was happy, like whatever was too tired in him had collapsed into this pile he was holding in his arms like it was the most precious thing anyone could ever be holding. He was wearing all black. I think he thought I was in a metal band. His girlfriend didn't come. I hadn't met her all those years he stayed away from us by being with her. I'm sure it was for the best, but I was disappointed since I wanted to meet her, but I thought it might be better that way since Opal said they had some news for us. We were all gonna go eat somewhere else after the show since they didn't give the musicians a meal and the food seemed too trendy for its own good. And hella expensive.

We got a decent amount of applause when we were done, and some dads came up and put money in the bucket we had there in front of the makeshift stage. All in all after we split it, it wasn't enough to even pay for breakfast, even if we went somewhere cheaper, but still, we got paid to play.

At the greasy-spoon diner we found nearby we ordered a big stack of pancakes and a bunch of bacon. There was a letter, Opal told us. A letter? Jacquie just sipped her coffee smiling a little. At first I couldn't imagine what it was. Who wrote letters?

—— • • ——

CHAPTER THIRTY-FOUR

Dead Letter Mail

I sent this with no return address to the last address I had, the one and only address I ever had in my head. Maybe I remember it wrong and you won't get this. I've been meaning to write you for a long time. Here now doing it, I'm already regretting that I hadn't before, while also regretting that I'm doing it now. Feelings are always so twinned, with opposite meaning.

It's not the future we imagined, right? I never really imagined a future. Thought it would stop somewhere along the way.

There's a good chance you aren't where this letter got to. That it gets lost in the mail, because if where I sent it they don't want it, I didn't put a return address because I don't have one yet. So maybe this won't get to you. D'you all know about dead letter mail? Where lost mail with nowhere to go or return to ends up? Grandma Opal, you must know. It's all of us, right? We the Native American diaspora. Dead letter mail.

I've been living outdoors for years, chasing the sun. I always meant to end up in the right place during the seasons I needed the sun. I didn't leave California. I had a phone off and on, which meant I got the news of the world off and on. On purpose. People living outside like me were more and more. Then once the pandemic came, it seemed like the best place to be. Outside. It was what I wanted, for reasons I'll never understand, since I was too young to want something so stupid and selfish. Selfish is the most likely thing to become if you've been abandoned, I think. Being abandoned means you don't think anyone else is really there for you when it comes down to it. So it's just you. Yourself. Being how you would be if there was no one else there.

I had a memory the weight of a body about you all and I carried it with me everywhere, slung over my shoulder.

Most weight you feel with time. By which I mean heaviness gathers itself.

I never could have guessed that living outside would end up meaning I'd use the word family in so many different ways, with so many different kinds of people since I left home. The word family will never feel the same as it once did, or maybe it never quite fit. Like we need new words for what we become, how much we change, how we wear words and names out, especially when your heart breaks about going from being a kid to being an adult because you have to, because the world isn't made for kids.

I write you from the mountains, in the foothills of the Sierra Nevada. It's one of the best places in the country to be homeless any season but the winter. You wouldn't recognize me if you saw me. Not right away. I got taller. I have a beard.

The truth is you didn't know me like I knew you. You all were already grown when I knew you. I wasn't even all the way here yet. Y'all only knew a seed.

I left and didn't ever tell you how gone I got. No word. No nothing. After what happened with Orvil, how we almost lost him again, and then the years that followed, how we lost each other to it, the thing that happens when you're just playing it safe enough to get by, but not really paying enough attention to wonder why we all got so gone about everything. I wonder if you all get together during the year for birthdays or Christmas anymore.

I can tell it better. I'm no cold monster for leaving and staying away. Once Orvil came home, and after Opal got better, I thought we'd already made it through everything we'd have to go through. I even thought that I'd done it, or was part of why it all got better. That's what I'd been doing with the blood and belief. But then you all stopped being yourselves. You were playing it safe. Playing. So I pretended the same. Until I couldn't anymore.

I'm not even that much different from the Lony you remember, except that I am. No one can get that far away from themselves if you've known them enough like you can with family, and you did, you did know me in ways I didn't even know you knew me, 'cause I was a fucking kid and didn't know shit but that growing up was some bullshit older people were on about to get you to stop complaining about the bullshit no one ever wants to admit is bullshit. I'm not mad. I don't feel that way, I'm just trying to explain real quick why I left, or what was up with me then, or what I think might have been up with me then.

It wasn't until after graduating from high school that I left, that I knew I could leave. I knew at least making it through to graduation meant a lot and I meant to get there and I did. I was smoking a cigarette with loud music I didn't recognize on the way up to the hills in Oakland, me and my friends used to go up there to smoke cigarettes and look at Oakland all lit up at night. No one was talking. Other kids were going to parties, but my friend group, we'd lived harder than parties by then. I barely graduated. It was the same for all of us, but we were graduating and we were all sober having gone too hard. That was better than having done well headed off for a promising college or whatever. Nothing felt certain about my or anyone's future then, but I could rest for that moment, my arm out the window, the music blasting out any thoughts that might distract me, a cigarette just the right kind of small buzz still with a decently long, lit embered end. You don't get many of these in life, I hadn't had that many anyway, this feeling like whatever else, anything, who cares for now, I could feel relief, and sort of lie back into the moment. I said thank you out loud. That night I was watching my smoke leave my mouth then stream out and float up, up into the night, into the sky, with just those handful of stars you can make out in a city. When I was done I flicked my cigarette out into the street and laughed at flight, the idea of flying, about how much I'd always loved the idea of it, but everything must come down. I knew I was coming down from something even then, that it would take a long time to come back from.

After I left for that road trip, when I was gone and didn't feel that bad about it, I realized my heart didn't really know loyalty, or if it did it died somewhere along the way. It was stretched to its breaking point and maybe mine wasn't as pliable or long or it was thinner than most, it broke like a rubber band and snapped back at me too, and that shit hurt. I didn't care if it *mended. I maybe even actively let it atrophy. I went for warmer weather. I'd met kids who lived on the streets and in parks and talked about the times when they lived where it was warm, how it was paradise, to hustle and not pay rent and figure food out however you could, a real adventure. A life in nature as it was, like some real Indian.*

I lived like Indians back when our world ended that first time. To be free and wandering and figuring it out because it all got so disfigured, this is what I wanted. I went north. I stayed in Sacramento for a while, that park and that river and that spread-out, flat-ass city. I grew up there. I stopped being sober. Did too many drugs. I was not being a good human or a contributing member of society, but I also wasn't contributing to the shit corporations and U.S. government which affect, which destroy so many more lives for there to be a count, and they wouldn't count it if they could, all what the corporations do to people and the earth. I maybe begged and I maybe stole but I was young and I was free. I really thought I was living like an Indian. I was hurting so bad but wouldn't have ever said that I was. I was doing what you do when you're hurting and can't say it. Digging another hole for myself.

Let me try again. I was a boy and our family had just started to feel all right like we were moving toward something bigger than we'd ever been, with Orvil dancing and us brothers riding our bikes together, it felt like the beginning of something. And I was okay with what happened. We had a chance to get better together. That's the only good thing about getting hurt is that if it happens together we have a chance to heal and get better together, which is a chance to get stronger than you ever were before. Healing is holy and if you have the chance to not have to carry something alone, with people you love, it should be honored, the opportunity, it should be honored, and you all got selfish about it, you all got scared it was gonna be bigger than our love and then it was.

To put it more simply, I wanted to be outside. That was what it'd been about. Not more than that. Not less. Just exactly that. Simply that. And I did live out in the country for hella long, always somewhere it was warm enough to where you didn't have to worry about freezing to death, where I could find a blackberry bush and maybe fish. I did. I told you I felt like a real Native out there. Walked country roads with no one on them. I left Oakland, headed farther north this time. Got out to where I saw more dirt than road. Saw the tagged ears of animals some consider holy. I became a vegetarian. I had a phone I'd plug in when I could. I remembered all your numbers. Could have called. I tried to forget them.

I thought about the things I used to think about when I was a kid. Wanting to be a bird and that make-believe magic was real. That I could fly.

I met young people like me, women and men, and had relationships with them. All different kinds. I never stopped thinking about you all.

I forgive you. You're not asking for it. Maybe you are. You probably thought I hadn't noticed. I was always too spacey to be paying attention. I knew the way you talked about me. A dreamer. I get it. Everyone thinks kids don't get what a world is, what this world is. But we feel it all. We want nothing more than to make-believe belief can be enough, and when we realize it isn't, when you make kids believe belief isn't enough, we take it all in under hooded eyes.

I've known what this world's about. I been running into it. We young ones do. We who hate that we still believe something good could come of it. We the young ones have always suffered, inherited, had to know what it means to be left behind and left with shit and left with weight and left without you or any form of help or helpful policy to bridge what's between the abyss and anything even resembling justice and equality.

If only the young survive the selfishness of this dying world, of old whites who always thought they owned the earth, to use and expend whatever they can grasp with their cold dead hands, who've always led this country down its hole, to its inevitable collapse. We who inherit the mess, this loss, this deficit, this is my prayer, for forgiveness, we the inheritors of a world abandoned. May we learn to forgive ourselves, so that we lose the weight, so that we might fly, not as birds but as people, get above the weight and carry on, for the next generations, so that we might keep living, stop doing all this dying.

This is the last thing I'll say here. I want to try to find a way for us all to be together again. I want to come home. That I even have one took me a long time being away to know. Maybe that's what we're all doing here. Alive long enough to get that when we die it's home we're going back to, and that we came here to know that when we die it isn't an end but a return.

I have to hope you're still there, up Fruitvale. On that other Fruitvale. Where we first made each other feel a part of something that made us better by becoming it. Family. Then got all *lost about it. Each other. I did too. I still don't know how to trust what I love.*

I hope I didn't stay away too long. It won't ever be the same as it was before. We all know that. I hope y'all haven't forgotten about us, about how we used to be when we were good. Of course you can't forget the bad shit even if you try. Even if you do it still comes at you. It can take superhuman strength to remember what was good. Don't be dumb I guess I have to say like don't make it worse that I came back. Okay? I hope you're there. Most of all I just I hope you're all there.

LONY

ACKNOWLEDGMENTS

Thank you first and foremost to my editor, Jordan Pavlin, for helping me see this through to what it became, for believing in the work when I did not, and for guiding my writing with a focus on readability and storytelling with such wisdom and grace.

And thank you to my agent, Nicole Aragi, for representing me with impeccable wit, warmth, love, and charm. For taking me on in the first place.

I could not have written this book without the big love and support of my family and friends. Thank you, Kateri, my first and best reader, for all your strength and love. Felix, for all the ways you don't know you lift and carry me. Thank you, Solomon, for the new strength and hope you have inspired. Teresa, Bella, and Sequoia, for living through the years we lived through together with renewed love. Mamie and Lou, for all your undying support and love to all of us. Thank you to Mario Diaz for being the amazing brother I never knew I needed, for reading an early, bad version of this book. And thanks to my mom for reading the same bad version, for always supporting and loving my work. Thank you to the Diaz family for taking us on and loving

Acknowledgments

us as family. And thank you Martha, Jeffrey, and Geri for all the love and healing support over all these years.

Thanks to early and later readers Kiese Laymon, Terese Mailhot, and Julian Aguon for reading my work at various stages of development and disrepair. Huge thanks to Kaveh Akbar for having written his novel alongside mine starting in 2019, for trading pages the whole impossible way through, and for all the immeasurable brilliance you give to this world.

Thank you to the city of Oakland and its people, for all the ways you have made me who I am, made this book and the first book what they became.

Thank you to any and all readers who gave their time to this book, who gave their own precious time in this life to read this.

Finally, I'd like to acknowledge my Southern Cheyenne people, who survived more than anyone should have to, and who made it possible for me to imagine the lives of the characters in this book.

Tommy Orange is an enrolled member of the Cheyenne and Arapaho Tribes of Oklahoma. He was born and raised in Oakland, California. He currently teaches at the Institute of American Indian Arts in Santa Fe. His first book, *There There,* was a finalist for the 2019 Pulitzer Prize.